LONG WAY HOME

MATTHEW RIKER BOOK 3

J.T. BAIER

1

Matthew Riker had only been back in his hometown twenty minutes before he got into a fistfight. It hadn't been his intention to get involved in a conflict. In fact, he'd done everything he could to avoid the situation. But the man with the scar over his left eye hadn't wanted to take no for an answer, leaving Riker little choice in the matter.

It had all started because of a little curiosity. Riker had walked past the Suds and Grubs Tavern hundreds of times during his first eighteen years, but he'd never set foot inside until that night. He'd been too young to order a drink the last time he'd been in Kingsport, Iowa, and he wouldn't have had enough money to order one even if it had been legal. So, on a whim, Riker decided to pull his car over, walk across Main Street, and go inside.

The place was brighter than he'd expected, and the faint scent of greasy food hung in the air. The crowd was sparse, as one might expect at eight o'clock on a Thursday evening. A couple of old-timers sat at the far end of the bar, and their eyes lingered on Riker as he entered, as if maybe they recognized him. It wasn't exactly surprising, he supposed. He'd made quite the memorable exit so many years ago.

Riker made his way to the bar and ordered a glass of whatever domestic beer was on tap. As he waited for the barkeep to draw his beverage, his eyes wandered, and that was when the trouble began. He hadn't been looking for anything in particular, just taking in his surroundings as was his unconscious habit. His eyes settled on a scene in a corner of the bar lit only by an old Pabst neon sign. A man in his thirties took a folded stack of bills from a boy who Riker suspected was not of legal drinking age. Then the man passed the boy a plastic bag filled with something white.

Riker wasn't close enough to make out what was in the bag. Could have been pills or powder or even a rock. Didn't matter. Riker had seen enough to know he was watching a drug deal go down. His eyes lingered just a little too long, and the man spotted him watching. Even in the dim light from the neon sign, Riker could see the man's face redden. Riker didn't look away. That would have been a mistake. Instead, he kept his face slack, disinterested, as if he were staring off into space.

The man whispered something to the boy who nodded and made a beeline for the exit. Then he stalked over to Riker.

"You watching me?" the man asked without preamble.

"Nope." Riker regarded the man. He was big. Solid. Like he probably worked for a living. And there was a large scar over his left eye.

"That's funny, cause it seems like you were watching me."

"I wasn't." Riker considered his next move. He could either stay stoic and silent or try to make nice. Maybe it was the nostalgia of being back in his hometown for the first time in so many years, but he decided to take the latter option. "How about I buy you a beer?"

It only took a moment for Riker to realize that had been the wrong move. The man's hands clenched into fists and he leaned toward Riker. "I don't want a beer. What I want is for you to mind your damn business."

"Fair enough." Riker turned away from the man and took a sip of his beer. It was watery; not at all the magical beverage he'd spent his teenage years imagining flowed from these taps.

The man took another step toward him. "Hey, I'm talking to you."

"Thought you wanted me to mind my business."

"It's too late for that. I'm your business now. Who the hell are you? I've never seen you in here before. You a cop?"

Riker sighed and set down his beer. "No. Look bud, I honestly don't care what you were doing in that corner. Whatever you've got going on here, it's got nothing to do with me." It was the truth, too. Riker had come to Kingsport, Iowa, for one purpose, and he intended to carry it out quickly and quietly. Small-time drug dealers operating out of the local drinking establishment were none of his concern.

Still, the man with the scar didn't appear ready to let it go. "Bullshit. If you didn't care, you wouldn't have been staring. I'll ask again. You a cop? Statie? DEA? Some shit like that?"

"And I'll answer again. I'm not a cop. I'm just a guy drinking a beer." Riker paused. If he'd stopped there, maybe things would have played out differently over the next few days. But he had just spent sixteen hours driving halfway across the country, and he was in a sour mood, so he spoke again. "Piece of advice. You go up to every stranger you meet looking for trouble, one of them just might give it to you."

The man flinched, surprised to be talked to that way. Then a slow smile played across his face, and he turned as if to go. It was a clumsy, obvious move, and Riker wasn't surprised in the least when he spun back around, swinging his right arm in a wild haymaker intended to catch the side of Riker's head.

Riker was ready, and he jutted forward, slipping inside the arc of the man's arm. He drew back his own right hand and brought it forward, delivering a sharp jab to the man's rib cage. The punch wasn't hard enough to break anything, but it was enough to let the man know that Riker meant business and wasn't in a trifling mood. The sharp pain that would accompany every breath for the rest of the evening should serve as a reminder for the man.

The man staggered backward, his eyes wide, and the bar fell silent. Riker suddenly realized he'd made another error in judgment. The bar wasn't crowded, but there were probably a dozen men in the place. And every one of them, from the old guy at the end of the bar to the bartender, appeared fully prepared to defend the honor of the man with the scar above his eye. Riker suppressed a curse. He'd made the rookie mistake of fighting with a man with more friends than him. He should have just taken that haymaker and been on his way. Now, there would be blood; some of it likely his own.

The man with the scar stood up straight, wincing, his hand on his ribcage. But the look in his eyes was one of delight. This stranger had hit a local, and now he and his friends had every right to make that stranger pay the price.

Riker was considering his options when the door to the men's restroom swung open and a man with a shock of chestnut hair and a thick beard stumbled out. The newcomer took a look at the situation and shook his head.

"The hell is all this?"

"This guy hit me, Luke," the man with the scar said. From the tone of his voice, it was clear that he saw Luke as his superior.

But Riker barely noticed that. He was busy staring at Luke, trying to see past the beard and shaggy hair to see if he recognized the face underneath it all. And Luke was staring right back at him, his eyes just as searching.

After a moment, Luke's face broke out in a wide grin. "It's okay, Scott. This asshole can't punch worth a damn, anyway. You get him on the wrestling mat, that's another thing entirely.

Riker couldn't help but smile just as widely as his old friend. "Luke Dewitt? Is that really you?"

"Afraid so." He approached, hand extended, and the two men shook.

At the touch of their hands, the tension seemed to dissipate in the bar, and everyone but the man with the scar seemed to exhale at once. The bartender went back to fussing with the ice maker and the old man at the end of the bar turned back to the TV.

The man with the scar looked on incredulously. "This guy punched me."

"You probably deserved it," Luke said. He turned back to Riker. "Welcome home, Matt. Jesus, it's good to see you."

"You too," Riker said, and he meant it. He hadn't told anyone he was coming back to town, and he'd planned on socializing as little as possible on this trip. But he had to admit that seeing his oldest friend felt pretty damn good.

Luke's face grew serious. "I guess I don't have to ask why you're back."

Riker shook his head. He swallowed, surprised at how hard the emotions were hitting him. He'd had three father figures in his life, not counting his biological father who didn't rate anywhere near the other three men in Riker's mind. Edgar Morrison, his former boss at QS-4, was the most recent. Before that, it had been James Halder, his commanding officer during his time with the SEALs. But Riker's first real father figure was the man whose memory he had returned to honor. His wrestling coach, Oscar Kane.

"I heard it was a carjacking," Riker said.

Luke grimaced. "Killing a man for a ten-year-old Nissan. That's just about the coldest thing I've ever heard."

Riker had seen men killed for far less, but he simply nodded.

"I'm glad you're here," Luke continued. "I would have called to tell you myself, but I didn't know how to get hold of you."

"Yeah. I haven't exactly been great about staying in touch."

"Understatement of the year." Luke nodded toward the bar. "How about we have a beer?"

Riker glanced down at his half-empty glass. "I'm way ahead of you."

"Good man. What do you say we toast to the old man?" Luke gestured to the bartender who handed him a beer.

"Absolutely." Riker raised his glass. "To Coach Kane."

The two men clinked glasses, and Riker downed the rest of his drink in one go. As the cold liquid ran down his throat, he thought about the man with the scar passing the drugs to that kid. And how the man with the scar spoke to Luke as if Luke were his boss.

He pushed these thoughts away. He was in Kingsport for one reason and one reason only: to mourn Coach Kane.

Whatever else was going on with his old friend Luke had nothing to do with him, and he wouldn't get involved. He promised himself.

He set down his empty glass and ordered another, the hollow sound of his empty promise echoing in his mind.

2

RIKER PARKED his truck on the street in front of a small ranch house and stepped out into the crisp night air. He took a deep breath, smelling the freshly cut grass and faint hints of the barbeques from earlier that day. He imagined that detergent companies had spent millions trying to replicate that scent.

The porch light cast a welcoming glow, but nothing about the moment felt welcoming to him. Even after the five beers he'd drank with Luke, his heart was racing, and he felt a drop of sweat slide down his back underneath his shirt. He was used to kicking down doors with warriors behind them, but he found the part of his past behind this door far more unnerving.

Steadying himself, he crossed the distance to the porch. He raised a finger and pressed the doorbell. It wasn't long before a silhouette darkened the shaded living room window and the door opened a crack.

The woman staring out at him was eight inches shorter than Riker, and her dark hair flowed down several inches past her shoulders. Her brown eyes inspected Riker from top to bottom, her expression one of disbelief.

"Matt?"

In Riker's mind, he still pictured his cousin Megan as the eight-year-old girl she'd been the last time he'd seen her. It took him a moment to recognize that girl's features in the woman before him.

"Megan?"

"Holy shit, I can't believe you're actually here."

"Yeah, it's been a while." Riker realized how silly the words sounded the moment he said them.

Megan laughed. "That's one way to put it. Another way to put it is you've been gone for eighteen years, and that everyone, including me, thought you were dead."

Riker smiled. "There were a few close calls over the years, but I'm still standing."

She reached out and poked him in the chest. "Looks like you're still flesh and blood. Come on in and tell me where you've been for half a lifetime."

Megan's house was neat and clean. The hallways were lined with pictures of Megan standing among smiling friends. The images showed restaurants, houses, beaches and dozens of other locations. Megan was in each one, but the people around her varied with some duplication.

She led him to the kitchen and poured a cup of tea for each of them. Then she took a seat across from Riker and gave him a piercing stare.

"Okay, where have you been for the last eighteen years?"

"I was in the Navy for a while. Then I worked as a consultant for a security firm. Now I am a beekeeper in North Carolina."

Megan sat waiting for a full minute in silence. "That's it? That's eighteen years?"

"I'm afraid so. No wife, no kids, no pets. I'm a pretty simple guy."

She took a sip of her tea. "Fine, keep your secrets."

"What about you? You were a kid the last time that I saw you."

She gave him a crooked smile. "You don't know? I assumed you'd been reading my emails. Why else would you be here?"

Riker's gaze fell to the floor. She was right, of course. Every Thursday for the past eighteen years she'd sent an email to his ancient AOL account, the one he'd had since high school. Riker never responded—for years he hadn't been allowed to —but she continued doggedly sending them. Usually, the emails contained life updates and minutiae, things that Riker had no reason to be interested in. And yet, the emails served as a sort of tether to his old life, and he looked forward to them.

He knew all about her life from those emails. She'd gone to college on a softball scholarship. After graduating with a teaching degree, she traveled the world for a year before moving back to Kingsport. The energy and joy with which she told tales of both her world travels and her daily life as a teacher at Kingsport High School always made Riker smile.

Over the years, the emails had morphed into a kind of journal for Megan, it seemed. They were written to a man she wasn't even certain was still alive, and she'd had no way to know if they were being read. He got the sense she was writing more for herself than for him.

But the tone of her most recent email had been different. Riker had been at home on the farm in North Carolina when he'd read it, only back from his adventure in California for a few weeks and finally settling into his old routine. The contents of the email had changed all that.

Matt,

I have some hard news that I think you need to hear. Oscar Kane was killed two nights ago. The police are saying it was a carjacking gone wrong.

I don't know if you're even getting these emails, but I thought I'd let you know just in case. I know how much Coach Kane meant to you.

If you are able to attend the funeral, you are more than welcome to crash at my place.

Love,

Megan

At the bottom of the email had been a link to the obituary with details on the funeral and burial arrangements. Riker had hopped in his truck and started the sixteen-hour drive back to Iowa the next morning.

Riker looked back up at Megan, his voice suddenly earnest. "I read your emails. Every one."

"Too much of a hassle to respond?" There was a glint of a smile in her eyes. This was a mystery she'd wanted solved for a very long time.

"No, it wasn't that." He paused, considering how to explain honestly without raising too many questions in her mind. "The line of work I was in... I had to be careful. I was dealing with highly classified situations, and I believe my communications were monitored. I didn't want to put you on their radar. And after I got out of that life... I don't know. Kingsport felt so long ago. I guess I wasn't sure how to even begin."

"Hi Megan, it's your cousin Matt, one of your few living relatives." She spoke in a low voice, doing a passable impression of Riker. "Just wanted to let you know I'm not dead. Talk soon!"

Riker couldn't help but laugh. "Okay, I get it. I'm a dick. I'm sorry."

She shrugged. "Lucky for you I always liked you. And seeing as we're family, I guess I have to forgive you."

They shared a moment of comfortable silence, each sipping their tea. Then Riker spoke.

"So, a carjacking?"

She didn't answer for a long moment. "That's what they're saying."

Riker raised an eyebrow. "You have a reason to question that explanation?"

"Aside from the fact that this is the first carjacking I've ever heard of in this little town? Yeah, I guess I do."

Riker leaned forward, his sadness suddenly giving way to curiosity.

She took another sip of tea, considering where to begin. "The first time I saw Coach Kane, he was jogging. Remember how he used to do that?"

Riker nodded. Long before Kane had been his wrestling coach, Riker had simply known him as the strange middle-aged guy who ran around town in a gray sweat suit, regardless of the season. But the strangest part was the way he'd held a stone clutched in each hand as he ran. Local legend had it that a kid who'd been cut from the wrestling team had once tried to run Kane off the road with his car. Ever since then, Kane had taken to the streets prepared to smash the windshield of the next person who tried something similar.

Riker had never asked Kane if the story was true. None of them had. Sometimes, it's better just to believe the legend.

"I remember. What's that have to do with the way he died?"

"Maybe nothing. Maybe everything." She shifted in her seat. "Things in Kingsport... I guess you could say they've changed recently. The town's gotten rougher. Crime's up. Income's down. The opioid epidemic has hit us especially hard."

Riker's mind flashed back to what he'd seen in the corner of the bar that evening. The drug deal he'd tried to ignore.

"Oscar Kane was a private person. I saw him around school, and we were friendly, but it's not like we were inviting each other over for dinner parties. Even still, I knew he was trying to do something about the drug problem. Going to city council meetings. Demanding the police do more. Stuff like that. He was trying to clean up the town, and I don't believe he would have given up, just like he wouldn't give up running after that kid tried to run him off the road. Then Gabe Sullivan died."

"Who's Gabe Sullivan?"

"Quiet kid. Polite. A pretty good wrestler, from what I'm told. Then he got into the drug scene. OD'd a week before his seventeenth birthday."

"Jesus," Riker muttered.

"The parents freaked out of course. Went to the police begging for help making sure it didn't happen to any other kids. Who knows how much effort they really put into it. But one person didn't give up on making sure something good came out of Gabe's death."

"Coach Kane." Riker knew how his old coach felt about his wrestlers. If something had happened to one of them, he'd move heaven and earth to make things right.

Megan nodded. "He got pretty obsessed with it. Stopped going to city council meetings and started spending his nights out on the streets, trying to talk to dealers, asking where they got their product. The last time I saw him was in the teacher's lounge. He looked like he hadn't slept in days. I asked how he was doing and he started talking about how it wasn't an accident that the drugs had suddenly moved into Kingsport. It was deliberately planned."

"What did he mean by that?"

Now Megan's gaze fell to the floor. "I don't know. I was running late and, honestly, the intensity in his eyes made me a little uncomfortable. I thought maybe he was losing it, so I got out of the conversation as quickly as I could." She paused, swallowing hard. "Three days later, he was dead."

"The supposed carjacking."

"It happened on the corner of Jackson and Randolph. You know the spot?"

"Yeah, over by Grant Park."

"Maybe I'm overthinking all of this. All I know is that Oscar never got to finish what he started, and that's a damn shame."

Once again, Riker's mind flashed back to the drug deal he'd witnessed earlier. Though he didn't want to consider the thought, he had no choice. If Coach Kane's death was related to the drug situation in Kingsport, Luke might know something.

"I'm glad you're back, Matt. Sorry the circumstances aren't better."

He reached out and touched Megan's hand. "I'm glad I'm back too. I came to pay my respect to Coach Kane, and now I think I know what that means."

Megan tilted her head in surprise. "How so?"

"The wake is tomorrow night, right? Maybe I'll spend a little time asking around about this Sullivan kid. Maybe I can dig something up, pick up the trail where Coach left off."

"I think you should probably pay your respects by going to the funeral. What happened to Coach proves we shouldn't be messing with this type of thing. Leave the dangerous work to the police."

For a moment, Riker considered telling Megan more about his past, about how the last eighteen years had prepared him for exactly this type of thing. Instead, he smiled at her. "You're probably right. That would be the smarter route."

Megan finished her tea. "I've got a bed made up in the guest room. You can crash there. I've got to get to sleep. I have to teach in the morning."

"I appreciate it. Do you mind if I go for a walk? My mind is racing and it will help me calm it down."

"Suit yourself. The key is hanging next to the front door. Just lock up when you leave."

Riker said good night and stepped out into the cool night air. Megan's home was on the outskirts of town and he easily found his way around. The streets led him back towards the main street and old memories crept into his mind. The past he'd left behind still lived in this town.

All at once, Riker suddenly realized where he was standing. The corner of Jackson and Randolph. The very spot where Coach Kane had died. It was as if his feet had taken him there of their own accord. There was nothing special about the corner. Nothing to mark it as the spot where one of the greatest men Riker had ever known had been murdered. It was as if the world was already forgetting Coach Kane.

Riker silently swore that he wouldn't let that happen.

He glanced at his watch and saw that it was almost one in the morning. He turned to head back to Megan's, but froze as a scream echoed in the night.

3

RIKER MOVED QUICKLY but carefully toward the source of the scream, resisting the urge to run. Chances were strong that it was just some kids goofing around or possibly even an animal his beer-addled brain had mistaken for a human voice. But if it wasn't either of those things, he needed to approach with caution.

Megan's words from earlier that evening rang in his ears. *Coach was trying to clean up the town.*

If Coach had been here, he certainly would have gone to investigate that scream, and he would have helped whoever had made the noise. Coach was gone now, but Riker was still here. That meant he didn't have much of a choice but to do what he could to help.

As he crossed through a yard and into a small neighborhood park, he heard another yell, this one more muffled. Then a voice. "Yeah, you'd better stay down, you little bitch."

Riker moved around a stand of trees and caught his first look at the speaker in the glow of the moonlight. Two young men—probably in their late teens—stood over a third young man who looked to be a few years younger. From the way the kid on the ground was huddled up in the fetal position and the way he was covering his head, Riker knew that he was catching a beating, and probably not his first.

"You gonna keep your mouth shut now, or do we have to break your jaw?" the man on the left asked the teenager. Before the kid could respond, the man drew back his foot and kicked him in the ribs, causing another scream.

Anger flared up in Riker at the sight. He'd seen a lot of death in his time with the SEALs and QS-4, but even after all that nothing made him lose his temper more than seeing someone strong attacking someone weak. For as long as he could remember, such things had filled him with rage, and he doubted that would ever go away.

Still, he forced himself to take a deep breath as he approached. It was difficult to tell their exact ages in the moonlight, and he wasn't about to go beating on teenagers. He also wasn't going to allow this to continue.

"Evening, gentlemen," he said. "Kinda late to be out on a school night, isn't it?"

The two young men turned, startled to see the large man approaching them. Then they exchanged a glance.

Riker nodded toward the kid on the ground. "Did your buddy slip? That can happen at night. Lots of roots and rocks out here. Easy to trip."

The two young men exchanged another glance, then the taller one took a step forward, puffing out his chest. "This is none of your business, man. You better keep moving."

"I will," Riker said. "I just want to make sure your friend's all right."

"He's not our friend," the tall young man said.

Riker took a step forward. "Maybe he's my friend."

The kid's hand went into the pocket of his sweatshirt. "Look man, I'm not going to ask again. Get moving."

"Not without my buddy." Riker took a step to the left, subtly shifting his position so the two young men wouldn't be able to flank him. "How about he and I go, and we forget this whole thing?"

"He's not going anywhere. Everyone in Kingsport knows to steer clear of this park after sundown unless you're looking for trouble. So either you're new around here or you're an idiot."

"Maybe I'm the first thing you said."

"What's that?"

"Looking for trouble." Riker turned to the kid on the ground who had rolled onto his back now. "You okay, son?"

The kid hesitated, then nodded weakly.

"Okay, I've had it with this shit." The tall kid pulled his hand out of his pocket and revealed a pistol clutched in it. "Last chance, man. Get to stepping."

Riker tilted his head at the gun, staring at it. "Glock 19. Nice weapon. Reliable. Good capacity. Easy to conceal. I do have one suggestion though, if you're open to constructive criticism."

The tall kid's mouth dropped open, and he stared at Riker as if he were an idiot. "Did you hear what I said?"

"Yeah, I heard. Thing is, you're holding your pistol incorrectly." In a flash, Riker surged forward, grabbing the kid's elbow with his left hand and his wrist with the right, so that he had total control over the arm. Then he squeezed and twisted with his right hand.

The kid let out a yelp of pain as his hand went limp, releasing the pistol.

Riker let go of the kid's arm and snatched the falling pistol out of the air. He ejected the magazine, letting it fall to the ground. He checked that there wasn't a round in the chamber and stuck the weapon in the back of his waistband.

"See what I mean? Your grip is a very important aspect of gun safety."

"What the hell, man?" the kid yelled, still clutching his injured hand.

Riker had only applied enough pressure to get him to drop the weapon, though he could have broken the wrist with that move if he'd needed to. There was no need here. Not only were these young men, likely under eighteen, but they were untrained. He was in no real danger.

Out of the corner of his eye, he saw the shorter young man stepping forward and reaching into the pocket of his sweatshirt. Riker didn't let this one get his hand out of the pocket. He slid forward and in one smooth motion, hooked his foot behind the kid's ankle and pushed with an open hand against his chest.

The shorter kid hit the ground with a thud. Riker was on him in an instant, quickly relieving him of the weapon in his pocket. He ejected the magazine from that one too.

"See what I mean?" Riker said. "Easy to slip out here."

He quickly frisked the young man and while he didn't find another weapon, he did find something else of interest —a number of small baggies filled a brown substance. Heroin.

Riker grimaced, thinking of the growing criminal element Megan had mentioned. And also of Luke.

"Well, I guess we've solved the mystery of why you are hanging out in the park at one in the morning. What do you say we place a call to the police? The four of us can wait here for Kingsport's Finest."

By the time he finished his sentence, the taller kid was already in motion, running toward the edge of the park.

Riker didn't even pause to think. Not only had the kid been beating on someone weaker than himself, but he'd also pulled a gun on Riker. While it hadn't exactly gone the way the kid had been hoping, it had succeeded in pissing Riker off. There was no way he was letting the kid get away.

Riker sprang to his feet and ran after the kid.

The young man was fast. He had the speed of youth and the long, lanky build of a runner. He also probably knew the area far better than Riker did. Much of this area had been cornfields back in Riker's day. The town had expanded, and the place he'd once known like the back of his hand was now unfamiliar territory.

Riker sprinted through the park, quickly shifting his gaze between the ground in front of him and the young man he was pursuing. Riker had been right—there were plenty of roots and rocks to trip over, and running full speed through the park at night probably wasn't the wisest idea, but the heroin dealer hadn't asked for his input before taking off.

Up ahead, the young man reached the edge of the park and the neighborhood on its border. Instead of heading for the front yard of the first house, the kid angled toward the back. He slammed into the six-foot-tall chain-link fence and quickly climbed it.

Riker couldn't help but smile. The hubris of youth, assuming no one over twenty-five could climb a fence. But the kid had made a tactical error. Climbing the fence had caused him to slow down, costing him crucial seconds and allowing Riker to close the gap. And Riker had no intention of slowing to climb the fence.

As Riker reached the house, he leaped into the air and grabbed the top of the fence, vaulting over. The kid was already at the fence on the far side of the yard, once again climbing. He risked a glance back and his eyes widened as he saw that Riker was already running through the yard.

Then he disappeared over the fence and into the next yard.

This time, Riker changed his angle slightly as he reached the fence. He jumped and kicked off the brick wall, sending him even higher. He cleared the fence even more quickly than he had the first time, using only one hand to guide him as he soared over the chain links. His legs were already in motion as he landed, and he raced forward.

Three steps later, he was within arm's reach of the kid. He put out a hand and shoved the young man on the back. The kid tumbled face-first into the grass. Riker was on him in an instant, pinning him with one arm while he retrieved the cellphone from his pocket with the other. He dialed the police while the young man futilely squirmed to free himself. But Coach Kane had taught Riker well. The kid didn't stand a chance of breaking free.

By the time he dragged the young man back to the park, both his drug-dealing buddy and the kid they'd been wailing on were gone. Riker sighed. At least he'd got one of them, and this kid had even more heroin than his buddy. Still, he didn't know how much progress he'd made toward Coach's goal of cleaning up the city.

He kept the young man restrained until a cop car pulled up five minutes later. A male officer in his forties stepped out of the driver's side, and a female officer in her late twenties got out of the passenger side.

Riker quickly explained the situation and handed over the drugs and the weapons he'd confiscated. As the male officer escorted the young man to the car, the female asked Riker more questions.

"You want to explain what you were doing at the park at one in the morning?"

He glanced down at her badge, which he could just

make out in the glow of the flashing police car lights. "Just out for a walk, Officer Alvarez."

"You live in town?"

"No. I grew up here, but it's been a long time since I've been back."

She gave him a long look. "In that case, a word of advice. The only people who come down to Grant Park this time of night are people who are selling and people who are looking to score. I suggest you steer clear of it."

Riker frowned. The young man had said something similar. "Let me ask you something, Officer. If you know there are drug deals going down in the park, shouldn't you be here putting a stop to it?"

She looked away, but only for a moment. Then her face hardened. "We're a small department. We're doing the best we can, but having an officer in the park full time to stop drug deals isn't in the budget. Is that all right with you, or do you want to tell me how to do my job some more?"

"Apologies. I'm not trying to criticize. Just getting the lay of the land."

Her expression softened. "And I'm not trying to be harsh. Do me a favor and be careful. While I appreciate what you did tonight, vigilante justice isn't welcome around here. Understood?"

"Understood."

Riker watched as the officers got back in the squad car and drove off. He waited until the lights faded into the distance, and he walked back to Megan's. The long day of driving, the alcohol, and the excitement all seemed to catch up with him at once, and he slipped into bed, bone-tired.

4

RIKER PULLED on the door handle to the high school entrance, but it didn't budge. He tried the other door with the same result. Confused, he took a step back to make sure that they didn't push open.

A voice came through a speaker next to the door.

"Can I help you?"

Riker looked around and saw a camera mounted in the corner above the doors. He smiled up at it. "Yes, I'm trying to get inside. I'm meeting one of the teachers for lunch."

"Which teacher are you here to see?" the voice inquired.

"Megan Carter."

After a short pause there was a buzzing sound followed by a click. This time the door pulled open easily. Riker stepped inside and approached a woman sitting at a desk behind a glass shield. She pushed a clipboard toward him.

"Sign in and I'll get you a visitor's pass."

"Is this standard procedure?" Riker asked.

"Of course." She could see the confusion on his face. "I'm guessing that you haven't visited a school recently."

"Not since I attended high school, so it's been a long while. People just came and went last time I was here."

She gave him a half-smile. "The world has changed a great deal since then."

"Yes ma'am, it has."

Riker thought that the idea of security made sense, but the implementation was laughable. He simply filled out his name on a sheet of paper along with the time and then the woman at the desk pointed him in the direction of Megan's room. He wanted to tell the school that their security protocols were close to worthless, but then he considered that the shoddy protections were simply there to make parents feel better in a world that made no sense.

He stood outside the open door to Megan's classroom for a moment, watching her as she instructed young minds. Her energy filled the room while she spoke about the root causes of the Revolutionary War. The teenagers were actually paying attention to her lecture.

Megan noticed the figure in the doorway and stopped her lesson. She waved for Riker to enter the room.

"Class, we have a special visitor today."

Riker stood in the doorway, hesitant to enter. He had intended to wait outside the room until the class finished up. Now he would be the center of attention, which was just about the last thing he wanted.

Megan moved across the room to Riker and grabbed his hand. "Looks like Mr. Riker needs a little assistance." She pulled him toward a spot in front of her desk.

"This is Matthew Riker; he is a former US Navy SEAL." Heads snapped to attention and a murmur went through the room. "If you don't mind me calling a bit of an audible, I thought we might end today's class with a little Q&A session."

Riker's eyes bore into Megan's. "I don't think that I am very relevant to your class. I can just wait outside until you finish up."

"Don't be silly." She continued before Riker had a chance to respond. "We've studied numerous wars in this class, but we never study the men and women who stand on the battlefield. This is a great opportunity for these students. I'll start things off. What country did you spend the most field time in?"

"I am really not allowed to discuss—"

Megan cut him off. "Please speak up and address the entire room."

Riker couldn't help but smile. He knew exactly what she was up to. After his reluctance to talk about his past last night, she was going to grill him in a place where he couldn't avoid her questions so easily. The small woman in front of him could have served as a commanding officer. He did as he was told and addressed the class.

"I'm sorry, but most of the missions were classified, so I really can't answer any specific questions."

"Fine, even though we collectively pay for all those missions I suppose you are bound to the rules of the military. Does anyone have any questions for Mr. Riker that are less mission-specific?"

A hand in the front of the class shot up, and the young man spoke without waiting to be called on. "Have you ever killed anyone?"

Riker gave Megan a look to see if she wanted him to answer the question. She nodded back at him.

"Yes," he said evenly. "It's not something I talk about much, but that is part of some missions."

The class was silent for a moment. The realization that a killer stood in front of them changed their attitude. A boy in the back of the room wearing ripped jeans called out, "Can you do something cool?"

"What did you have in mind?"

The kid gave a mischievous smile. "I don't know. Chop a board in half with a karate move or throw a knife through something. If you're such a badass killer then do something cool."

The class stared at Riker and waited.

After a moment, Riker said, "Megan can I borrow your scarf?"

She handed it to him and he wrapped it around his eyes, using it as a blindfold. Every student leaned in towards Riker.

"There are twenty-seven of you in this room including Ms. Carter. Of the twenty-six students, twelve are male. There are five windows in the room, three on the west wall, and two on the south. The window in the southwest corner is most vulnerable to a sniper positioned on the building across the street. There are large steel scissors on the right side of the desk and there is a paper cutter on the east side of the room. Either could be used as weapons. The fire suppression system has a strobe light two feet from the door. This could be used to temporarily blind a target.

"The kid sitting in the second row over, three seats back is wearing a hoodie that could conceal a weapon as is the girl in the back center seat. The top of Ms. Carter's desk is metal and should be able to stop a small-caliber handgun bullet if used as a shield." Riker took off the blindfold. "The coolest thing that the SEALs taught me was awareness. I am alive because I know my surroundings. I am always aware of possible dangers and potential weapons. This is how we survive."

The class was silent again. Megan stood with her mouth slightly open as Riker handed her the scarf.

Then the student who'd asked the question said, "A backflip would have been way cooler."

The class burst out laughing.

The student continued. "What do you do now? I mean what could compare to being a SEAL?"

Riker smiled. "I'm a beekeeper. I tend to my hives and sell the honey."

Another round of laughter came from the class.

"That doesn't sound very exciting."

"No, it's not, and that's the point."

The bell rang and students grabbed their belongings and flew out the door. Megan and Riker grabbed some food and found a spot outside to eat their lunch.

"Thanks for coming here today. I really wanted you to see the school and my class."

"Thanks for putting me on the spot in front of said class. I don't think that was my finest moment."

Megan tried to cover her smile with a drink of soda. "Probably not. You came close to impressing them for a moment, but I don't think making honey impresses the kids like it used to."

"Say what you will, taking care of the hives is a responsibility that I take very seriously. I certainly don't do it to impress a bunch of teenagers." He looked around at the students eating their lunches on campus. "I have to confess, seeing you wasn't the only reason that I wanted to come here for lunch."

"What other reason did you have?"

"I'd like to meet the kids on the wrestling team. I know that sounds a little strange, but they might have information about what Coach was up to in his last days. If the team was as important to him as it was back in the day, those kids probably saw him more than anyone else."

"You just can't stay out of trouble can you?" She pointed to a table with a dozen kids sitting around it. "Those kids sitting over there are wrestlers if you want to give it a shot."

"Don't worry. I'll stay out of trouble." Riker stood up without waiting for a response and walked over to the table. The kids' conversation stopped and all eyes turned to the strange man standing next to them.

"Hey sorry to bug you guys, but I used to be on the wrestling team here."

The kids continued to stare.

A kid who had been in Megan's class spoke. "This guy is the Navy SEAL that I was telling you about." He turned back to Riker. "I recognize you. Matthew Riker. Your picture is up in the wrestling room on the Wall of Honor."

Riker smiled at that. The Wall of Honor displayed all the wrestlers who'd made it to the state championships over the years, so he should have known he'd be on it, but hearing that he was warmed his heart.

A couple of kids scooted over, making room for Riker on the bench seat.

"It was a long time ago, but yeah this is my hometown."

Another kid shook his head in disbelief. "I can't believe that this podunk town produced a Navy SEAL."

"It wasn't the town that gave me the ability to become a SEAL. It was Coach Kane. That's why I'm back in town, to pay my respects."

The kids all looked down. The loss of their coach was still fresh and one of the boys quickly brushed some moisture from his eye.

"I can see that he meant a lot to you guys," Riker continued. "He meant a lot to me too. I want to do anything I can to honor his memory." He paused for a moment. "I'd like to make sure that his death isn't meaningless. I'm trying to figure out why he died."

"He died because some asshole shot him." It was the kid who'd wiped away the tear, trying to sound tough now.

"I know, and I like to figure out who did it and why. I heard he was trying to get rid of a bad element from town. Do you guys know anything about that?"

Most of the kids looked down again. One of the smaller boys spoke up. "Don't be a bunch of pussies." The kid looked Riker in the eyes. "We all know why Coach died. He didn't roll over when bad things happened, unlike everyone else in this town. Like with the drugs. He was always trying to get the police involved. Anytime he caught a student with any of that shit he would make them tell him where they got it. Then he would give that information to the police."

"That must have pissed off the people selling the drugs," Riker said.

"Not really. The police never arrested anyone."

Riker shook his head. "Let me guess, when the police questioned the dealers it was his word against theirs."

"Pretty much. And the dealers kept selling that stuff to anyone who would buy."

"What about Gabe Sullivan? I heard Coach was looking into who sold him the drugs that killed him."

The kids exchanged nervous glances.

The first boy, the one who'd been in Megan's class, spoke again. "Oh come on, you guys. It's not like it was a secret." He turned back to Riker. "Yeah, Coach got deep into it. He questioned each of us multiple times. He hounded the police about it. Talked to every dealer he could find. He was hell-bent on figuring out who got Gabe hooked."

"Do you think he ever found a lead?" Riker asked.

The kid shook his head. "I don't know, man. But he did seem different the last couple of days. Maybe hopeful or something. It's gotta me wondering if maybe he found somebody who knew--"

"Matthew Riker," a gruff voice behind Riker called, cutting off the younger man. "I can't believe that you came back."

Riker hadn't heard that voice for eighteen years, but he knew it immediately. He'd sat in the principal's office enough times to recognize the occupant's voice. He stood up and turned to face an elderly man.

"Mr. Harlen, I didn't know that you still worked here."

"Yes, some of us support our communities and the people we grew up with. Your father was one of those people."

Riker met the older man's gaze with a cool stare. "That man was far from an upstanding citizen."

"Your opinion doesn't hold any weight with me," Mr. Harlen said. "You shouldn't be on school grounds. Hell, you shouldn't be anywhere but a prison cell."

"You're entitled to your opinion. I'm here at the invitation of my cousin."

"Consider your invitation revoked. You can leave now or I will call the police."

Riker turned to the kids at the table. "Thanks for letting me sit with you for a minute. I'm glad that Coach was still the same guy that I remembered." He turned back to Harlen. "Though some people could probably do with a change."

"No one really changes, Mr. Riker. That's how I know you are still a piece of trash."

Riker took one step towards the old man. Harlen flinched and backpedaled two steps. Then Riker gave him a nod and left the school grounds.

5

Dewitt Construction's headquarters was a squat brick building on the edge of downtown Kingsport. The company had another location just outside town where they stored their heavy equipment, but here was where the deals got done. And here was where Riker went looking for the owner of the small company.

From the conversation at the bar the previous evening, Riker knew that Luke had followed through with his high school plan to one day take over his father's construction company. And, as much as he didn't want to, Riker knew that this was his next step in finding out the truth.

He paused at the door for only a moment, his hand resting on the cool metal handle as the memories came rushing back to him. Luke's father had started the construction company before his son was born, and he'd somehow managed to eke out a modest living despite the few construction projects even available to bid on in his hometown. Riker remembered that he'd often take work on other crews out of town, sometimes being gone for weeks at a time. Thankfully, rent in downtown Kingsport was low enough that he kept his small office—which just so happened to be a great place for his son and his friends to hang out away from the prying eyes of adults.

Coming back here so many years later felt odd to Riker. The fun-loving kid who'd spent so many hours here during high school felt like a completely different person than the man he was today.

After pausing for another moment, Riker pulled open the door and stepped inside. The familiar old bell chimed as he crossed the threshold. Riker was surprised by how little had changed. The carpets were the same color as in his memory. The three desks were arranged as they had been back then. Even the smell was the same—a unique combination of sawdust and cleaning product.

Only one desk was occupied this afternoon, and the man behind it looked up as Riker entered. Luke smiled at his old friend. "Didn't expect to see you again so soon."

Riker made his way across the room and sank into the chair before answering. "I'm trying to get the lay of the land. Hoping you could help me out."

"Sure. What are you looking for?"

"Grant Park. Can you point me in that direction?"

Luke's smile faded as he looked at his old friend. "I heard you already found that last night."

"I guess I did." He paused, regarding his friend. The fact that he already knew about the arrest spoke volumes, confirming Riker's suspicions. "What are you mixed up in, Luke?"

Luke's face flushed, and his eyes went to the desk, but to his credit he didn't bother lying. "I'm no saint, Riker. Things around here have gotten tough. I've done what I needed to in order to get by."

"But selling drugs?"

Luke didn't answer for a long moment. "Is this going to be a problem for you? Are you some kind of narc now?"

"No. But I'm not going to pretend it's not happening either. Whatever you're mixed up in, I might be able to help you get out of it. I owe you that much."

Luke scratched at his beard, then looked back up at his old friend. "That kid you shoved into the dirt? His name is Randy Howard. He spent the night in jail, but he's out this morning."

Riker's face betrayed no expression. "You bail him out?"

"No. They dropped the charges."

"Why would they do that?"

Luke shrugged. "Point is, he stopped by here after he got out. He told me the story."

"Did he tell you he pulled a gun on me?"

"Guess he might have left out some details," Luke said with a smile.

"Are you his boss?"

Luke considered that a moment. "No. More like his co-worker."

Riker frowned. He didn't much like where this was headed. "I'm going to say it plain. Coach changed my life. For better or worse, I wouldn't be the man I am today if not for him."

"No argument there." Luke shifted in his seat.

"Megan told me Coach was fighting the drug problem. Sounds like he may have been getting somewhere, too. I'm starting to think maybe his death wasn't a random carjacking. You know anything about that?"

The uneasy expression on Luke's face dissolved into anger. He answered through gritted teeth. "You're really going to ask me that? You know I loved that man as much as you did. I wouldn't have hurt him. Not ever."

Riker looked at Luke for a long moment. He was pretty good at discerning when someone was lying, and Luke seemed to be telling the truth. And yet, Riker had been fooled before. "So you wouldn't hurt him, but you're part of the very problem he was trying to clean up."

"Things in Kingsport are complicated."

Riker leaned forward. "I'm going to try to finish what Coach started. I owe him that."

Luke's eyes were flashing with anger when he looked at Riker again. "You're just going to sweep in and solve all our problems, is that it?"

"Not all of them," Riker said flatly. "I just need to understand what happened to Coach. His killer is walking around out there, and I can't sleep easy while that's the case."

"Matt, Coach Kane isn't the only person you owe a debt of gratitude."

Riker didn't answer, though he felt a wave of memories wash over him again. *A blood stain. A broken plate on the floor. Johnny Cash skipping on the record player.*

"When you needed help, I was there," Luke continued. "I didn't ask questions. I just trusted my friend and did what needed to be done."

"And I'm grateful for it," Riker said.

"Well, I'm calling in that chip now. Go to the wake and the funeral. Pay your respects. Then go home. What's going on in Kingsport doesn't concern you."

Riker met his friend's eyes. "I'm sorry. I can't do that. That's not how I'm wired."

Luke's expression hardened. "Then we're done here. See yourself out."

A twinge of regret prickled Riker's skin. Here was his oldest friend asking him for a favor that was definitely owed, and Riker was saying no. He wished Luke had asked him for something else. *Anything* else. He would have done it without question. But this...this would mean betraying both Coach's memory and his own code of honor.

He stood up and made his way to the door. As he was reaching for the handle, Luke spoke again.

"Matt, I'm going to ask you one more time. Please. Leave this alone."

"I'm sorry, Luke. You have my answer." He pulled open the door and left the office.

Riker headed west down Main Street, crossing in front of the window of Dewitt Construction. He kept his eyes in front of him, but he felt Luke's cold stare on his back.

He circled the block, making his way around to Grady's Coffee. He walked inside, ordered a tall black coffee, and took a seat near the window—a seat that just so happened to give him a clear view of the front door to Dewitt Construction. The only other exit to the building led to a small alley, and Riker knew it was rarely used; at least it had been in the old days. When Luke left, Riker would see him go, and he'd be able to follow him. As much as he hated to admit it, his old friend was likely his key to understanding the criminal enterprises going on in Kingsport.

As he watched, a bit of sadness crept up in Riker. His oldest friend was now in the drug game. If things had gone differently Riker's senior year of high school—if he'd stayed in Kingsport or gone to college and then come back home—maybe things would have worked out differently for Luke. Maybe all he'd needed was one friend to help nudge him off the dark path he'd taken.

Riker pushed such thoughts away. Playing out the possibilities of what might have been was a sure path to misery. Riker had spent plenty of time traveling that road, and he now did everything he could to avoid it. Besides, Luke was a smart, capable person. The choices he'd made were his own.

"Matthew Riker?"

The voice came from behind Riker, and he instinctively cursed himself for not watching his own six. A rookie mistake he wouldn't usually make.

He swiveled around and stared blankly at the older man behind him.

The man looked to be in his late sixties. He was nearly bald, and the little hair he did have was shock white. He stood about five-ten and he was so thin that he looked like a stiff wind might blow him over.

Then Riker recognized the man, and he broke out in a smile. "Doctor Hanson?"

"You remember me! I'm impressed."

"How could I forget?" Riker shook his head, surprised it had taken him even a few seconds to recognize the doctor. Hanson had treated him for every childhood ailment he'd had as well as given him the annual sports physicals required for wrestling.

"I take it you're in town for the funeral?"

"Yes."

Doctor Hanson shook his head. "Sad what happened. Coach Kane touched a lot of lives in this town." He gestured to the seat across the table from Riker. "Do you mind if I sit? I'd love to hear what you've been up to these many years."

Something out the window caught the corner of Riker's eye. He saw Luke step out of the door and head to his car, hands jammed into his pockets. Riker's heart sped up as he watched his friend disappear from his line of sight.

It wasn't too late. He could have made some quick excuse and went after Luke. But he'd have to hurry and his chances of being caught were high. He turned back to Doctor Hanson, a man who knew just about everyone in town. Perhaps the source of information he'd been looking for was standing right in front of him.

"Sure, Doctor. Have a seat. Let's talk."

6

MEGAN TOOK a sip from her coffee mug without looking up from the paper she was grading. When the room temperature liquid hit her lips, she grimaced.

"Okay, girl," she muttered to herself. "Time for a break."

She stood up, grabbed her coffee mug, and headed out into the empty hallways of Kingsport High School. Though this was technically called her free period, it was usually anything but free. She spent the hour grading papers and prepping for the next class. Like every other public school teacher she knew, she was facing a less than ideal student-to-teacher ratio and found herself working late into the evening most nights, even on the days she wasn't coaching the debate club or the volleyball team. But unlike some of her colleagues, Megan truly loved the work.

She'd stumbled into teaching, picking the major in college almost on a whim when most of her energy had been focused on softball. But whether it was happenstance or fate, she'd quickly realized that working with kids was her true calling. She felt truly privileged to spend time with young people at such a pivotal stage in their lives. A few of her coworkers told her that was just the overly sunny outlook of youth and it would fade with time. But six years in, she still felt the same way.

The sound of her boot heels clicked on the linoleum floor as she made her way to the teachers' lounge, and her mind wandered back to earlier that day when Matt had stood in front of her class and awkwardly answered their questions. She smiled at the mental image of her Navy SEAL cousin squirming. He could face enemy soldiers, but somehow a room full of teenagers was his undoing. She let out a soft chuckle and reminded herself to give him a hard time about it that evening.

She had to admit, it felt pretty good having him back in town, even though the reason for his visit was heartbreaking. For years, she'd blindly sent her Thursday emails off into the ether, never expecting them to be answered or even read. She'd once considered adding a read-receipt to her messages so that she would receive a notification when the email was opened. She'd ultimately decided against it, knowing that if Matt was reading the emails and not responding, he must have his reasons.

But here he was, back in Kingsport. It was surprising how quickly they'd reconnected. After all, she'd just been a kid when he'd left town. But their conversation had been comfortable and easy the previous night, the family connection strong enough to overcome their years apart, and she was very glad.

As Megan rounded a corner to the hallway that led to the teachers' lounge, a loud voice stopped her in her tracks.

"You'd better keep that name out of your mouth!"

Megan stared in disbelief for a moment, not just at the volume of the words, but the person who was speaking them.

David Underwood was only a few inches from Blake Mullins, and his face was beet red as he shouted at the other boy. Both of them had their hands balled into fists. Megan had been at this job long enough to know when a fight was about to break out.

"Aren't you two supposed to be in class?" she asked, marching briskly forward.

Neither of them answered. Their eyes were locked and both looked ready to throw a punch at any moment.

"Hey, I asked a question."

They stared at each other for another moment, then David broke eye contact and looked at Megan.

"Sorry, Ms. Carter. I have a pass." He fished a piece of paper out of his pocket and handed it to her.

She quickly read it and frowned. "This is a pass for you to go to the library. I don't see anything here about you being allowed to yell in the hallway."

Blake let out a laugh.

"And how about you? You have a pass, Blake?"

His smile faded, and he shook his head.

"Where are you supposed to be?"

"Chemistry."

She raised an eyebrow. "Then I suggest you get there fast."

He gave David one last angry look, then turned and disappeared down the hallway. Megan watched him go.

Blake Mullins was the kind of kid she would have expected to find wandering the halls and picking fights during class. He was a junior, and his grades were somewhere between below average and horrible. This semester it seemed he was absent more days than he was in class. As much as she hated to admit it to herself, she fully expected Blake to drop out sometime in the next six months. She just hoped he'd find his way and not disappear into the prison system, though that outcome wouldn't exactly surprise her.

David, on the other hand, was not someone she'd expect to find fighting in the halls. He worked hard, was always polite, and managed to pull down top grades while being one of the best wrestlers in school. He started to walk away, but Megan held up a hand.

"Wait. You want to tell me what this was about?"

"Not really," he said.

"Okay. Fair enough. Thing is, you were yelling, which makes me think you wanted someone besides Blake to hear."

His eyes were on the floor. "No. He just made me so mad. I was minding my own business and he walked by. Started talking crap."

"Crap?"

"About Coach Kane."

With that, everything fell into place for Megan. David had been more distant than usual since Coach's death. And Blake...again, she hated to think poorly of any student, but there was a good chance that Blake was involved in the very drug problem that Coach had been fighting to solve.

"I'm sorry to hear that," she said. "I guess he didn't know Coach Kane very well. I can't imagine anyone who knew the man having anything negative to say about him. He was a good man."

"Yes, he was." David's voice was hollow.

"And nothing can change the man he was. Certainly not some crap Blake Mullins said in the hallway to tick you off."

A slight smile touched the corner of David's lips. "Yeah, I guess not. You going to be at the wake tonight?"

"Yes. I'll be there."

"I'm not looking forward to it."

"Me neither. But it will give us the chance to say goodbye and pay our respects."

David nodded. For a moment, it seemed like he was going to walk away, but then he spoke again. "Do you think it was worth it, Ms. Carter? What he did? Standing up to the drug dealers?"

"That's a tough question. I wish he wasn't dead. I wish he was standing right here with us now. But I'm not going to say he was wrong to do what he did. He stood up for what's right, and that's never the wrong thing to do."

David sighed. "That's what I thought. I agree on both counts. Maybe it's time for me to do the same. Thanks, Ms. Carter."

He turned and headed toward the library. Megan watched him go, wondering if she'd said the right thing. His parting words troubled her. She hoped the young man was all right, and that he wasn't planning to do anything stupid.

7

MOMENTS AFTER DOC Hanson took a seat a young barista placed a cup of coffee in front of him.

"Thanks, Tim. Did you put two sugars in it?"

The young man laughed. "I hope I can get your order right, Doc. It's the same every time you come in here."

"Sorry, I always like to double-check."

"Maybe someday you will trust me."

Tim placed a spoon next to the cup of coffee and moved back into his position behind the counter.

"Looks like you are every bit of a fixture in this town as you were twenty years ago," Riker observed.

Doc smiled. "More than ever. The kids that I used to take care of have kids of their own now. I'm two generations of this town's history."

"Are you getting close to hanging up the spurs?"

Doc's face soured, "I'm still a long way from retirement." He puffed his chest out a bit. "I'm old, but there is still a lot of life in me."

"Sorry Doc, I didn't mean any offense. I guess I've never been that good at interacting with people."

"I don't think that's true at all. I still remember the first time we met. You were at the ice cream parlor with your mom. I was the new doctor in town back then. I didn't know anything about your family, or anyone in town for that matter. Your mom was at the counter paying for an ice cream cone that you held in your hand. She realized that she didn't have enough money with her. She was flustered and didn't know what to do. Little Matthew Riker handed the cone back to the attendant. You told him that you were worried about cavities and could not take the ice cream. I still remember the look on your mother's face. It was a mixture of pride and sorrow. She knew that you were a good kid at heart. Willing to sacrifice to protect other people." Doc took a sip of his coffee and set it back on the table with a smile.

"You forgot to tell the end of that story. A young doctor stepped forward and paid for the cone. You said that you were the new doctor in town and that you gave permission for an occasional cone of ice cream. In fact, you said that it was doctor's orders when you handed me the cone." Riker sipped his own coffee. "My mom retold that one often over the years."

"Those were simpler times. It was easy to know what the right thing to do was."

"For you and me both, Doc."

"Your mother was a good woman. It's a shame what happened to all of you."

Riker looked down at his lap for a moment. "It feels like all of that stayed with this town. If you don't mind, I'd like to move on from that topic."

"Of course." Doc paused for a moment. "Where are you staying?"

"With my cousin Megan."

"That's great. There's nothing more important than family. Will you be in town long?"

"I'm not sure. I was going to leave after the funeral, but I may stick around for a little while."

"Why's that?"

"Coach Kane meant a lot to me. He meant a lot to this town. The way he died doesn't sit right with me. I'd like to make sure it doesn't happen to anyone else."

"Be careful, Matt. There is a bad element in this town now. I don't want to see you end up like Coach Kane."

"I was actually hoping to talk to you about that."

Doc's eyes widened and he set his coffee down on the table. "Me? Why?"

"You know the people of this town better than anyone. What can you tell me about Gabe Sullivan?"

"That's a sad tale, if I've ever heard one." The doctor shook his head. "I gave him his annual physical in January, blood work and everything. He was clean then. Six months later, he was dead. My heart goes out to his parents. To be honest, they're not doing very well."

"I heard that Coach Kane was looking into who his dealer was."

Doc nodded. "That was Oscar Kane. He charged head-first into situations, trying to right any wrongs he saw. He had a big heart."

"And how about you? Any thoughts on what might have happened to Coach? Was he asking too many questions to the wrong people?"

Doc shifted in his seat, clearly uncomfortable about the direction the conversation was taking. "Oscar turned over every stone in his investigation, including speaking with Gabe's doctor."

"Oh? And what did you tell him?"

"The same thing I'm telling you. But it's what he told me that might be of interest. He implied that he had a source with inside knowledge of the drug operation who was willing to share information with him."

"Who was it?"

"He didn't say and I didn't ask. I'm not a detective, and I'm smart enough to know I can't change the world. I try to stick to making a difference in small ways. Helping my patients is enough for me."

"I take it you've seen the impact of the drug problem more than most."

"Indeed. I remember about ten years ago when I saw my first overdose. I thought it was an isolated incident, but it turns out it wasn't. There have been many since then. More and more people came in with opioid issues. Some were trying to get prescriptions. Others were looking for help with withdrawal. I did what I could to help them kick the addiction. None of it mattered. I have seen the same men and women dozens of times. I hate to say it, but it's more than I can handle."

"Doc, it sounds like you've given up."

He shook his head. "I'm not going to stop fighting. I've just become a realist about it. I know that the police feel the same way. The problem is just too big."

"Sometimes a fresh perspective can make the difference. I have some experience dealing with bad people, and I think I might be able to help here." Riker paused as a car pulled up to Luke's building across the street. It was a large black SUV with tinted windows. Two men in tailored suits stepped out. Both checked the area and then went into the building. One of the men had a tattoo that flowed up from the collar of his shirt and wrapped around his neck.

Doc turned to see what Riker was looking at. "Did you

find yourself at this coffee shop by chance or are you playing detective?"

"I was just visiting an old friend."

"Luke Dewitt? He is an old friend, isn't he? Have you had a chance to catch up with him?"

"A bit. We still have things to discuss. I'm surprised that you know where Luke's office is. Are you two friends?"

"He and the men on his construction team are frequent patients. I've patched them up a lot over the years, everything from puncture wounds to crushed hands."

"Does he seem okay?"

"What do you mean?"

"I think you know exactly what I mean."

"All I know is that life is complicated and Luke is a good guy at heart. When the school wanted to put in tennis courts, Luke did the job at cost. He helps out in the ways that he can."

"Have you considered that guilt may be the driving force behind his good deeds?"

"Does it matter? A good deed is a good deed."

"Yeah Doc, it matters a lot. I have dealt with some truly evil men. They all found a way to justify the things they did. But they still made the choice to hurt others for their own gain. That 'complicated world' stuff is always a bullshit excuse for them to do what they knew was wrong."

"That is a very simple way to view the world."

"What can I say? I'm a very simple guy."

Riker watched as the two men in suits came out of the office across the street. When they exited the building each man checked their blind spots. They did it on instinct, and Riker knew how much training it took to make that level of caution happen automatically.

Riker made a show of checking his watch. "I didn't realize what time it was. I've got to go meet up with Megan."

The doctor gave him a long look. "If you're serious about following up on this, I would investigate who Oscar's source was. If you find that person, maybe you'll find the information that got Oscar killed. And that could lead to who killed him."

The men across the street were already getting into their car. Riker couldn't see the plates from his angle.

"I appreciate that, Doc. Maybe we can catch up later, but I really need to go."

"It was good to see you, Matt."

"You too, Doc."

Riker headed out the door in pursuit of the men from the office.

8

Riker stepped out of the coffee shop, and the humidity of the early afternoon hit him in the face like a wet towel. The sun was high overhead, and it beat down on him with surprising intensity. He'd forgotten how sometimes even October afternoons in Iowa could feel just as punishing.

He strolled casually up the sidewalk, headed in the same general direction as the men in the tailored suits. The men reached their SUV and continued past it on foot. Apparently they had business with someone besides Luke.

As he walked, Riker considered what Doc Hanson had told him about the growing opioid problem. Riker had read plenty of articles and seen numerous news stories about the opioid epidemic in recent years. About how it was tearing communities apart, particularly poorer, rural communities. He'd read reports of cops and paramedics who carried Naloxone injections and regularly had to use them on overdosing citizens, sometimes multiple times on the same day.

Was that what was happening here? Was Kingsport just another victim of the opioid epidemic like so many other small towns in the United States? Had the world really changed this much over the past six years while he'd been living on his small, isolated farm?

And if so, what could he possibly hope to do against such a large-scale problem? Some of the best minds in the country had tried their hand at ending the crisis, and so far all of them had been unsuccessful. What chance did Riker have?

He didn't know. But he did know that Coach Kane had been trying to fight the problem. The Coach Kane he remembered was a practical man who looked at the world in realistic terms. He wasn't the type to go tilting at windmills. That led Riker to believe there must have been an angle he thought he could work. A loose thread to pull on that might improve the situation, at least here in Kingsport. Kane had died without completing the task, so now it was up to Riker to find the end of the thread and do a little pulling of his own.

Up ahead, the men were walking with long easy strides, watching their perimeters but not really expecting any trouble. They strode through town like they owned the place. Riker's hands clenched into fists at the sight, and he was surprised at the sudden anger he felt. Apparently he was still a little possessive about his hometown.

The men were nearly a full block ahead of Riker, and he kept pace, maintaining the distance between them. In his mind's eye, he inspected the map of downtown Kingsport as he best remembered it, visualizing each shop that they passed. After another half-block, they turned and walked into one of the establishments. It was a flower shop, or it had been in Riker's day.

He hesitated for a moment, considering his next move. His best bet would be to find a place to observe inconspicuously. Then he could either follow them when they left the shop or head into the shop and question whoever was inside. Moving a bit closer, he scanned the area. Unfortunately, there was no coffee shop across from the flower shop. But there was a jewelry store. He could duck inside, play the nervous boyfriend looking for a gift, and keep one eye on the window. It wasn't perfect, but it would work for his purposes.

When he reached the corner, he stepped off the sidewalk and into the crosswalk. He was only two steps into the street when a flash of sunlight off metal caught the corner of a car, along with the throaty roar of a V-8 engine. His head swiveled to the left, and he saw a pickup truck careening toward him. His body reacted without the need for conscious thought, leaping back onto the sidewalk.

The driver angled the wheels toward Riker, but Riker was still in motion, scrambling backward until a street lamp was between him and the truck. The truck's front wheel hopped the curb, but the driver angled it back to the road and stepped on the gas, sending the truck racing into the distance.

Riker's heart raced as his mind sifted through the details of what had just happened, connecting dots and drawing conclusions for him to consider. The truck had been a recent model. Iowa plates. The driver had been wearing a flannel shirt, not a suit and tie like the men Riker had been following. The way he'd angled the vehicle onto the curb left no doubt that he'd purposefully been trying to hit Riker. And, assuming the driver wasn't just out joyriding trying to take out random pedestrians, that indicated there was probably another person watching Riker, someone who'd called in the truck at the moment Riker was preparing to cross the street.

He scanned his surroundings, looking for possible

suspects. What he saw made him grimace and curse himself for having been so focused on the men he was following that he'd missed the clear signs all around him.

A man in a John Deer baseball cap, leaned casually against a car, cell phone to his ear. Two other men chatting on the sidewalk across the street. All three of them carefully not looking at Riker, a man who'd almost just been run down by a pickup truck. All three wore jeans, work boots, and T-shirts. Was it possible that these were Luke's guys? Had his old friend sent someone to hit him with a truck?

Riker glanced at the flower shop one more time. The men were still inside, which meant he had a decision to make. Keep watching for the men in suits or find out more about the men watching him? After a moment, he made his decision and started walking.

He turned the first corner he came to, and then stopped. Ten seconds later, the men who'd been chatting on the sidewalk rounded the corner as well. They froze when they spotted Riker, and their hands went to their waists.

Riker gritted his teeth. He really didn't want to fight these men, not while he was still trying to figure out who they were and why they were after him. Kicking their asses wouldn't win him any friends, and he might need friends in the coming days. Instead, he returned his mind's eye to the map of the downtown area. It only took him a moment to locate a spot that would work. Once he had it in mind, he took off running.

He didn't bother looking back as he headed up the street. He didn't have to--the men would be following him, running as fast as their heavy work boots allowed. Pumping his arms, he pushed himself farther down the block until he spotted what he was looking for--an alley between a pair of three-story brick buildings.

As he ducked into the alley, he smiled. An eight-foot-tall wooden fence still stood at the end of the alley, blocking it from the next street over. He thought back to the previous night as he charged forward. This fence was taller than the chain-link one he'd vaulted over, but the daylight and clear path gave him greater confidence.

As he reached the end of the alley, he heard the breathless voices of his pursuers. He leaped into the air and planted his left foot against the brick wall, pushing off hard and sending him higher. He grabbed the top of the fence with both hands and swung his legs over.

He landed cleanly on the other side and jogged out onto the street. His pursuers would either have to climb the fence or circle around the block. Either way, he'd bought himself some valuable time.

As he was trotting back toward the flower shop, a female voice called to him.

"Riker!"

He turned and spotted a uniformed woman standing in the doorway of a small shop. After a moment, he recognized her as Officer Alvarez, the woman who'd arrested the drug dealer the previous night.

With a reluctant glance toward the cross street that would lead him back to the flower shop, he paused and turned toward the police officer. "Officer Alvarez. Good afternoon."

"Same to you." She looked him up and down. "You okay? You seem a little out of breath."

"Fine. Just out for a little jog."

"Okay." She looked him up and down again, taking in his jeans and T-shirt. "I'm glad I ran into you. I wanted to talk about last night."

Riker glanced toward the corner one more time, then

pushed it out of his mind. If she wanted to have this conversation, he was more than willing. "Yes, let's talk about last night." He heard the anger in his voice, and he didn't bother trying to hide it. "I understand the drug dealer is already back on the streets."

Alvarez stared at him for a long moment, her face unreadable. "That's correct."

"You wanna explain that one to me?"

"Not that it's any of your business, but we didn't exactly have a lot of evidence. A gun and some drugs that he claimed were yours, not his. In the end, it's your word against his. Add to that the fact that he was physically assaulted by a former Navy SEAL, and Chief Myers felt it wasn't worth the legal exposure. We dropped the charges."

Riker's eyes narrowed. "Are you kidding? He pulled a gun on me."

"Was he pointing a gun at you when you chased him through the park and tackled him to the ground?"

"No. But it was a shove, not a tackle."

Alvarez cracked a smile at that. "Look, I know it's hard to swallow. That's part of life in law enforcement. You don't always get the bad guy. And sometimes you're the one who sets him free. You just hope that in the balance of things you are making the town a safer place."

"Quite the system you have here."

"It's not perfect, but it's the one we've got." She paused. "Actually, that's what I wanted to talk to you about."

"Yeah?"

"I got to thinking about it, and you were right. We should be doing more about the drug problem in Grant Park. I asked Chief Myers if he could assign somebody to patrol the area at night. At least drive past every hour or so to keep the dealers on their toes."

"What did he say to that?"

Alvarez shrugged. "He said it wasn't the worst idea he's ever heard. Next week's schedule comes out Friday, so I guess we'll find out then how seriously he took the suggestion."

The officer's face was tough to read, but she looked sincere to Riker. He got the sense that she took her job seriously. That was the kind of ally Riker needed. And if the last ten minutes were any indication, he was going to need all the allies he could get. He wasn't sure that he trusted Officer Alvarez completely, but he trusted her intentions. For now, that would have to be enough.

"Thanks, Officer. I appreciate you letting me know."

She nodded. "Stay out of trouble, Riker."

"No promises, but I'll do my best."

With that, Riker headed up the sidewalk and back toward Main Street. When he reached it, he paused and looked in both directions.

There was no sign of the men who'd chased him into the alley. But there was also no sign of the men in the tailored suits. The SUV with the tinted windows was gone.

9

Megan walked in the door and put her bag down. She stepped into the kitchen where Riker was getting a snack.

"Hey Megan, how was school?"

"Good, but we need to get ready for the wake."

"I am ready."

Megan stopped and took a closer look at Riker. "I mean we need to get changed."

Riker looked down at his clothes. He was wearing black dress shoes, his best pair of jeans and a shirt with a collar. "I'm already changed."

Megan slapped the palm of her hand to her forehead. "Let me guess, those are your 'nice jeans'."

"Yeah. No rips or bullet holes."

Megan gave him a skeptical glance. "No bullet holes?"

"These are the best clothes that I have. I just found out about the funeral and drove straight here. Shopping wasn't on my list of things to do."

"It is now. You said you wanted to honor Coach Kane. I

think you should start by showing a little respect at the wake."

Forty minutes later the two walked into a locally opened clothing store on Main Street. A bell chimed when they entered and a young woman in a form-fitting dress greeted them. She looked to be in her early twenties and had long sandy blonde hair with light highlights.

"Good to see you Megan. Who's this handsome fellow?"

"Hey Grace, this is my cousin Matthew. We are headed to Coach Kane's wake and we need some dress clothes. Shirt, tie and some slacks."

Riker glanced around the small store, feeling like a child who'd been dragged out to buy school clothes at the end of the summer Women's clothing lined one wall and men's clothing lined the other. The faint smell of leather came from the dress shoes next to the door.

"You came to the right place," the woman said with a smile. "I'll grab some things for you to try on."

"Thanks, Grace, you're the best."

Riker gave a nod to Grace and she smiled back with a wink. Riker couldn't help but notice the way her outfit hugged the curves of her body.

Once Grace was out of earshot Megan nudged Riker with her elbow. "I think she might be a little young for you."

Riker raised an eyebrow, "I agree, I have no intentions towards Grace, aside from purchasing clothes."

"You sure, it seems like there could be some intentions coming from both parties."

A slight red tone touched Riker's cheeks. "I was just being friendly. Besides, I'm sort of involved with a woman that I met a little while back."

Megan's smile grew a little bigger. "Do tell. Is it serious?"

Riker's smile faded a bit. "We both felt something

special, but the timing wasn't right. We met under some intense circumstances and both of us had some things we needed to deal with."

"There's always going to be excuses to put things off, but if you like this woman you should go for it."

"You're wise beyond your years. I really hope that our story isn't over yet."

"I am wise beyond my years," Megan replied. "Speaking of wise, that was something in the classroom today. You always look for weapons everywhere you go?"

He shrugged. "I guess it's habit at this point. But it's not difficult. Plenty of things can be weapons."

"Yeah, like what?"

He nodded toward a nearby rack of belts. "Those, for one. Especially the ones with the bigger buckles. You swing that hard enough, and you'll be surprised at what it can do."

"Huh. What else?"

Riker thought a moment. "Can I see your car keys?"

She gave him an odd look, then pulled her keys out of her back pocket.

"You keep your keys in your back pocket?" he asked with a laugh.

"When they start making women's pants with appropriately sized pockets, I'll carry them elsewhere." She tossed him the keys.

He gripped the keyring in his hand, letting the keys protrude between his fingers. "See? Not as good as a knife, but if you punch someone with this, especially if your adrenaline is flowing, you can do some real damage." He tossed the keys back to her.

She caught them and shook her head. "You live a very strange life, Mr. Riker."

Riker caught motion out of his peripheral vision. He

turned in time to see a small girl pulling on a dress. The child, who couldn't have been more than four years old, pulled harder on the dress, tipping the display stand.

Riker sprinted, quickly crossing the twelve feet between him and the girl. His hand closed around the metal rack just before it crashed down onto the girl's head. She froze, a guilty expression on her face, with the dress still clutched in her hand. Riker returned the clothing stand to its proper position as the child ran off with the dress.

She reached one of the changing room doors and yelled, "Mommy, mommy, I got you another dress to try on."

Megan stared at Riker. "Wow, nice reflexes. You totally saved that girl."

"Only from the most minor of injuries." Riker shook his head. "I need to start charging for that."

"What, saving kids? Is that something you do often?"

Riker smiled. "Not really, forget I said anything."

"Uh, I don't think so. You can't mention saving a kid and then not tell the story."

Riker hesitated. He knew that he shouldn't discuss Li, the girl he had saved in New York, but there was something about Megan that made him want to open up.

"There was a girl who was separated from her parents. I helped her get back to them."

Megan was silent for a moment. Her mind worked at filling in the details that Riker had left out. "I'm guessing that this wasn't just a girl lost in a store."

"No, it was a little more complicated than that. When I was helping her I really didn't think about why I was doing it. I mean I knew it was the right thing to do, so I just did it, but now I've had a little time to reflect. She was in danger and I helped her out of it, but I think I was in danger too and she helped me."

Megan gave her full attention to Riker. "What do you mean?"

"I had forgotten that there are people worth saving. I was in a dark place, alone and distant from everyone. She reminded me that people start off good. I saw an innocent kid who was full of life and wonder. Saving her was the right thing to do. There was no gray area, no questions about future implications. I had spent a lot of time in the gray area and I had forgotten that there is a true north. I think she saved me as much as I saved her."

"It sounds like you really care about her."

Riker gave a nod. "I do."

"Do you get to see her often?"

Riker took a breath, thinking about how to answer the question when he was saved by an interruption.

Grace walked up to them with several shirts and pants in her arms. She looked at the two standing in silence. "I can come back if I'm interrupting."

Riker shook his head. "Not at all. I was just telling an old story. Megan has a gift for getting people to say too much. Let's focus on the task at hand so we can get to the wake."

Grace's eyes widened. "Oh my gosh, I didn't realize that was tonight." She handed the dress slacks to Riker. Then she took a pink and purple shirt out of the stack of clothes. "I think darker colors will be best."

"I agree. Besides, pinks aren't really my style on any occasion."

Riker put on an outfit and came out of the dressing room. Megan looked him over.

"Much better than jeans and a T-shirt."

"I'm glad you approve. Do you think they will let me wear this out of the store?"

"Of course. I already told Grace we are heading straight

to the wake." Megan walked over to Riker and straightened his tie.

"I'm glad you came back to town. It's just a shame it took Coach Kane's death to get you here."

"Sorry. I did have some very valid reasons for not coming back."

"I get it. After the way your dad died, it would have been tough for anyone to come back."

"It wasn't just that. My career demanded a lot of me. In fact it demanded everything. Coming home wasn't an option."

"Well, that sounds like a dumb career."

Riker smiled at her. "I suppose it was sometimes, but it had its moments."

"Yeah? Like what?"

"Some of the guys that I worked with were like brothers to me. We shared a bond that most people will never know. I also served under some exceptional men."

"That's good. I think that if you spend a little time with people in the real world you might like some of them too."

"Maybe, but I think there are some people I will not like." Riker remembered the man who had almost hit him with the truck earlier in the day.

"You need to learn to focus on the good people."

"That may take a little effort. I spent my entire adult life focusing on the bad ones. All the skills that I have are designed to deal with them."

Megan stepped back. "You really think you can clean up the town, don't you?"

"I think that I have the ability to finish what Coach started. I may not succeed, but I definitely have the required skills."

"Have you ever considered that you might want to work

on a new set of skills? I mean, it sounds like your new life as a beekeeper will leave you more time for social events. Practice finding good people. You might even enjoy their company."

"How about I try a little of both. I can tell that you aren't going to let me be a grumpy loner while I'm here, but I would like to finish this mission."

"I'll accept that as a first step."

Riker smiled. "I'm glad that I have your approval. I'm also glad that I'm getting to know my cousin. You certainly have the Riker family spirit."

Riker paid for the clothes and put his old outfit in the bag.

Grace put her card in the bag with the other clothes. "If you need help with anything else my number is on the card."

"Thanks, Grace."

Megan grabbed Riker's arm and pulled him towards the exit. "Come on lover boy, we've got to get to the wake."

As he got into the passenger seat of Megan's car, Riker noticed two men sitting in a truck one block down. As they drove away, the truck started its engine and followed them down the street.

10

St. Mary's Catholic Church was located on the east side of Kingsport, with a nice residential neighborhood on one side and a cemetery on the other. As Megan pulled her car into the crowded parking lot, Riker mused that at least the processional to the burial wouldn't take long. But that was for tomorrow. Tonight was the wake, the time for friends and family to gather and remember the departed.

And based on the number of cars in the parking lot and along the street, there were plenty looking to pay their respects.

Megan shifted the car into park and turned to him. "You ready to do this?"

"I am. Are you?"

Megan bit her bottom lip and thought a moment before answering. "You know, when I started working at the high school, Oscar Kane just seemed like this muscle-bound meathead. I knew what he meant to you and all of his wrestlers, but I didn't think I'd connect with him. What could I have in common with a guy like that? He quickly proved me wrong, of course. At first I thought maybe it was just because I'm related to you, but then I realized he was like that with everyone."

Riker put a hand on Megan's arm. He'd been so concerned with diving into his self-assigned mission of cleaning up Kingsport that he'd almost forgotten that Megan had lost a colleague. She was dealing with her own grief.

"He had a way about him," she continued. "He connected with people. When he talked, you felt like you were the most important person to him. He gave you his full attention in every conversation, you know?"

"Yeah, I do. I'm sorry you lost your friend, Megan."

"Me too." She looked down at the steering wheel. "I believe in what you're trying to do, Matt. Coach would have been proud."

"Thanks."

She drew a deep breath. "Okay. Let's do this."

As they trudged through the parking lot toward the church, Riker tried to remember the last time he'd been to a wake. There hadn't been any sort of ceremony for his fellow operatives who died in QS-4. He'd been to his share of military funerals in his Navy SEALs days. But an actual wake in a church? It had been a long time.

When they reached the door to the church, Riker pulled it open and let Megan enter first. He followed her inside through the entryway and into the back of the church where people were huddled in small groups, talking in hushed tones. A table near the entrance to the sanctuary held a stack of folded paper. The cover showed a picture of Coach Kane with the words "At rest in our Lord" at the bottom.

Riker stifled a chuckle. Whatever it was Coach was doing in the afterlife, he doubted he was resting. He wasn't one for sitting around.

Through the open door to the sanctuary, Riker saw a line of people queued center aisle. And at the front of the church stood Patricia Kane, Coach's wife. A closed coffin was next to her.

Riker watched for a moment while the man at the head of the line walked to the coffin, paused a moment to pay his respects, then shook Patricia's hand and spoke to her.

Riker's eyes went back to the coffin. Perhaps the fact that it was closed was for the best. He didn't want the image in his mind of the strong, lively Coach Kane to be replaced by that of a corpse. Though the shut lid also spoke to the violence of the man's death.

He felt Megan's hand on his arm.

"Should we go up and pay our respects?"

"In a minute," he answered.

A group of men and women was gathered on the left side of the church. Riker recognized a few of them, and realized it was all the high school teachers. One of them spotted Megan and waved her over.

"Go ahead," Riker said. "Be with your friends."

"Thanks." She squeezed his arm again. "I'll be right over there if you need me."

As Megan joined her co-workers, Riker's eyes wandered to those seated in the pews. Most were in small groups, but he noticed one young man sitting alone. It took Riker a moment to recognize the boy—it was one of the wrestlers he'd met at the high school that morning. The kid's face was drawn and pale.

Riker strolled over and took a seat next to the young man. "Hey. Mind if I sit here?"

The young man just shook his head.

Riker held out his hand. "I'm Matt."

"I remember. I'm David."

The two of them shook hands.

"These things can be rough. You holding up okay?"

David shrugged. "I don't know. I didn't think coming here would be a big deal. I already knew he was dead. But being here...knowing he's in that box up there..."

"Yeah, I got it. This makes it all real."

"It's not just that. Coach Kane was so intense, you know? It almost seems like he was more alive than other people. To think of him having to lie still for all eternity, I guess it's messing me up a little."

"You're not alone, man. I feel the same way."

David looked at Riker hard, as if maybe he couldn't believe that a Navy SEAL was experiencing the same deep emotions that he was. "Did you know he coached at Kingsport High for twenty-four years?"

"I did," Riker admitted.

"Can you imagine all the kids whose lives he changed?" David shook his head in amazement. "He used to tell this story about one guy who kept getting in fights his freshman year. Coach recruited him for the wrestling team, and he ended up going to the state championship and even getting a scholarship to the University of Iowa. Coach said he'd never been so proud as when he got the call telling him about the scholarship."

Riker swallowed hard. He knew all too well who that young man had been. It touched him to know that Coach was still talking about him so many years later. "Thanks, David. It was nice talking to you. I'm going to see if I can find the bathroom."

Riker stood up from the pew and headed toward the back of the church, blinking back the tears in his eyes. He was surprised at how hard the kid's story had hit him. He'd always felt a special connection to Coach Kane, but part of him had assumed that to Coach he was just another kid on the wrestling team. To know that he'd had an impact on Coach meant a lot to him.

He left the sanctuary and instead of heading toward the restrooms off to the right, he headed straight for the doors. He still needed to stand in that awful line, see Coach's coffin up close and pay his respects to Patricia, but he needed some fresh air first. He needed to get his head right.

He left the church and headed out into the Iowa dusk.

11

THE CRISP EVENING air chilled Riker's skin, and the gentle breeze dried the streak of salt water on his cheek. He stood on the steps of the church and looked at the red clouds over the horizon.

The world felt very strange to Riker. He was used to constantly being in control of his mind and his body. At times he felt rage or anger, but he used them to his advantage. Now, standing on the steps of an old church, he felt anything but control. It felt as though he was in a boat at sea, tossed in a storm. The waves of his past crashed against him. He questioned the path that he had taken while his compass spun wildly and he no longer knew what direction to go.

In that moment of anger, panic and uncertainty Matthew Riker saw two men standing across the street. He recognized one of them. He was the man who had been driving the truck that tried to hit him.

The man from the truck was of medium build, and he had a cigarette hanging loosely from his lips. Next to him stood a behemoth of a man. He had no definition, but Riker guessed he stood six foot five and crested three hundred pounds. Both wore jeans, T-shirts, and heavy work boots.

They stared at Riker from across the street without any effort to conceal their reconnaissance. The tip of the cigarette glowed for a moment and smoke drifted up from the smaller man's lips. He tipped his hat at Riker.

Riker didn't weigh his options or consider his surroundings. The storm of emotions blowing through his head pushed him forward. He moved one foot in front of the other without any thought or rationality. He didn't look for traffic as he crossed the street, but no one was present except for the two men on the other side. If someone had been there, they would likely have noticed that Riker moved like a force of nature. Something beyond the control of mankind.

As he drew closer, the smaller man spoke. "You're the legendary Matthew Riker? You just look like a dick wearing cheap clothes to me."

Riker continued moving towards him. He didn't say a word or respond to the insult. He just put one foot in front of the other and closed the gap at an even pace.

The man continued talking. "Here's what's going to happen. We are going to have a conversation with my boss. You are going to do whatever he tells you to do. If you give him any shit at all, you will regret it in ways that you can't understand."

Riker stayed silent. He was now only ten feet away from the two men.

"I need to hear that you understand me, boy."

Riker continued to approach in silence.

The smaller man saw the blank depth of Riker's eyes. He seemed to shrink two inches and he took a step back, turning to the big man next to him. "Floyd, this guy doesn't seem to get it. I think you may need to help him understand."

The big guy, Floyd, stood straight up and uncrossed his arms. He started to move towards Riker. Riker didn't seem to notice him. He kept his gaze locked on the smaller man. He continued his silent march. He was only five feet away.

Floyd spoke in a deep voice that matched the size of his body. "Okay tough guy. You asked for it." He drew back a bulbous fist and stepped towards Riker.

Without breaking his stride, Riker shot out a right jab. The punch seemed to explode out of thin air. Floyd didn't even have time to flinch let alone block the punch. The shot landed in the center of Floyd's throat. The big man staggered for a moment and grabbed his throat with both hands. A wheezing sound squeaked out of his mouth, and he dropped to both knees, still holding his throat.

Riker paused for one brief moment. He turned to Floyd and twisted his body, firing off a left uppercut. A crack echoed through the empty street when the fist connected with Floyd's jaw. The big man's eyes rolled back in his head and his body went limp. Riker stepped to the side, and the big man fell like a tree onto the sidewalk. Another crack rang out as his head bounced off the ground.

Riker shifted his focus to the other man. The man had dropped the cigarette from his mouth. His hands fumbled at the back of his waistband, his eyes wide and scared.

The man pulled a pistol from the back of his waistband and swung it in Riker's direction. Riker was already in arm's reach. He grabbed the man's wrist and pulled it down and to the side while he brought his right knee upwards. The knee hit the wrist with enough force to add a new bend to the arm. The man dropped the gun and it clattered on the sidewalk.

The man's scream echoed down the street, and Riker released the wrist. The man held his broken arm close to his chest, tears streaming down the sides of his face. He looked up at Riker and saw that his eyes still held the same blank expression. The injured man was out of tough things to say. He turned and ran up the street.

Riker glanced back at the large man on the ground. A small pool of blood was forming around his head, and his unconscious face was slack. Then Riker turned his gaze at the man running down the street. He took one breath and then gave chase.

Riker's arms pumped and he lengthened his strides. The movement was familiar; he had lost track of the number of men he had chased down on foot. Yet everything about this chase felt different. It felt wrong. Riker's eyes focused on the man fleeing towards the north end of town, but his mind was distant. Memories fogged his thoughts and the image of Patricia Kane's sad, bloodshot eyes as she stood next to her husband's coffin filled his mind. Fear and sadness clawed at him, so he ran harder. He tried to push everything but the task at hand to the bottom of his mind, but those memories refused to go away. Riker cursed aloud and moved his legs faster. He felt his heart pound in his chest.

Up ahead, the man turned a corner, and Riker reminded himself that he needed this man alive. He needed to keep some level of control. As he turned the corner himself, he saw the man cut in between two buildings. Riker pushed on, closing the gap. He cut in between the two buildings and shoved the fleeing man from behind. The man tumbled to the ground, skidding to a stop on the concrete. Then the man looked back toward Riker and smiled.

Pain exploded in Riker's brain and his vision tunneled. He fell forward, landing on one knee. He focused on staying conscious, ignoring the feeling of blood flowing down the back of his neck.

He forced himself to turn, and he saw three men with baseball bats coming at him. He tried to stand but staggered and fell to both knees. One of the men swung a bat hard at his face. Riker got his hands up just in time to deflect the blow. He moved away from his attackers and staggered to his feet. The man on the ground was laughing now, and the sound seemed to be coming from miles away.

"Break his fucking wrist, Harry!" the man on the ground said as he got to his feet. "He owes me that much."

Riker's vision was still blurry, making it difficult to track the man who was coming at him. Harry swung the bat at Riker's wrist, but Riker anticipated the move. He stepped toward the attacker. Closing the distance took the force out of the blow. The handle of the bat smashed painfully into his ribs, but nothing broke. Riker lunged forward, grabbing the man's legs and tackling him to the ground.

Another man brought his bat down hard on Riker's back. A fresh wave of pain shot through Riker's system, but it brought keen awareness back to Riker's cloudy mind. As the man raised the bat like a tomahawk, preparing it to strike again, Riker rolled off the man he had tackled. The bat was already in motion by the time the attacker noticed, and his bat crashed in Harry's chest. Something inside of Harry cracked and he gasped out for air.

Riker tried to get to his feet once again, but as he stood the last man slammed his bat into Riker's shin. The force swept Riker's foot back and searing pain exploded in his leg. He dropped to the ground and immediately felt more blows raining down on his back and sides. The world was growing black.

He silently cursed his own stupidity. He had forgotten

his training and run blindly into a trap. Morrison would rip him a new one for not checking his blind spots, for not being aware of his surroundings. He realized that Morrison would not get that chance since he was about to die here in this dim nameless alley in a town he'd thought he'd left behind forever.

Riker tried to protect his head as the blows continued, but his body moved sluggishly, barely responding to his commands. After everything that he had been through he would meet his end here.

"Stop!" a voice yelled from the end of the alley.

Riker thought that voice sounded familiar, but his cloudy mind couldn't place it. Who it was mattered less than the result of the command. The hits stopped.

Riker heard footsteps approaching, and he turned his head in their direction. It took all the willpower that he had left to open his eyes. The world was out of focus, but he could make out the figure of a man walking towards him, a revolver in one hand. Or was it two men? Hard to tell with the world swimming around him so wildly.

The man knelt down next to Riker. He thumbed back the hammer of the revolver and it clicked into firing position. Riker fought to stay conscious as the cool metal of the barrel pressed against the side of his head.

"Hey, Matt," Luke said. "Sorry that it came to this, but you just weren't hearing me when I asked you to leave. The boss told me that I had to put a bullet in your head to be sure that you would get the message."

Riker blinked hard and his double vision cleared, leaving a single image of his old friend kneeling before him. He tried to speak but coughed instead. He tasted blood in his mouth, and he hoped that it wasn't coming from his lungs.

"Hey, Luke." The words came out in a whisper. "What do you say we talk about this over a beer?"

"Sorry, buddy. I don't think we will be breaking bread any time soon. I am going to do you one last favor. I convinced my boss that I could give you a final warning. If you don't get the message I can't help you anymore."

Luke slowly thumbed the hammer back down and pulled the gun away from Riker's head. "Leave town and forget that you ever came back here. If anyone from our organization sees you again, we will kill you. I can't say that Megan will be safe either."

"Don't threaten Megan," Riker said with all the strength he could muster.

"Buddy, you are not in a position to make demands. Get the hell out of Kingsport."

Luke drew back his fist and punched Riker in the temple. The world went black.

12

Eighteen years earlier

The bus ride home from Garland High School was long and quiet. All told, the tournament had gone well for the wrestlers of Kingsport. They'd had some unexpected wins and even a few true upsets. The reason for the somber atmosphere was the one match they hadn't won. The star of the team, Matthew Riker, had been soundly defeated by his opponent.

Matthew Riker sat near the back of the bus, staring out the window. It was dusk, and soon he wouldn't even be able to see the cornfields rushing past as the bus sped down the state highway. Not that Riker was watching them closely anyway. His mind was elsewhere. Losses had been rare his sophomore year, and almost non-existent his junior year. Now that he was a senior, he'd hoped to go undefeated. He'd known that his dream would be put to the test that afternoon by Chuck Mason.

Mason was the only kid in the state who was being

recruited by colleges as aggressively as Riker, and the fact that the two of them wrestled in the same weight class had made their eventual faceoff inevitable. Riker had prepared for the contest all week, wrestling against guys in bigger weight classes at practice to get used to the strength he knew his opponent possessed. He'd put in long hours and prepared in every way he knew how.

But it hadn't been Chuck Mason who'd defeated him that afternoon. It had been another kid, one he'd never heard of. A farm kid with a crooked smile and massive hands. Riker hadn't been worried going into the match. In fact, most of his attention had been focused on Mason, sitting on the bench across the gym. Riker knew Mason would be watching in preparation for their later match, and he'd intended to put on a show. Then the match began, and everything went to hell.

The country boy caught him off-guard with a lightning-quick takedown, scoring the first points. Then he'd taken top position and unleashed a leg ride that utterly controlled Riker, flipping him onto his back for points and eventually securing a pin. It had been over fast, and Riker had left the mat shell-shocked. Even his win over Mason later in the day hadn't taken away the sting. In some ways, it had made it worse. It had proven he could beat the best. So how had he been taken down by some no-name wrestler he'd never even heard of?

An elbow nudged his side and he looked over at Luke Dewitt, who sat next to him as he always did on these bus rides. Luke had won both his matches that afternoon, and they had been hard-fought battles, as evidenced by his swollen right eye. But to his credit he wasn't gloating about his victories. He understood the gravity of his friend's loss.

"Look, man, that kid got lucky. Don't even worry about it."

Riker didn't answer. He knew that wasn't true. There had been nothing lucky about that leg ride move. It had been pure artistry.

Luke's voice was lower when he spoke again. "If it'll make you feel better, I can ask around. Find out what kind of truck he drives. We can go smash out the tail lights."

Riker couldn't help but grin a little at the notion. "How do you know he drives a truck?"

"Guy like that? It's always a shitty old truck."

"You should know," Riker said with a laugh. "Trucks don't come much shittier than yours."

"Very true. My old Bronco doesn't hold a candle to your ten-speed Schwinn."

"Find a new seat, Luke," a growly voice in front of them said.

The blood drained from Luke's face, and he quickly did as asked. There were few people whom Luke respected enough to immediately obey, but Coach Kane was on the list.

"You okay, Riker?" Coach asked, looking back at him over the seat.

Everyone else in his life called him Matt, but he sort of liked how Coach addressed him by his last name. It made him feel older. Stronger. He was even starting to think of himself as Riker rather than Matt.

"Yes, sir. I'm good."

Coach shot him a crooked smile. "You don't have to lie to me. You take every loss hard, and this one was harder than most."

Riker didn't bother denying it. "I just don't understand

how I let it happen. I was ready for Mason. Beyond ready. I was laser-focused."

"Yeah," Coach agreed. "Maybe that's the problem."

Riker knew Coach was right. He'd looked past that first match, just assuming it would go his way.

"Look, Riker, don't tell these other schmucks I said it, but you're one of the best I've ever coached. Not because of raw talent, though you've got a little. It's your work ethic. Your dedication. That's the unfair advantage you have against all those other jokers on the mat, and this time you let it slip away from you."

"Yeah." Riker looked back out the window. He could barely make out the cornfields in the dim light now.

"One piece of advice. Use this. It's a good lesson. You might be tough, but all it takes is one bad day. You might be able to take out the big threats, but don't look past the smaller ones, or they are the ones that'll get you. You have to be one hundred percent focused every time you step out onto the mat. Understand?"

Riker nodded. "What about that leg ride move? How do I beat it?"

"Practice, and a lot of it," Coach said with a grin. "You have to tuck your foot up so he can't grab it."

"Won't that put me off balance?"

"That's the part that takes practice." Coach sighed. "But not tonight, of course. Practicing the day of a tournament would be strictly against the district's policies. We'll all be heading straight home after this. Won't be a soul in the high school for the rest of the night." He paused, glancing at Riker. "By the way, remind me to put in a maintenance ticket on Monday. The way the latch sticks on the wrestling room door, anyone could walk right in there. Gotta get that taken care of next week. Help me remember, Riker?"

"Yes, sir," Riker said, stifling a grin.

After a few more minutes, Coach moved to another seat to talk to more wrestlers, and Luke slid back onto the bench.

"What was all that about?"

Instead of answering the question, Riker asked one of his own. "How's your leg riding technique?"

Luke raised an eyebrow. "Strong as hell. Why?"

"I need practice."

When they got back to the high school, they got into Luke's truck and circled the neighborhood until all the cars in the parking lot were gone. Then they rolled back into the lot and Luke parked his truck.

"You're damn lucky I feel sorry for you," Luke said as he got out of the truck. "I was hoping to meet up with Stacy tonight. I would much rather be rolling around with her than with you."

"Then you should be thanking me," Riker said. "I saved you from an evening of listening to Stacy talk about her college boyfriend."

"Whatever. After ten minutes in the back of my truck, she'll forget all about that loser."

"Ten minutes? You'd be lucky to last thirty seconds."

They reached the exterior door to the wrestling room, and Riker pulled on it. Just as Coach had indicated, the door swung open. Riker inspected the latch for a moment, then pulled off the piece of duct tape that had been placed there. "Guess I can tell Coach he doesn't need to put in a maintenance ticket."

Luke walked over and flipped on the lights while Riker took off his shoes and stepped onto the mat. When everything was in place, he turned to his friend.

"Seriously though man, thanks. I might have to face that kid again, and I want to be ready. I won't be able to sleep until I figure out this counter move. I appreciate you helping me out."

Luke shrugged. "You're probably right about me not having a shot with Stacy anyway. But answer me one question."

"Sure. What is it?"

Luke gave him a serious look, a rarity for him. "Is this really about mastering the counter move and not about you avoiding your old man?"

Riker paused, considering the question. He had to admit that hanging out at the high school gym beat going home to his cramped little house where his dad was surely a quarter bottle in at this point in the evening. That was in the back of his head, as it always was, but he was certain that wasn't the prime motivating factor. The anger inside of him might have had its embers built in the situation at home, but it was that leg ride move that was currently stoking the flames. "Avoiding the old man is just a side benefit. I'm here to wrestle. And I'm not leaving tonight until I get this thing figured out."

Luke took off his jacket and tossed it onto the bleachers. "Okay then. It sounds like we're going to be here for a while. Let's get to work."

13

Riker opened his eyes, and his conscious mind was greeted with pain that seemed to come from every part of his body. He tried to organize his thoughts but a haze had settled over his brain. He was reduced to basic ideas and commands.

He blinked and immediately started to drift towards unconsciousness. He pushed that desire for sleep away and forced his eyes open again. He needed medical attention, and he wasn't going to get it sleeping in an alley. He focused his mind and his will on one thought: get up.

As he struggled to his hands and knees, pain screamed at him from his head, back, ribs, and leg. His body begged him to lie back down and go to sleep. Riker paid no attention to that. Instead he used the wall for support as he got to his feet.

He took one step on his right leg and a blast of pain exploded from this shin. He stumbled, but was able to balance himself with the wall. Looking down, he saw that the lower part of his right pant leg was soaked with blood. He suppressed a shudder at the memory of the bat slamming into his shin. From the pain, he guessed that the leg was broken.

Riker suddenly thought of Morrison, and a small smile curled the corners of his lips. He knew that his old C.O. wouldn't waste a moment pitying him in his current, pathetic condition. He imagined the gruff voice in his head. *I hope this is enough of a lesson to get through that thick head of yours. When I tell you to always be mindful of your surroundings, I mean always.*

Riker silently promised himself that he would never drop his guard again. He took another step. This time when the burst of pain came, he welcomed it. It put a keen edge on his mind and taught its lessons well.

As he reached the end of the alley, he steadied himself against the buildings along the street slowly, making his way back to the street with the church. When he rounded the corner he saw a man standing with a brown paper sack in one hand. Riker figured the man was likely homeless—his clothes were old and it was clearly not lemonade in the sack.

"Holy shit," the man said. "Are you okay?"

"I could use a little help." The words took more effort than Riker had expected, and he felt himself slowly slide to the ground, his back against a brick wall behind him.

After that, time passed in flashes. He vaguely remembered handing the man his phone. There was a car ride, and Megan might have been there. There were bright lights. He spoke to someone, but he couldn't remember who or what was said.

"Matthew, are you still with us?"

Riker opened his eyes and the world came back into focus. He looked around the room, no idea how he'd gotten there. Doc Hanson stood next to the bed he was lying on, shining a light in his eyes. Megan sat anxiously in the corner of the room. The homeless man was there as well.

He drew a deep breath, trying to orient himself. It appeared he was in a doctor's office. Doc Hanson's most likely.

"I'm here," he said. "How long have I been out of it?"

"It's been an hour since you left the wake," Megan answered. "I didn't realize you were missing, and then Donnie called me."

"Donnie?"

"Hey Matt," the homeless man said. "I guess you don't remember the conversation we had on the ride over here."

The name and the face seemed familiar to Riker, but he couldn't quite place it. "Sorry, but no. Everything after the wake is a little foggy."

Doc Hanson put a gentle hand on Riker's shoulder. "Who did this to you?"

Riker smiled. "I just stumbled and bumped my head. I'm clumsy, I guess."

The doctor did not return the smile. "You have a concussion, bruised ribs, a fractured leg, and I put twenty-eight stitches in various lacerations. I'll ask again. Who did this to you?"

"So it's just a fracture on the leg? I was worried that it was a full break." Riker touched the back of his head and felt a row of stitches. "Thanks for patching me up."

"You still aren't answering my question. Do you know who attacked you?"

The answer came from the back of the room. "I think we all know who did this. The same assholes who killed Sam."

Riker stared at Donnie. He looked ten years older than Riker. His body was slouched and his skin was wrinkled from a hard life. Underneath the worn exterior was a familiar face. The pieces of the puzzle started to form a picture in Riker's mind.

"Donnie Wagner? Is that you?"

"Yeah, it's me. We had this conversation in the car on the way over."

Despite his appearance, Donnie Wagner had been a year behind Riker in school. He'd been a wrestler, though not an especially good one. But off the mat, Donnie and his brother Sam had been quite the hell-raisers, causing trouble and getting into fights just about every weekend. Even Riker and Luke hadn't wanted to mess with those two. To see him now, looking so different from the fierce young man he remembered, was disconcerting.

"Sorry my brain was still a little rattled. You look... different than I remember."

Donnie gave a weak laugh. "You mean I look like shit. It's okay. You can say it."

"It's been nearly twenty years. I'm sure we all look a little rougher around the edges." He paused, pushing himself into a sitting position. "Sam died? I'm so sorry to hear it."

"He didn't just die. He was murdered." The bitterness was thick in Donnie's voice. "They did it right in front of me, too. Since then... Well, things have been tough."

"I'm sorry for your loss, Donnie."

The thin man nodded, fighting back tears.

Doc Hanson stepped forward and put a hand on Donnie's shoulder. He turned to Riker. "Why would they attack you? Did you find out who killed Oscar Kane?"

Riker shook his head. "Apparently asking questions was enough for them."

"Then I think we all know what needs to happen."

Megan spoke up. "What do you mean?"

"We need to get you out of town, Matthew. After what

happened to Coach Kane and considering that you were just beaten within an inch of your life, the threat couldn't be any more real. I don't want to see you die."

Donnie reached down and picked up a paper bag, the same one that Riker had seen him drink out of on the street. "He's right, man. You can fight them and die, or let it go and drink."

Megan stared at the two men, her eyes wide with disbelief. "This is bullshit. How can we let these people just get away with it?"

"I know that it is not fair, but what can we do?" Doc asked. "If the police can't stop these guys, how could we?"

"I don't know, but we have to do something. They attacked my cousin. They are sucking the life out of our town. We can't just sit around and do nothing."

Riker smiled at Megan's will and sense of justice. They were cut from the same cloth. It was a different type of bond from what he'd had with his brothers in arms, but it was no less real. He wasn't sure, but he thought this might be how family was supposed to feel.

"I think there is something that we can do." Riker turned to Doctor Hanson. "You told me yourself that Coach may have had an inside source in the drug ring. If we can find that person, they might know the details of what happened to Coach Kane. Then we can make sure justice is done."

The room was silent for a moment. Then Doc spoke.

"Matt, you were just beaten within an inch of your life. What you are talking about is suicide."

"I may have gotten off to a rough start, but I'm a long way from finished with this. Tonight was a reminder for me. I was unfocused and undisciplined. If I'm going to get justice for Coach, I need to remember my training."

"You need to be realistic. You're badly injured. I know that you used to be a soldier, but you are clearly outmatched." Doc glanced toward Donnie, who was staring down into his paper bag now. "You want to tell them what happened to Sam? I know it's difficult, but he needs to hear it."

Donnie swallowed hard, his eyes still on the bag. "Sam and I got it into our heads that we were going to do something about the drug problem. We worked at it for weeks, trying to figure out the structure of the ring, where they kept their stash, all sorts of stuff. Then one night, we had a few beers and decided to take a more direct approach. We decided to burn the whole thing down."

He paused, looking down at his feet.

"We didn't think there'd be so many of them. They overpowered us, tied us up. There was this guy there I'd never seen before. Huge Colombian guy. He bent down and stared at me with these cold, dead eyes, like he was trying to see into my soul. Then he did the same to my brother. The Colombian nodded toward Sam. The guys rolled out this steel drum and shoved Sam inside. They poured gasoline on him and dropped in a lit match. His screams went on for a long while. When they finally stopped, the guys untied me and let me go. It was like they didn't even think I was worthy of a bullet."

"Jesus. I'm so sorry, Donnie."

"So you see, Matt," Doc said, "you can't go after them. No good can come of it."

"I'm truly sorry about what happened to Sam." Riker met the older man's gaze. "And I appreciate the input, Doc, but I didn't ask for a vote."

Donnie looked down at his feet, unable to make eye contact with Riker. Doc stood with his mouth open, unable to believe what he'd just heard. Only Megan was smiling, a proud expression on her face.

Riker stood up on his good leg. Crutches were waiting for him next to the bed. He grabbed them and moved to the supply drawers along the wall of the room.

"What are you doing?" Doc asked.

"I'm going to need some materials to make a good splint."

"You have a fractured leg. You need a cast, and you need to stay off of it for a minimum of six weeks."

"No, that's what I *should* do. Just like I should tuck tail and run. But that's not what I'm going to do. I'm going to rig up a splint for my leg so I can be as mobile as possible. Then I'm going to get to work."

The doctor said nothing. He simply watched as Riker gathered supplies and wrapped a splint around his leg.

Megan helped Riker. She followed his instructions and secured the injured limb.

"You're a fool Matthew," Doc Hanson said. "But at least let me give you something for the pain." He pulled out a small pad and started to scribble a prescription on it.

"If you've got some aspirin I'll take it, but I don't need anything else."

"You can't be serious."

"I've played hurt before, Doc. The pain helps me focus and I can't risk the haze that drugs will put over my mind."

Doc Hanson walked over to a cabinet and pulled out a bottle of aspirin. He tossed it to Riker. "Suit yourself. I hope you'll reconsider. I don't want to bury another good man."

"Thanks for the help Doc, but don't count me out yet. I've been known to beat long odds from time to time."

"Don't get cocky, tough guy," Megan said. "But I do like your attitude."

Riker used the crutches as the two left the office. Just before they walked out the door, a voice called from behind them.

"If you need help let me know," Donnie said from the corner of the room.

Riker looked him in the eyes. "Don't offer if you don't mean it."

Donnie kept eye contact with Riker. "I would have made a move against those bastards a long time ago if I wasn't such a chickenshit. I'm done being scared. I've got nothing left to lose."

Riker gave him a nod. Then he and Megan headed out.

14

RIKER SHOVED the crutch under his armpit and forced himself to his feet with a grunt. He was careful to keep most of his weight on his left side and the rest on his crutch; even still, his fractured leg buzzed with fiery pain.

"You sure I can't change your mind about those pain pills?" Megan asked. "I could call Doc."

"I'm sure." Riker gritted his teeth and hobbled forward. He wanted to keep his head clear tonight. He didn't expect he'd be sleeping anytime soon, but he wanted to lie down in bed, stare up at the ceiling and think about things. Those long, dark hours were when the truth often came to him. Pieces that seemed unrelated in the daylight worked themselves together in his mind, forming a clearer picture.

When he finally reached the door to his bedroom, he turned back to her. "Thanks, Megan. For everything."

She let out a chuckle. "You kidding? I've been trying to get you to visit for years. This is great."

"All the same, I'm sure you didn't imagine having to nurse me back to health when you asked me to visit."

"No, that's just an added bonus." She paused a moment.

"You were serious about what you said at Doc's, weren't you? You're going to keep going? Keep looking for answers?"

Riker turned his head, shooting her a crooked grin. "It'll take more than a couple baseball bats to stop me." Now it was his turn to pause. "It's going to get more dangerous before it's over, Megan. Not less. Maybe you should consider leaving town for a while."

"Maybe you should consider biting me."

"Very mature," he said with a laugh.

"Don't ask me to leave my town, Matt. I'm in this just as much as you are."

"All right. I won't ask again." With that, he hobbled off to the guest room, eased the door shut behind him, and collapsed into bed.

Just as he'd predicted, sleep did not come easily. As he lay still, the sharp pain in his leg dulled into a steady, almost rhythmic throb. His ribs felt a bit worse, reminding him of their injury with each inhale. He let his mind drift, hoping it would find something to catch onto. The item that grew in his thoughts and ultimately took over his brain surprised him—Donnie Wagner.

Riker hadn't known the Wagner boys well, but everyone in school knew better than to mess with them. They took any perceived slight as a welcome excuse for a brawl. Donnie and Sam hadn't been the greatest wrestlers on the team, and in fact, probably should have been cut. But off the mat, they were some of the fiercest fighters in school. The last three years of high school, Riker tried to focus his aggression toward the wrestling team and avoid any outside altercations. The Wagner boys were the complete opposite. They lived to tussle; wrestling was just a way to blow off a little steam when they couldn't find a real fight.

Their wrestling careers, such as they were, came to an

abrupt end after a tournament in Des Moines. A kid had quickly pinned Donnie, and he had made the mistake of whispering some trash talk about Mrs. Wagner into his ear while he had him on the mat. After the match, Donnie and Sam proceeded directly to the nearest janitor's closet where they grabbed two heavy wooden broom handles. They then went straight to the home team's locker room. They beat the trash-talking kid and two of his teammates bloody with those broom handles. After that, they'd turned in their singlets to Coach Kane, walked out of the gym, and hitch-hiked home.

It was difficult to see how that scrappy kid who was always looking for a fight was even the same person as the broken man Riker had spoken with at Doc Hanson's. For a moment, he wondered what could have caused such a change, but he already knew the answer. He thought back to Donnie's story of how his brother had been burned alive. That would probably be enough to break any man.

Riker shifted his position, ignoring the subsequent jolt of pain in his leg. It seemed that the deeper he dug into this, the more people he found who had been hurt. The Wagner brothers. Gabe Sullivan, the boy who'd OD'd. And of course, Coach Kane. He couldn't bring back the people who'd died, but maybe if he proved who killed Coach Kane he could bring about some justice.

The thought was still running through his head when he heard something outside his window. It was a small sound--a twig snapping, maybe--but knew immediately it had been caused by something large. He remembered the half-spoken threat against Megan, and he wished he had his SIG.

He rolled out of bed, grabbing a crutch and getting to his feet, pushing the pain aside. Another noise came from the window, this one louder than the last. Someone was tapping on the glass.

Riker lumbered over, instinctively standing to the side of the window as he pushed the curtain open and looked out. Luke's face glared back at him. Riker's eyes searched the darkness for other figures, maybe men with bats, but there were none. Luke appeared to be alone.

"Open the window."

Luke's words were muddled through the glass, but Riker heard them well enough to understand. He hesitated only a moment before opening the latch and pushing up the window.

"Where are your buddies?" Riker asked. "I was thinking maybe you stopped by for a rematch."

"They're not my buddies. I came to talk. That's all."

Riker shifted his weight a bit, putting it onto his good leg. "You'll have to forgive me if I'm not in a chatty mood. I've had a weird night."

"Yeah? I was part of a gang that jumped my oldest friend. It's been a weird night for me as well."

Riker inspected Luke's face. The only light was coming from the streetlamp behind Luke, and it was difficult to read his expression in the darkness. "Is that why you came here? You feel bad about kicking the shit out of me?"

"Of course I feel bad."

"Well, if it's any consolation, things won't go that way next time."

"I feel bad, but that's not why I'm here. I came to make sure you got the message. That you're leaving town."

"No can do, buddy. I've got a funeral to attend tomorrow."

"Pack up in the morning and leave. Don't spend another day in this town."

Riker looked at his old friend for a long moment before speaking again. “You know, people keep telling me that. Telling me to leave. You want to know why I’m not leaving?”

Luke crossed his arms in front of him. “Cause of some misguided belief that you’re this big hero who’s going to come back and save your poor hometown?”

“No. Because what I’m seeing here doesn’t make sense. Beating me up just for having the audacity to ask a couple questions? Killing Coach? Burning Sam Wagner alive? These are not the moves of small-time drug dealers looking to protect their territory. Something bigger is happening here.”

“That’s not a road you want to walk down,” Luke said, his voice low.

“Coach walked it. I’m starting to think he found some answers. And if he found them, I can find them too. That’s why I’m not leaving. And I won’t until the job is done.”

Luke was quiet for a long moment before he answered. “Matt, what I said about Megan in the alley, it wasn’t a threat. It was a warning. I don’t want anything to happen to her.”

“It won’t. Not while I’m around. And if you’re running with guys who would hurt an innocent woman, you need to take a good hard look at what your life has become.”

“Yeah?” There was anger in Luke’s voice now. “Maybe I should have just run out on my town and my family like you.”

“That’s not what happened, and you know it.”

“No? Seems to me you could have come back. They give you leave, even in the SEALs, right? You had working phones. Or maybe you just thought the people you left behind weren’t worth keeping in your life.”

“So it’s my fault that you’re a damn drug dealer?”

"No. Not your fault. Not your business, either. Go home, Matt. Kingsport doesn't need your help, and neither do I."

"Tell me about your boss, Luke. Tell me who you work for."

"Matt, go home." Luke turned and walked away.

Anger surged through Riker. The answers to so many questions were right there in front of him. Maybe he just needed to ask a little harder. "Don't turn your back on me!"

Luke just kept walking.

Riker let out an angry grunt. If Luke wasn't going to stop on his own, Riker would have to stop him. He turned and hobbled to the door, pushing on through the living room, his teeth pressed together in pain. By the time he opened the front door and looked out, Luke was halfway down the block.

Peering out, Riker could see a line of fences not that different from the one he'd so easily vaulted over earlier that day or the ones he'd hopped near Grant Park the previous night. Even climbing over that fence would be a herculean task in his current condition.

Fists clenched in frustration, Riker watched as his old friend disappeared into the night.

15

RIKER WOKE with a sense of purpose the next morning. He wrapped a tight splint around his shin. A look in the mirror revealed areas of black and blue all over his body. He grabbed four aspirin and headed out to the kitchen.

He was greeted by the smell of coffee and freshly cooked bacon. He was glad to see that Megan was an early riser as well. He put his crutches next to his chair.

"Looks like you survived the night," she said as she put a steaming cup of coffee in front of him.

"Yep, there is still a little life left in me. Thanks for cooking."

"I figured that you could use some sustenance to help the healing process." She set a plate of eggs and bacon next to his coffee. "Do you think you will be okay to make the funeral today?"

"Not an issue. I actually have a lot more than the funeral that I am hoping to attend to today."

Megan raised an eyebrow. "I figured that you would rest up and lick your wounds. I know you tough guys need time to recover from a bruised ego."

"My ego is fine. I wasn't beaten by the guys in the alley; I was beaten by my own mistakes. I was acting careless. Blinded by emotions."

"Huh. I thought that you were beaten by baseball bats."

Riker smiled. "Okay, I was beaten by my own mistakes and baseball bats." He took another sip of coffee.

"What else do you have to do today?"

"I've got to file a police report."

"Really? It seemed like you didn't have any faith in the police. Why the change of heart?"

"No change of heart. I don't think the police are going to do anything."

"Then why file the report?"

"I want to take a look around the station and meet some of the officers."

Megan looked at her cousin. Her eyes narrowed as she put the pieces together. "Do you think they are doing more than just losing the battle against the drug ring?"

"I think that it's a good possibility. The criminal element here seems much stronger than the police in the town. I'm guessing that they have someone on the take. I'd like to know who that is and how deep they are."

"That sounds exciting. I'll drive."

"I've got it. I can work the gas and brake pedals with one good leg. You don't need to involve yourself."

"I'm already involved. I live in this town, my friend was killed, and my students are in danger. Besides, right now I'm tougher than you are."

Riker saw the look of determination in his cousin's face and knew that this battle had already been lost. She really was cut from the same cloth as he was. "Okay, we'll head to the station after we finish up this wonderful breakfast."

The police station would have been easy to miss if you

didn't know the town well. The unassuming brick building nestled between several other nearly identical structures had a small police sign over the main doors, but even that would be easy to miss. When Riker hobbled in on his crutches he noticed that the interior was as nondescript as the exterior. An older, out of shape man sat behind a reception desk. If he had not been wearing a police uniform, this place could have been mistaken for a dental office.

The fluorescent lights made the man behind the desk look pale and sickly. The scent of cigars filled the room.

Riker was standing directly in front of the desk before the man looked up from his paper.

"What can I do for you this fine day?" He did a double take when he saw Riker's condition. Then his eyes lit up as he spotted Megan.

"Megan, you didn't beat this fella up, did you?"

She gave a polite laugh. "What can I say? He got out of line, and I had to show him how to treat a lady."

Riker's glare let them both know that his injuries were still a little too fresh for jokes.

"All kidding aside Ed, this is my cousin, and he was attacked last night. We came in to file a report."

Ed shook his head. "I'm sorry to hear about that. I just don't know what this world is coming to. Officer Alvarez is here. She can take your statement and open up a file."

Riker regarded the elderly police officer. "Ed Peterson. You don't remember me, do you?"

Ed cocked his head and looked closely at Riker. Then his eyes widened. "Matthew Riker. I remember you. It looks like you grew up. I don't think I've seen you since--"

"I remember," Riker said, cutting him off. He didn't like to think about the night when he'd last sat in this police station. "I joined the military right after graduation. I haven't been home since."

The three stood in awkward silence for a moment.

"We'd better get that report filed. Thanks, Ed." Megan walked down the hallway towards the main part of the station, and Riker followed on his crutches.

The hallway led to a large room with four desks in it. Three of the desks were empty. Officer Alvarez sat at the fourth. She looked up from her computer screen when they came into the room.

"Oh my God. What happened to you?"

Riker made his way over to her desk, trying not to grunt with each exhausting step. "That's what I'm here to discuss. I think that drug dealer that I brought in the other night has some buddies who were not too happy about the incident."

"Have a seat. Tell me what happened."

Riker leaned his crutches against the desk and slid into a chair next to her. Megan sat in a chair across the desk. Riker looked around the small station and saw the three of them appeared to be alone.

"Are you the entire police force?"

"It sure feels like I am some days, but no. At the moment, we have two officers in the field, and the chief is in his office." She nodded her head towards an office in the corner with a brass plaque that read Chief Myers.

"I'm guessing that with such a small force everyone is pretty involved."

"Yep, it is a group effort, but the chief really runs the show." She typed a few strokes on her keyboard. "So, are you going to tell me about the attack?"

Riker told his story as matter-of-factly as possible, leaving out most of the details that could help identify the men who'd attacked him. He didn't mention Luke's involvement at all. As he finished his story, he paused, and he put his hand on the desk to steady himself.

Alvarez stopped typing. "Are you okay?"

"I'm fine." He let out a deep breath and shook his head to clear it.

Megan got up from her seat and put a hand on his shoulder. "Are you sure you're all right?"

"I think I just need a glass of water or maybe some soda. Do you have anything?"

"I'll grab you a Sprite." Alvarez got up and went out a door in the back of the room.

As soon as the door closed Riker grabbed the keyboard and turned the screen of the computer to face him.

Megan's eyes widened. "What are you doing?"

"I just wanted to get a peek at the files before she had time to close out of the program."

"You sly dog. I'll keep an eye out. Just hurry. She could be back any moment."

Riker clicked through the software looking for open case files. Each case was listed with a number as the file name. There was no way to tell what each one was without clicking on it and looking at the report inside.

He looked at the first file which was an open hit and run. He closed it out and proceeded to the next file.

"You need more time." Megan stood up and walked towards the door that Alvarez had gone through.

"You think you can stall her?"

"I'm known to be a bit of a chatterbox. I'll just tell her about what a pain you are. That'll buy us a few minutes."

Riker continued going through the files as fast as he could. They appeared to be in chronological order from the newest to the oldest. He clicked through, but nothing helpful caught his eye. Most were about petty crimes like car break-ins. By the time he was a couple weeks back into the files, he noticed there wasn't one on the drug dealer he'd stopped in Grant Park.

He switched his focus from the open files to the closed ones. There were a few drug-related charges, but most of them had been dismissed quickly. No major busts, only small fines or cases dismissed due to insufficient evidence.

Riker started to type Oscar Kane into the search bar, but he heard someone moving around in the corner office and closed the files, restoring the one Alvarez had been working on. The office door opened just as Riker tilted the monitor back to its original position.

Chief Myers was younger than Riker had expected him to be, maybe forty. He looked as if he was in good shape for his age and his uniform was pressed and clean. His eyes locked on Riker, then scanned the room for Alvarez.

"Has someone helped you?" He kept his eyes on Riker and moved his hand to the side of his holster.

Riker put on his friendliest smile. "Yes, Officer Alvarez is helping me. She just stepped out to grab me a beverage. I'm not getting around so well today." Riker put his hand on his crutches.

"You must be Matthew Riker."

"At your service. How did you know who I was?"

"Word spreads fast in a town like this. I heard that you were running around causing a little trouble. Looks like the trouble caught up with you."

"I'd say trouble ran right into me. I was just telling Alvarez all about it."

The door in the back of the room opened and Megan and Alvarez came out chatting about the new school track. When they saw the chief standing there, the conversation stopped.

Alvarez broke through the moment of silence. "I see you've met Chief Myers."

"Not officially." Riker used the desk and chair to push himself to his feet. He extended a hand towards Myers. "Nice to meet you, Chief."

He shook Riker's hand. "You can call me Joe. Only Alvarez needs to call me Chief. You staying in town long?"

"No, I'm really just here to pay my respects to Coach Kane. Once I do that, I'll be on my way."

"He was a good man. He did a lot for this town."

"Have you had any luck finding his killer?"

"We haven't had any major breakthroughs yet, but the case is still open. I'm sorry to say that cases like that usually go unsolved. It appears to be a random act of violence. We might get lucky and have some idiot shoot his mouth off about killing the Coach, but there just isn't much physical evidence."

Riker shook his head. "That's a shame. I'm sure you'll do your best."

"Of course. I just like to be realistic about things."

"I always appreciate a man who is upfront about the way things are."

"Nice meeting you. I'm sure Officer Alvarez will take care of you. I've got to run."

Ten minutes later, Riker and Megan were back in the car, their report filed.

"Well, did the charade pay off?" Megan asked. "Did you find anything useful?"

"Yes. I confirmed that things are even worse than I thought. Chief Myers is working with the criminals."

16

MEGAN DROVE in silence for nearly a minute. Her voice was tense when she spoke, her eyes fixed on the road ahead of her. "You're wrong. Joe Myers can't be working with the criminals. That's insane."

Riker didn't bother replying to that. Megan clearly needed a moment to work through the implications.

"Joe is one of the few people in this town fighting for our safety. He coaches Little League. His son was in my class two years ago, and now he's off studying at Brown. There's no way."

Riker stayed silent, the hint of a smile playing on his lips as he watched his cousin consider this aloud.

"If he were on the take... Lord, the entire law enforcement budget goes through him. He's in charge of hiring, firing, where the police patrol and where they don't." She turned to Riker, anger in her eyes now. "Are you going to say anything?"

"You're figuring it out just fine on your own."

She thought for another moment. "How do you know? That he's working with the criminals, I mean."

"I had my suspicions going in, but a couple things confirmed it for me."

"Such as?"

"He recognized me right away, and not from when I was a kid. His eyes went right to my leg. He recognized me by my injuries, which means he knew about the attack before I reported it."

Megan opened her mouth to speak, but no words came out. She clearly didn't have another explanation for what they'd seen.

"And then there were the files on the computer," Riker continued. "I wasn't able to look very long, but I could see that most of the cases were assigned to Alvarez or one of the other officers. All the drug-related ones I saw were assigned to Chief Myers, and every one of them was marked closed. Most without any charges ever being filed."

"Jesus." Megan let out a weary sigh. "Okay, I'll admit, that's more than a little suspicious."

Riker looked out the window as the car rolled past the high school. It looked empty on this Saturday afternoon, the parking lot deserted but for a single pickup truck parked near the dumpsters. Apparently the wrestling team had canceled their usual Saturday practice due to their coach's upcoming funeral.

"Tell me about Chief Myers," he said.

Megan thought for a moment. "He came to town about ten years ago. Worked on the force until Chief Raynor passed away, then took his place."

"Married?"

"Divorced. One son."

"The kid at Brown. How about the ex-wife? She still in town?"

Megan nodded. "Works at the library." She glanced at

Riker. "You're not going to interrogate that poor woman, are you?"

"No," Riker said, though the thought had crossed his mind. He wouldn't act on it; at least not now. "Here's what's bothering me. A town Kingsport's size, five thousand people or so, there's money to be made in the drug trade. Especially with the opioid crisis in full swing. But enough money to incentivize a police chief to bury every drug case, not to mention a murder? Send your kid to Brown type money?"

"You think there's something bigger going on?"

"I think it's possible." He glanced at the clock on the dashboard. They still had a couple hours before the funeral. "Do you know where Chief Myers lives?"

She shot him a confused look. "About a mile from here. Why?"

"I wouldn't mind taking a look around his house. And I'd prefer to do it when I know he's not there."

Megan shook her head and smiled. "You've been back two days, and you've already got me breaking and entering."

"Correction. I'm breaking and entering. You're waiting in the car."

To her credit, she didn't argue. Two minutes later, she circled the block, pointing out Myer's house to Riker. Then she dropped him off at the end of the block.

Riker approached the house casually, walking down the sidewalk until he reached Chief Myer's home. Like all the other houses on the street, it was a squat, two-story residence that had probably been built in the 1940s. It was well-maintained, and the yard was well-kept, but it was nothing fancy. Nothing that screamed that the owner was on the take from a drug organization. Riker knew that didn't mean anything. He'd seen millionaires living in cheap, one-bedroom apartments. That scenario was even more likely with those who had made their money illegally and were afraid to spend it. Which was exactly why Riker wanted to get inside the house.

He approached the front of the house, intending to walk right up to the porch, but something next to the door made him keep walking. It was one of those digital doorbell systems. The kind with a camera built in.

He cursed softly. For all he knew, Chief Myers could be watching him right now through an app on his phone, wondering why Matthew Riker had gone straight from the police station to his neighborhood. And it wasn't like the chief would need a good look at his face. The way he was hobbling along on his injured leg would be enough for the captain to recognize him.

Still, chances were the chief would need to realize someone had been in his home for him to check his app for suspicious passersby. Riker kept walking until he was out of sight of the doorbell camera. Then he checked to make sure he was alone on the street, and he slipped around the house to the backyard.

His hand was already in his pocket pulling out his bump key before he reached the back door. He had a moment of doubt when he saw the deadbolt--it was a brand he was unfamiliar with and clearly an upgrade over the usual residential fair. Still, he inserted his bump key and gave it a hard rap with the back of his pocket knife. The key turned easily, and Riker was inside a few moments later.

The house practically screamed divorced man in a way that was so obvious that it made Riker shake his head. The fridge was stocked with beer and frozen pizzas. The pile of unwashed dishes in the sink threatened to topple over and send dirty plates crashing to the floor.

Riker made his way through the kitchen and got to work.

He knew he couldn't risk spending a lot of time here, so he needed to move fast. If he found what he was hoping to, it would reveal a lot about the chief of the Kingsport police and exactly how deep he was into the criminal world.

He started in the living room, looking behind the large painting that hung over the mantle. He carefully moved the couch away from the wall far enough to look under it. He checked the mantle for any loose or false bricks, but found none. Then he moved on, heading toward the second story, where he figured the master bedroom would be located.

As he reached the top of the steps, he paused at an open door to his left. A bedroom had been converted into a home office. And there was a laptop sitting closed on the desk in the center of the room.

Riker stared at that laptop long and hard. If Chief Myers had any correspondence or records that might implicate his involvement in the drug trade or in Coach Kane's death, it would likely be on that laptop. He lifted the laptop's lid and dragged his finger across the touchpad. The screen lit up, prompting him to enter the password.

He sighed and closed the laptop. As tempting as it was, Riker knew he needed to leave it alone. He wasn't skilled enough to get into the computer without spending way too long here, and if he took the laptop with him, it would be missed and send Chief Myers into a panic that would quickly lead to him inspecting his door camera footage.

Riker found the master bedroom at the end of the hall and gave it a quick search. Nothing under the bed or behind the dresser. When he opened the door to the walk-in closet, he smiled. A full-length mirror stood on the wall at the end of the closet. Riker approached, running his hand along the edge of the mirror until he found what he was looking for--a small latch. He pressed it, and the mirror swung open, revealing the large wall-safe hidden behind it.

Riker stared at the safe for a long moment. He wouldn't try to crack it--that would take far too long. Simply knowing it was here was enough to give him insight into Chief Myer's worldview. It told him two important things.

First, Chief Myers had something he felt was worth hiding and protecting. Possibly information, but more likely cash. Ill-gotten cash he was too afraid to spend, at least all at once.

Second, it told Riker that Chief Myers was paranoid. As a police officer, Myers would know that the two places burglars spend the most time are the living room and the master bedroom. Someone with that knowledge who really wanted to hide a safe would put it anywhere except those two locations. But Myers didn't. He wanted the money close to him. He was paranoid about it. Maybe even afraid it would be taken from him.

Riker gave the safe another long look, then carefully shut the mirror. He needed to find out more information about Chief Myers and his possible connection to the death of Oscar Kane. But that would have to wait. Riker had a funeral to attend.

17

AFTER RIKER GOT out of the car and headed for Chief Myers' house, Megan drove out of the residential neighborhood and back toward the high school. Her mind was reeling from the revelations of the past few minutes, and she needed to be somewhere familiar. If Chief Myers was working with the drug dealers, what did that mean for their town? Did any of her students really stand a chance in life if the system that was supposed to protect them was actually in league with the people who meant them harm?

When she reached the parking lot, she noticed something that had first caught her eye when she and Riker had passed the school. She hadn't given it much thought then, but now it seemed more important. A lone pickup truck was sitting in the high school parking lot. Megan recognized that vehicle. It belonged to David Underwood.

Pulling her Mazda into a parking spot not far from the truck, she got out and approached the other vehicle. She found David lying in the truck's bed, reading a beat-up paperback. Megan couldn't see the title of the novel, but she could tell from the portion of the cover she could see that it was science fiction.

Though she made no attempt at being quiet, David didn't look up from the book until she spoke.

"If you're trying to be early for class Monday morning, you're overdoing it."

He pulled the book down and looked up with a start. He visibly relaxed when he saw it was Megan. "Oh sorry, Ms. Carter. I was just hanging out here doing some reading."

"Good book?"

"Not really." He tossed the book down into the truck's bed. "This alien civilization has the power to travel millions of light-years across the galaxy, and yet they don't wear clothes?"

Megan laughed. "Maybe their physiology is different from ours and they don't need clothes for warmth."

He considered that a moment. "I don't buy it. They'd still need to protect themselves. Seems like they are just as susceptible to bullets as humans. Invent some body armor or something."

"A fair point. Is that why you're hanging out in the school parking lot on a Saturday morning? To criticize old science fiction novels?"

David shifted his position, leaning against the wall of the truck. "No. I'm used to coming here every Saturday for wrestling. My parents didn't know it was canceled, and I had a few hours to kill before the funeral. Guess I wasn't sure where else to go."

Megan's mind flashed back to when she was a little girl, and her cousin Matt was always hanging around, looking for excuses not to go back to his house. He'd help with chores, mow their lawn, and even help her with homework. She'd loved having him around, and at the time she'd not thought there was anything odd about it. It was only looking back years later that she'd realized his true motivation.

"Is everything all right at home, David?"

He didn't answer immediately. "Yes. Er, no. I'm not sure. It's my dad." He looked up and saw the concern in Megan's eyes. "It's not like he hits me or anything. He's a pretty cool guy, overall. But his job. I don't know. I've had trouble dealing with it lately."

Megan raised an eyebrow. "What's he do for a living?"

"Officially? He works for Dewitt Construction. Unofficially…" He trailed off, then his face reddened as if he couldn't believe what had just come out of his mouth. "Look, I'm not saying he's a criminal or something."

"Okay," she said evenly, though she knew that was exactly what he was saying.

He let out a weary sigh. "You won't tell anyone, will you?"

"No. Not unless you want me to."

"Well, I don't." He drew a deep breath, and his voice was much calmer when he spoke again. "I'm sorry. It's just, this is my dad, you know?"

Megan hopped up and sat in the truck bed, her legs dangling off the edge. "Have you talked to him about how you feel?"

"Yeah. We've got into some pretty heated arguments about it since Coach died. He says he didn't have anything to do with that and doesn't know who did. I believe him or I'd be going to the police, family or not. Still, I can't understand how he works with the people who might have done it."

"What's he say when you ask him?"

"He won't get specific. I get it, he's trying to protect me. But still. All he ever says is that it's not that easy to leave."

Megan sat quietly, letting the last couple days play in her

mind before she spoke again. "You know, I might have someone who can help. He's pretty good at dealing with sticky situations."

"You mean your cousin."

A surprised smile blossomed on her face. "Am I that easy to read?"

"Come on," David said, cracking a smile of his own. "A former Navy SEAL comes to town, starts asking questions about the drug ring, and you *might* know someone who can help me? Who else would it be?"

"Fair enough." She gave the young man a long look, her expression more serious now. "Do I have your permission to talk to him about this?"

David considered that, the indecision clear on his face. For a moment, it seemed that he was going to agree. Then he looked away and she knew he was going to decline. "No, please don't. At least not for now. I'm going to talk to my dad again before the funeral. Maybe I can talk some sense into him."

"And if that doesn't work?"

"Then we'll see."

"Fair enough." Megan started to get up, but she stopped when David spoke again.

"I told you what I'm doing here, but you never told me why you're in this parking lot on a Saturday morning, Ms. Carter."

"Same as you, I guess," she said with a smile. "My cousin needed a ride somewhere, and I'm killing time before I have to pick him up. He's going to text me."

"Ah, I see. Official Navy SEAL business? Or was it a beekeeping emergency?"

"It was both, actually. An invasion of terrorist honey bees." She hopped down, and her feet hit the pavement with a thud. “Remember what I said, David. If you need my help, or my cousin’s, just say the word.”

“Thanks, Ms. Carter.”

Megan went back to her car and drove off, hoping she was doing the right thing for her student.

18

WITH HIS ONLY dress clothes in ruins after the previous night's beating, Riker was forced to brave the clothing store once again. He kept the visit brief this time, carefully ignoring Grace's advances as he picked out an outfit very similar to the one he'd worn the previous evening. After that, he asked Megan if they could visit the hardware store. She questioned the stop, but Riker simply told her that he needed a few supplies. He bought a timer switch, a fan, some duct tape, a two-foot section of rebar, and a few other small items.

The two arrived at the church an hour before the funeral started. Riker used the time to bring his supplies inside and set them up as he needed. It didn't take long. Shortly after, people started to arrive for the service.

Patricia Kane came in just before the funeral was supposed to start. Riker got up to go speak with her, but he saw that she was already surrounded by friends and family. He decided to wait for a better time.

After a brief prayer led by the priest, the procession started. Several pallbearers carried the casket from the church to the cemetery a few hundred yards away. The large crowd followed them to what would be Oscar Kane's final resting place. Riker used two crutches and seemed to struggle to keep pace with the slow-moving crowd.

The immediate family sat next to the open grave while the priest spoke. Riker told Megan he would be more comfortable standing and urged her to join her fellow teachers. She reluctantly agreed, leaving Riker alone behind the last row of chairs. He stood looking over the sea of people dressed in black. He guessed that there were more than three hundred in attendance. He listened as the priest spoke of eternal happiness and a time of celebration. He knew that the words were meant to comfort the living, but he didn't see any reason to celebrate in the wake of a murder.

While the priest gave his sermon, Riker scanned the crowd. He was here to pay respect to Oscar Kane and he intended to do so in the best way that he could. He found his targets in the back of the crowd. Luke stood with five other men close to him. They all wore black, but their suit coats didn't do a good job of hiding the bulges from the weapons tucked into their waistbands.

Luke's eyes met Riker's. Riker simply shook his head. Luke looked down at his feet. Riker assumed that they would come for him shortly after the burial. Anytime you knew the time and place that a target would be it made sense to take advantage. Still, he had hoped that he was wrong and their respect for the deceased would prevent them from attacking today. That hope disappeared with the sight of the armed men.

The priest finished up and the principal of the school stepped in front of the gathered crowd. He was the first to eulogize Coach. He spoke with the authority of a man accustomed to addressing large auditoriums of people.

"I've known Oscar Kane for ten years. I met him the day I became principal. I've always known him the same way most of you have, as Coach Kane. The title of Coach has never been so fitting. He saw that I was nervous about my new position in a new town and he took me under his wing. He helped me learn the layout of the community. He gave me advice about the school and the parents. He and Patricia invited me into their home multiple times." He turned to Patricia as he spoke. "His nature was to help people become better in every way. He was a true coach to me and to the people of this town.

"Over the years I have seen him transform young boys with bad attitudes into respectable young men. There were no lost causes for him, just people who needed a little extra help. He never gave up on anyone or anything."

Those words stood out to Riker. He knew that they were true. He looked over at Luke, the words still ringing in his ears, and wondered if there was anything good left in his old friend. He doubted it, but Coach Kane would have tried to get him to change his ways.

The principal continued. "Coach was the heart of this town. He didn't just lead our school to victory on the wrestling mats; he started the food bank and looked after kids who needed it. I worry about where this town will be without him."

Riker checked his watch. Then he hobbled back towards the church using his crutches. He held up his injured leg preventing it from touching the ground. It pained him to leave before the end of the service, but he needed some alone time with Luke and his friends.

When Riker was halfway back to the church, he looked

over his shoulder and saw Luke and five other men walking towards him. Riker needed to reach the church with enough time to put his plan into action, but he resisted the urge to move too fast. He wanted to make sure that his injuries seemed so serious that they thought him no threat at all.

Riker entered the doors of the church. The foyer was long and narrow. The restrooms were to his left, and a loud noise emanated from the men's room. The loud clicking sound made Riker smile—the fan he'd set up on the timer had started running, and the cards he'd secured to the blades were making even more of a racket than he'd anticipated.

Now that he was out of sight from Luke, he moved more quickly, hurrying toward the bathroom. The splint on his leg did its job, and he didn't need the help of the crutches. Each step on the injured leg shot a wave of pain through Riker, but the limb functioned properly. He ducked into the women's bathroom which was a few feet away from the men's room.

He retrieved the two-foot piece of rebar he'd left behind the trash can. He hefted it, feeling its weight, glad to have a weapon that could quickly disable an opponent and help him keep his balance if needed.

Now the hard part. He drew a deep breath, focusing his mind, taking it to that place that had earned him the code-name of Scarecrow. He was injured, but he was still a predator who had laid a pretty trap for his prey, one that they wouldn't be able to resist.

He pressed his ear to the restroom door, listening. It wasn't long before he heard footsteps in the hall. He heard Luke tell one of the men to lock the doors, and then he heard the slide of a bolt.

"What the hell is that noise?" one of the men asked.

"It's coming from the bathroom."

"He's trying to get out through the window." This last voice was Luke's.

Riker heard the steps of the men running towards the bathroom. He waited, listening to them rush through the door next to the one he hid behind. His pulse quickened as adrenaline surged through his body. The familiar feeling told his body that it was time for battle. He held his position, gripping the doorknob in one hand and the solid piece of metal in the other.

A muffled voice came from the room next to Riker. "What the hell is that?"

Riker turned the knob and slowly emerged from his hidden position. One man stood in the doorway of the men's room, looking in at his friends. Riker swung the rebar down, slamming it onto the man's right shoulder. A crisp crack came from inside of the man's body as his collar bone split in two. Riker surged forward and dropped a shoulder into the middle of his back. The hit lifted him off his feet and knocked him into the middle of the other men.

Three of them stumbled forward, crashing into each other like dominos. Luke was the only man unaffected. He was standing a foot to their right, inspecting the fan. He turned to see the other men stumbling to the ground as Riker rushed into the room. The injured man whimpered, his hand on his shoulder. His shirt bulged from the shard of bone trying to push its way through the skin.

Luke stood frozen in shock for a moment. That moment was more time than Matthew Riker needed.

Riker swung the bar again. This time he hit Luke in the midsection, just below his ribs. The force of the blow made Luke double over as the air rushed out of his lungs and diaphragm. He tried to yell orders to the other men, but he had no breath left inside to generate the sound, and he dropped to his knees, struggling to draw in air.

One of the men on the ground reached for the pistol in his waistband. Riker turned towards him, spinning his body and using the motion to generate momentum with the bar. He brought it down on the man's forearm. The steel bar held its shape, but the man's arm gained a forty-five-degree bend.

The remaining two men attempted to get to their feet. One was halfway up when Riker gave him a swift kick with his good leg, swinging hard as if Riker were trying to make a long-range field goal. The tip of his shoe caught the man under his chin, and his teeth snapped from the force. His eyes rolled back, and he collapsed to the ground.

The last man made it to his feet, wavering as he took in the carnage around him. He tried to grab his gun, but his eyes were on the mangled bones of his friends, and his ears were filled with their cries of pain.

Riker brought the bar around again and connected with the man's knee before he could free his weapon. Bone crunched and the man fell to the ground, grabbing the injured leg. Riker kicked again, slamming a foot into the side of the man's jaw, and the man went limp.

Riker heard a sucking gasp and turned to see Luke finally get air back into his lungs. He was on his knees, doubled over, holding himself up with one hand and the other hand holding his stomach.

Riker grabbed the pistol from the back of Luke's belt and turned it towards the other men on the ground. Two were unconscious. The other two were holding their broken bones and each was close to ghost white.

"I'm going to take your weapons," Riker said. "If any of

you try to put up a fight, I will make sure to break both arms and both legs. Do you understand?"

The men grunted their agreement, and Riker grabbed all of the weapons without any resistance.

Riker turned back to Luke, leveling one of the confiscated 9mms at his old friend. "Luke, I need to know. Did you kill Coach Kane?"

Luke looked up past the gun and directly into Riker's eyes. "Fuck you. I told you I didn't have anything to do with his death." The words came out just above a whisper.

"Considering that you just tried to kill me at his funeral, your words aren't worth all that much."

"I gave you a fair warning. I told you to leave. I'm trying to protect you."

"Did you protect Coach in the same way? Did you try hard not to shoot him?"

Luke didn't break eye contact. "If it will help you feel better, go ahead and pull that trigger, but I didn't have anything to do with his death. I may be a piece of shit, but I would rather die than hurt Coach."

Riker looked into his former teammate's eyes. He saw only truth there. Luke was ready to die on the floor of this bathroom and he felt no guilt about the death of Coach Kane. He lowered the weapon. "Get your men out of here. I don't want to cause any more of a scene than we already have. I'm letting all of you live. You can consider us even now. If we have to do this again, I promise that it will end in death."

Riker stepped around the injured men and left the church. Then he limped his way back to the grave site to pay his respects.

19

Riker found Megan standing near the graveside and slid in next to her. She gave him a quick look up and down, taking in the state of his clothing, and shook her head. "Really? At the funeral?"

He shrugged and gave her a half smile. "I didn't start it, if that helps."

"Well let's hope you finished it. I have a feeling Oscar would have appreciated that."

Riker said nothing, but he couldn't help but silently agree. He shifted his attention to the grave, where the closed casket sat. Though it was draped in tasteful cloth, Riker knew what hid beneath--a metal rigging that would lower the casket into its dark, eternal home.

The priest took a step forward, placed a hand on the casket, and spoke in a loud voice. "Oh God, all that you have given us is yours. As first you gave Oscar to us, now we give Oscar back to you. Receive Oscar into the arms of your mercy. Raise Oscar up with all your people."

Perhaps in some other time or place, these words would have been comforting, but they felt rote and distant to Riker.

The priest delivered them without any of the fire that had been so critical to Coach Kane's life. Riker's eyes drifted from the coffin and the priest, back to the crowd. Something about it seemed off to him, and it took him a few moments to realize what it was, but when he did, it hit him hard.

The ratio of males to females was off. The majority of the crowd was men. Some in their teens. Some in their twenties. A few even in their thirties. As Riker observed the men, he realized that most of them must have been like him. Wrestlers. People who'd been shaped at an early and crucial stage by the guidance, discipline, and philosophy of the man who now lay dead in that casket, waiting to be lowered into the dirt.

Coach Kane had touched so many people. To see them all gathered here, the sorrow clear on their faces, hit Riker hard. If it had been him lying in that coffin instead of Coach Kane, how many people would gather to send him to his eternal rest? The people he knew from his time at QS-4 wouldn't be able to attend. Jessica? Perhaps Simon? A few acquaintances from back in North Carolina? Megan, if someone thought to pass her the news that he was dead. But certainly not a crowd like this.

Riker had saved lives. He'd toppled dictators and taken down terrorists. But he hadn't touched as many people as Coach Kane had, at least not directly. If that was the sign of a life well-lived, then Coach Kane had lived very well indeed.

The priest finished speaking, gave the benediction, and invited the attendees to pay their final respects. The mourners began to file past the casket, some touching it, some just staring at it for a moment before moving on. When it was their row's turn, Megan touched Riker's arm.

"You ready?"

He hesitated, not yet ready to say goodbye. "You go ahead. I'm going to hang back here for a minute."

Megan nodded, then headed up to join the queue.

Riker waited as the mourners filed past him. His thoughts turned once again to his high school days and the time spent on the mats. A realization struck him. He'd never really seen Coach Kane wrestle. Sure, the coach had demoed plenty of moves, showing glimpses of his speed and strength, but Riker had never really seen him cut loose. He'd only known a thin sliver of the full man that had been Coach Kane. The thought made him sad.

When there were only a few mourners left, Riker forced himself to get moving. He limped up to the casket, rested his hand on it for a moment, then walked away. He made a silent vow to Coach Kane. *I'll finish what you started, Coach. I promise.*

As Riker turned to go, he saw a thin figure huddled near a tree, one hand rested on the trunk. Even from this distance, Riker could see the tears streaking the man's face. It took Riker a moment to recognize him, but when he did, he limped his way over to him and put a hand on the man's shoulder.

"You okay, Donnie?"

The thin man wiped at his cheek with the back of his hand. "I don't know, Matt. I'm going to miss him." Donnie's whiskey-scented breath wafted into Riker's face as he spoke.

"We all are," Riker said. He gave Donnie a long look. Back in the day, Donnie and his brother had been the toughest guys around. It hurt to see him so broken.

"Can I tell you something?"

"Yeah, of course," Riker said.

"I've been scared for a long time. Ever since those guys set my brother on fire. But Coach wasn't afraid. He was the only person in this town with the balls to stand up to these assholes." Donnie met Riker's gaze for the first time. "I don't know what I believe about all this afterlife stuff. But if Coach is out there somewhere, I hope he's looking down on us, watching. Because if I ever get the chance, I'm going to make him proud. I'm going to be brave."

He let go of the tree and took a step forward, nearly losing his balance.

Riker steadied him with a hand on his back. "Donnie, maybe you should go home."

"Yeah. That's a good idea."

"You need a ride?"

"No. It's only a few blocks, and I could use the fresh air."

Riker watched as Donnie wandered off toward the edge of the cemetery only swaying back and forth a little as he walked. He was still watching Donnie when a voice came from behind him.

"Guess you managed to get the better of Luke's crew this time."

He turned and saw a man standing in the shadow of an oak tree—a man he'd last seen in the alley holding a baseball bat. Riker's face grew taut, but the man held up his hands, showing them empty.

"Chill. I'm just here to talk. I wanted to apologize for last night. Things got way out of hand."

Riker inspected the man and saw sadness in his eyes. "I take down your buddies and suddenly you're filled with regret?"

"It's not like that. My name's Eric Underwood." He held out his hand.

Riker hesitated a moment before shaking it.

"When Luke told me they were going to jump you after the funeral, I told him I was out. He was pissed, but I didn't care. I wasn't going to disrespect Coach Kane like that."

"Were you a wrestler?"

"No. But my son is. Coach meant the world to David."

Riker tilted his head in surprise. "David? I met him at the wake."

"He told me. Said you were a good guy. He also seems to think you might be able to help me. I guess that's why I came over to talk to you. After what happened to Coach... I don't know, maybe I've been looking for someone to talk to. Someone who can maybe do something about all of this."

Riker inspected the man more carefully, now spotting the way he kept shifting his weight and glancing past Riker to make sure no one was watching.

"You're him," Riker said. "You're the guy who was giving Coach information about the drug organization."

Eric didn't respond, but he didn't deny it either.

"Help me finish what Coach started," Riker said. "Who do you work for? What's really going on in Kingsport?"

"That's not why I'm here. After what they did to Coach, there's no way I can give up any information. I'm sorry, but it's just too dangerous for my family. In fact, we're seriously considering leaving town. I don't think they'll mess with me if I just go. You should think about doing the same. The organization has got a real hard-on for you."

Riker kept his face blank, carefully hiding his frustration. He'd finally found the source he'd been looking for, and the man wasn't willing to talk.

"I can't give you any information on the organization, but I can tell you what happened the night Coach died."

"You were there?"

"Not when they killed him, but before. I guess it was my fault, in a way. Coach was there to meet me that night. I drove up and saw him parked near Grant Park, but there was another vehicle there too. I got spooked and drove away."

"Can you describe this other vehicle?"

"I can do better than that. I can tell you who owns it. Hell, I've ridden in it myself plenty of times."

"Tell me," Riker said.

"It was Luke Dewitt's truck. Luke was there the night Coach died."

20

THE SUN WAS DOWN WHEN RIKER and Megan arrived back home. Riker limped into the living room and collapsed onto Megan's soft green sofa. He rubbed his injured leg, trying to dull the constant throbbing pain. At the same time, he tried to reconcile what Eric had told him. He'd known Luke was far from a saint, but he'd never truly believed he would have hurt Coach. If Luke really had murdered Coach, Riker needed to take off the kid gloves.

"Let's take a look," Megan said as she pulled a chair up next to him.

"That's not necessary," Riker said.

Megan shook her head. "Don't be a tough guy. Let me see it."

Riker rolled up the leg of his dress slacks to the knee. He unwrapped the splint, exposing a black and blue shin. A scab had formed where the baseball bat had struck and the entire lower leg was swollen.

Megan shook her head. "I'm guessing that feels just as bad as it looks."

Riker gave her a smile. “It’s just a scratch. I barely noticed it all day.”

“Oh good. Then I don’t need to get you anything to help with the pain or swelling.”

“Okay, I could use a couple Ibuprofen if you have them.”

Megan got up. She returned a moment later with four white pills and a glass of water. “That and a good night of rest should help a bit.”

“Rest sounds nice, but today is far from over.” Riker looked Megan in the eyes. “Unfortunately neither of us will be getting any rest tonight.”

“Why is that?”

“I basically gave a big eff you to a drug gang today. They will be coming for me soon, and I’m sorry to say that they will be coming for you as well. I’ll take care of them, but I need you to get somewhere safe. You need to pack a bag with at least a week's worth of clothes and drive somewhere that you have no connection to. I should have this taken care of in a few days, but be prepared for the whole week.”

“And what will you be doing while I cower in some shady motel?”

“It doesn’t need to be a shady motel. You can go anywhere you want. Just don’t tell anyone, including me.”

“Okay then, what will you be doing while I kick my heels up on a beach?”

“In this case the best defense will be a good offense. They will expect me to hole up or run. I plan on bringing the fight to them. Picking apart the organization before they understand that they are under attack is the best option.”

“So you plan on going up against an unknown number of armed men who almost killed you once all ready? Do you even know where to start?”

“I know someone who does.”

"Go on."

Riker hesitated. He had already involved Megan more than he wanted to. Her life was in danger and he was just dragging her in deeper and deeper. "It really doesn't matter. You need to start packing and get out of here. They could come for us tonight."

"I'm not doing anything until you tell me what your plan is." Megan crossed her arms.

Riker saw that she meant it. She wasn't going to move a muscle until she got more information. "Fine, I intend to find and destroy their drug stash. It will accomplish two goals. First off it will be a big hit to the local operation, and second it will draw out the remaining members of the organization."

Megan's mouth dropped half-open. She took in a breath to respond, but she pondered what Riker said instead. He waited for her to process the plan.

"Okay, I see how that could work, but there is one major problem."

"What's that?"

"You'll die. I mean, I know you have training, but you're just one man. Don't they have armed guards wherever they are holding the drugs?"

"It will be very dangerous, and yes, I could die. If I die fighting to save this town, it will be a better cause than half the things I've fought for. Still I have no intention of meeting my maker any time soon. That's why I need to make this happen now. If I attack tonight, I can catch them off guard. They'll have no choice but to respond quickly. Most likely a full assault with lots of armed men. That's why I need you to leave town."

"If it has to be tonight, then you'll need all the help you can get. Where do we start?"

Riker tilted his head, not sure if he'd heard Megan correctly. "You start by packing some things and heading out of town."

"I appreciate your whole army of one thing, but I'm not a damsel in distress. I may not be able to run into a drug lab shooting up the place, but I can help." She gave a soft kick to the side of Riker's injured leg. He grimaced. "You need all the help you can get."

"Look, Megan—"

She cut him off mid-sentence, "I'm going to save you some time. You are going to try to convince me that it's too dangerous and I need to leave. That it will be easier if you don't have to worry about me. The thing is, you convinced me that this is worth the risk. I've been turning a blind eye to this cancer in our town. I always told myself that there is nothing that I can do about it. Except I have a chance to do something now. I'm going to help you in any way that I can. I'm not leaving town, so you may as well accept my help."

Riker heard the determination in her voice. It sounded familiar. It sounded like him. "You're sure? This will get ugly."

"I'm sure."

"Okay. Welcome to the team."

Megan laughed. "Two people isn't much of a team."

"Like you said, it's better than one. We actually need a little more help to get started."

"Is this the part where you sort of know the location of the stash house?"

"That's exactly what this is. When Donnie told us the story of his brother's murder, he said they were on their way to burn the whole operation down. At the time I thought that he meant that figuratively, but they were literally going to burn down the place."

"That's not exactly proof that Donnie knows where the stash house is."

"No, we need to talk to him to be sure."

"Okay, I'll drive. You get that splint tightened up." Megan stood up and went to get her car keys.

"One more thing, do you happen to own a gun?"

Riker examined the small pistol on the drive over to Donnie's house. It was a Taurus G2c. He had never used this model before—it was a budget 9mm. Although it wasn't what he would have preferred, beggars couldn't be choosers. The weapon was small and easy to conceal.

When they arrived at Donnie's house, Riker pounded on the door for almost five minutes before he answered. This gave Riker plenty of time to examine the exterior of the home. It matched the occupant very well. The lawn was unkempt and covered with dead patches of grass. The paint was peeling, and a few boards hung loose on the siding. A paint can next to the front porch was overflowing with cigarette butts with many scattered on the ground around the container. A stale, ashy smell filled the area around the can.

Just as Riker pulled out his bump key to see if Donnie was passed out on the floor, a light turned on inside the house. Donnie opened the door and blinked his eyes like a man still dreaming.

"What are you doing here?"

"Good to see you too, Donnie," Megan said.

He shook his head, pulling himself further out of sleep. "Sorry, I didn't mean to be rude. I took a nap after the funeral and I wasn't expecting to see anyone."

"You said to let you know if I needed your help," Riker said. "Can we come in?"

Donnie led them into the house. He put on a pot of

coffee and the three sat at his kitchen table. Empty beer bottles stood like soldiers guarding every part of the kitchen. They lined the counters and the table itself. Megan kept her hands in her lap, trying not to touch any surfaces.

"Sorry, I don't get many visitors these days," Donnie said.

"I'm not here to judge your housekeeping skills. I'm here because I need your help. At the funeral you said you wanted to do something. You said you wanted to be brave again. Did you mean that?"

"Every word of it. What do you need?"

"I just need some information. Where were you and your brother going the night that he was killed?"

"We were going to the source of the problem. You know where they make the drugs."

"Wait, what do you mean by make the drugs?" Megan asked.

"I suspected as much," Riker said. "This drug organization is up to more than just distribution. They are producing heroin. Maybe even growing it somewhere near town."

He turned back to Donnie. "Do you think the lab is still there?"

"I know that it is."

"How do you know they haven't moved it?" Megan asked.

"It's an old farm west of town. I go to the woods and watch the people come and go from there sometimes. I think of the way my brother screamed when he was burning. I remember the way his hair and skin smelt when he burned. I sit there and watch and drink until I wake up in a puddle of my own vomit. That's how I know they still use the place."

Megan's eyes narrowed and her voice grew cold. "If you know where they've been making the drugs the whole time why didn't you tell the police? How could you let them get away with it?"

Donnie lowered his gaze to the floor. "When they burned my brother, they told me I would be next if I ever said anything. I wish I would have said something. It would have been better to burn alive than live like I have been."

"Don't judge yourself too harshly, "Riker said. "Great men have broken under less. Can you tell me about this factory? I will need all the intel that I can get if I'm going to have a chance at this."

"I can do better than tell you. I'll take you there. I want to help with whatever you are doing."

"I respect that, but this will be dangerous. You know exactly what can happen if things go wrong."

"I do know, and if that's how I go out it will be better than the life I'm living right now. I need to do this for Sam and for myself."

Riker knew that he should try to talk him out of it. He wasn't even sure if a drunk would be more harm than help. But he couldn't deny a man his chance at redemption. It may be the only chance for Donnie to truly save his own life.

Megan turned to Riker. "I guess a team of three beats a team of two."

"Okay Donnie, tell me everything you know."

21

Riker crouched low in the woods, his eyes fixed on the road in front of him. An imposing figure stood just off the dirt road, in the middle of a wide driveway. There were tall trees and dense foliage on either side of the drive, but they did little to hide the chain-link fence around the perimeter of the remote property, or the barbed wire atop that fence. Quite a bit of security for a place in the middle of the woods north of town.

Riker watched in silence, his breathing falling into the slow steady rhythm it always did when he was on recon duty. His mind went to a strange place, both observant and passive. He instinctively kept his eyes angled away from the lights inside the property beyond the gate, preserving as much of his night vision as possible.

The man who stood guard at the gate had a relaxed posture, but he wasn't being sloppy. Riker had to give him that. Though he couldn't make out the man's face in the darkness where he crouched, he would have been willing to bet this was one of the guys who'd attacked him outside the wake the previous night which made him feel a bit less hospitable toward the man.

Back at Megan's house, Donnie had given them as much information as he knew about the layout of the facility. It was on an old farm that had belonged to the Warrens back in Riker's day. He'd gone to school with Harmony Warren--a nice girl, if not exactly the brightest. Back then, there had been no fence around the property. No armed guard either. Apparently things had changed.

Donnie had been stoic as he gave the details. He'd told them about the fence and the guard. And a bit about what lay beyond. He hadn't seen much before the men had stopped Sam and him. Understandably, his attention had been focused on his dying brother from that point on rather than on potential weaknesses in the drug dealers' fortification.

There had been one point where his eyes had lit up though, and for just a moment Riker had caught a glimpse of the old Donnie from high school. It was when he'd told Riker about the game trail that ran along the side of the property and about how he and Sam had often illegally hunted these woods. That was how they'd discovered what was going on out here, though it hadn't been until a few years later that Sam had decided to burn it to the ground. Still, Donnie had given Riker enough of the general layout to form the rough structure of a plan. It wasn't exactly subtle, but it might just work.

As Riker waited, his mind shifted to Luke. His oldest friend. The man who'd had a part in beating him unconscious. The man who'd lied to his face and said he'd known nothing about what happened to Coach. Now Riker knew that wasn't true.

And earlier this afternoon, Riker had let Luke walk

away, but that wouldn't happen again. On the way out to the farm, Riker had driven past Dewitt Construction as well as Luke's house. The truck wasn't at either location. He hoped his old friend was here tonight. Even if he wasn't, the attack would be sure to draw him out. Riker had promised himself that he would see justice, and he intended to do so, old friend or not. And God help Luke now that Riker knew he had something to do with Coach's death. Regardless of what Luke had done for Riker in the past, he swore that Coach Kane would not go unavenged.

He'd been waiting in the woods for no more than ten minutes when he heard someone whistling as they walked down the road. A moment later, the whistler staggered into sight, cutting a zig-zagging path along the road as he came. The man at the gate tensed up immediately, his hand going to the butt of the pistol at his belt. But as the approaching man came closer, the guard relaxed a little.

"You gotta be kidding me. Donnie, is that you?"

"You're damn right it is!" Donnie answered in a slurred voice. "And walking on public property too, so don't give me any shit about not coming around here. This is America!"

Riker raised an eyebrow, impressed at the man's ability to accurately portray a drunk. He considered that Donnie had had plenty of practice, but then pushed the uncharitable thought away. Donnie was not only risking his life but also returning to the site of his most profound trauma, the one that had pushed him into the bottle in the first place.

The guard sighed loudly and took a step forward. "Jesus man, you know better than this. Why don't you go home and sleep it off?"

Donnie stumbled forward a few steps and raised a finger, pointing it at the man's chest. "I will. I'll do just that. But there's something I want first."

"Yeah? What's that?" There was a hint of amusement in the guard's voice now.

"My brother's watch. It was a—whaddya call it—family heirloom. And it was on his wrist when that psychopath cooked him. I'm not leaving til I get it back!"

"Man, you think we kept that shit hanging around?"

"Well you'd better find it! I'm not leaving til I get it. Otherwise, I'm going on one of the Ghandi things. A hunger strike!"

The guard was slowly growing tenser again. Whatever amusement he'd felt at Donnie's appearance was quickly fading. "If you want to starve yourself, go right ahead. You just can't do it here."

Donnie gave him a defiant glare, then he sank to the ground, sitting cross-legged on the hard dirt.

"Seriously man?" The guard's hand went to his waist, but not to his gun. It went to the radio clipped to the other side of his belt. He lifted it to his mouth. "Yo, Phil, you there?"

There was a pause and then a crackly voice came through the radio. "Yeah, what's up?"

"Donnie Wagner just stumbled up here."

"So? Get rid of him!"

"I tried. The guy's drunk and he's not leaving."

Another long pause. "Alright, I'm on my way."

Riker waited a few more moments. Donnie was singing now, some old Rolling Stones song, loudly and very off-key. When two more men appeared at the gate, Riker slipped back into the woods.

He moved quickly and quietly through the brush, heading for a spot he'd scoped out twenty minutes earlier--a section of fence far from any of the lights inside the complex. He gave a thought to his teammates as he moved, hoping that Donnie would keep the distraction going a bit longer but not push so hard that he'd end up getting hurt. Donnie had already pulled two men away from the interior of the complex, which would make Riker's job that much easier. Megan was in the car, waiting for the text that was already typed into Riker's phone and ready to send. When the text came through, she'd come speeding down the road, doors open and ready for a speedy pickup. Riker had made her keep the pistol over her protests. Though he was going into the belly of the beast, he much preferred that she be armed over him. Besides, in his experience criminal compounds had no shortage of weapons inside. If he was spotted before he was able to successfully acquire a gun, he was likely dead anyway.

As he approached the pre-selected section of the fence, he reached into his back pocket and pulled out the hand-held bolt cutters he'd gotten from Megan's shed. He paused, listening to the commotion Donnie was still causing near the gate. Then he began to cut. He was through the fence in less than two minutes.

He made his way south across the compound, picturing in his mind the loose structure Donnie had drawn for him. If the drawing had been anywhere close to accurate, the main building should be straight ahead. In addition to the main house, there was a large barn and two grain silos on the property.

Riker didn't see another person before the building finally came into sight. A couple of pickup trucks with loaded beds stood just to the east of the building. Hoping their contents might provide him some insight, he angled toward the trucks. When he reached them, he saw the items in the beds were barrels. Using the carefully shielded glow of his phone's screen, Riker inspected the labels. Acetic anhydride. Sodium carbonate. Hydrochloric acid.

Riker grimaced. He'd seen these chemicals in a similar facility once before, but that one had been in Afghanistan. This all seemed unthinkable. Heroin production in rural Iowa? In his hometown? What kind of a cover-up would be necessary to make such a thing possible? And why here?

And yet, the evidence was right there in front of him. This was why Donnie's brother had been killed. Why Coach had been killed.

Anger rose up in Riker's chest. He'd never thought he cared that much about his hometown, but seeing what these bastards were doing to it made him truly angry.

He drew a deep breath. There were three men at the gate and an unknown number of men inside. He was unarmed, outnumbered, and crouching in the bed of a truck filled with highly-explosive chemicals. It was time to go to work.

22

THE FARMHOUSE WAS ONLY two hundred yards from the truck. Past the house was the barn. Both structures looked as if they belonged on an old farm in Iowa. They were slightly run down and in need of a fresh coat of paint.

The grain silos that stood at the back of the fenced-in area looked brand new. The metal they were made of glistened in the light from the house. Riker guessed that the silos were fifty feet tall with a base diameter of twenty-five feet. Even though they were tall, the silos looked squatty with the large diameter.

Riker stayed low in the shadows as he moved toward the barn. He had his leg wrapped tight, but the fracture still gave him a painful reminder with each step. The pain fueled him and kept his mind crisp. He reached the side of the barn and saw the two men returning from the front gate. Riker kept his back to the side of the barn around the corner from the door. He could hear the conversation of the approaching men. He stayed low and allowed himself a small glance at the men. Each had an assault rifle slung over his shoulder.

"I can't believe that guy came back here. He must have a death wish."

"You're overthinking it. He was so drunk I doubt that he'll remember being here in the morning. I'm just glad that he stumbled away on his own. I'd hate to have to make him disappear." Riker recognized the voice from the radio. They had called him Phi.

"Is there any chance we would actually have to kill some drunk guy?"

Phil stopped walking for a moment. "I know you haven't been with us long, but you need to understand that we work for serious men. They would absolutely kill anyone who caused a problem. Even if it's just a small problem. Do you get me?"

"Yeah man, I know who we work for and I know that I'm not going to cause any problems. If they say make some drunk disappear, I'll make him disappear. It just seems like that would be major overkill."

The two continued their walk towards the barn. "Just remember to take everything that we do seriously. I've seen these guys in action, they don't joke around."

They reached the door and Riker could hear the beeps of a code being entered into a keypad. Riker held his ground, readying himself to move quickly.

He heard the door open and the men start to move again. Riker sprang forward from his position and almost stumbled. The pressure on his shin from the run lit up his pain sensors. He forced himself to accept that constant pain would be a part of this mission and continued moving towards the door. He reached it before it swung shut and slid inside just behind the two men.

Both men turned towards the unexpected presence of an unknown party.

"What the ..." Phil started to say, but Riker grabbed the back of his head with both hands. He pulled down and brought his right knee up. Phil's chin snapped hard and Riker heard the crushing sound of a tooth crumbling in his freshly broken jaw.

For a moment the other man just stared in shock. Then he tried to get his rifle into position. It was hanging loosely around his shoulder. Riker was only a foot from him and the man fumbled to turn the weapon towards him. At the close proximity he never stood a chance at effectively using the rifle.

Riker saw his opportunity while the man had both hands on the rifle. He shot out a hard jab into the center of the man's neck. The loud slapping sound of the fist on the skin of his neck was followed by a harsh sucking sound as the man grabbed his throat and struggled to get air into the collapsed trachea.

Once again Riker brought his knee up and the head of the man down. The impact caused him to collapse next to Phil.

Riker picked up one of the assault rifles and grabbed the clip from the other. He stood in the entrance of a normal looking barn. Tools lined the walls and a tractor was parked in the back of the room. At first glance it was just a normal barn.

Riker looked closer at the double doors. They were lined with diamond plating and had two large bolts securing their position. Every wall was lined with diamond plating. The structure was much more secure than a normal barn. He looked at the concrete floor and could see a dusty path that led to a steel plate in the back corner of the room.

Riker tried to lift the handle of the plate, but it didn't budge. On the wall next to the access panel was another keypad. Apparently he needed another code to access whatever was beneath the floor.

He glanced back at Phil and his friend. Neither of them would be able to give out information any time soon. He would need to get someone to open the hatch from the inside.

Riker moved both of the unconscious men to the corner of the room and tossed a tarp over them. Then he took Phil's radio and crouched down behind the old metal tractor. It gave him perfect cover behind old American steel.

Once he was in position he screamed into the radio. "We are under attack at the front gate! I need everyone up here now!"

A response came from the handset. "What's the situation?"

"Get you asses out here now! I mean everyone!"

A moment later Riker heard the latch under the hatch click. The panel rose and five men came up from a ladder underneath and hustled toward the door. Each man had an assault rifle at the ready. Riker steadied his weapon at the center of their backs.

"Drop your weapons! I have you dead to rights."

All five men stopped and turned towards the voice. A large man with a dark beard pointed his rifle in Riker's direction and took aim. The other men leveled their weapons towards the tractor.

Riker squeezed the trigger of his weapon. He aimed at center mass of the bearded man and moved in a steady line across the five men. He squeezed the trigger controlling the pace of fire putting one round into the chest of each man. Three of them had fallen before the first of them got off a round. The shooter was panicked and missed Riker by three feet. Riker's shots were true and the next two men fell to the ground. The last man sprayed bullets in the general direction of Riker as he ran towards the door.

Riker fired once hitting the man in the elbow of the arm that held the rifle. He screamed and the rifle fell to the floor. Riker sent a second bullet into the shoulder of the other arm. The man screamed and collapsed to the floor. He continued to cry out and pushed himself backward with his feet, away from Riker.

Riker held his position and watched the other men on the ground for movement. He also waited to see if anyone else would come up from the hatch. After a minute he moved over to the man he had shot.

He leveled his weapon pointing it directly between the man's eyes. "If you don't want to end up like your friends you need to listen to me."

The man looked up at Riker. Both arms were lying limply at his sides and blood flowed from his wounds. His face was pale, but he had stopped screaming and Riker was surprised to see that there was no fear in his eyes.

"You have no idea what you just did, do you?"

"I'm actually still in the process of doing. Are there any more men down that hatch?"

"No, but that doesn't change anything. You are already a dead man. The men you are stealing from will make the remainder of your short life very painful."

"I'd worry a little more about your life and a little less about mine. Are you sure there isn't anyone else in the basement?"

The man gave a cold smile. "No men down there, but a lot of women."

"What?"

The man's eyes rolled back in his head and he slumped

to the side. It appeared that the shock from multiple gunshot wounds had gotten the better of him.

Riker approached the open hatch cautiously. He looked down and saw a ladder in a shaft that was twenty-feet deep.

He yelled down the opening. "If you want to live, lay down your weapons and come out one at a time."

A woman's voice responded in Spanish. "Estamos desarmados. Por favor, déjanos ir." *We are unarmed. Please let us go.*

Riker responded. "Estás a salvo ahora. Necesito que todos salgan." *You are safe now. I need everyone to come out.*

One by one, the women came out from the hatch. There were twenty of them in total, and all were Latin American. He guessed Colombian by the accent. All of them were around thirty years old. They stood in a group staring at Riker. "Espera aqui." *Wait here.*

Riker climbed down the ladder and entered a large room. It was sixty feet long and thirty feet wide. The ceilings were ten-feet high and everything was stainless steel. Large vats of liquid were in some kind of machines lining the walls. The tables held large deep bins filled with powder. Air flowed through the room and Riker could hear the soft hum of a ventilation system.

There was a door in the back of the room. Riker approached it with his rifle at the ready. He opened the door to find a room with a dozen pallets. Each pallet had a five-foot stack of bricks of heroin on them.

The size of the operation shocked Riker. It rivaled production facilities of South American drug lords. This was no local shop. The size of the operation sickened him. He wanted to find out who was behind it and to make sure they were stopped. He knew the best way to meet the boss was to mess up the operation.

There were two large barrels of chemicals in the main

room with a flammable symbol on the side. Riker took a deep breath and opened the lid. Then he tipped the barrels over. He climbed up the ladder as the contents spread across the floor.

Riker emerged and found the room empty. Apparently the women who worked in production didn't want to wait around and find out if he was dangerous. Riker looked out the door to the barn and saw the women running towards the house. Several armed men were exiting the building and yelling at the women in Spanish. He saw some of the women looking back towards the barn and pointing. It seemed they were not entirely grateful for their release.

He ducked back inside the barn and saw a can of gas next to the tractor. He grabbed it along with an old rag that hung on the wall. Riker shoved the cloth in the cap of the can and pulled a lighter from his pocket. He thought of Donnie's brother and felt a sense of justice as he lit the rag. Riker tossed the can across the room and into the open hatch.

The moment he let go of the can he raced out the door of the barn. From one hundred yards away someone yelled, "Stop right there!"

Riker didn't slow down. Instead he raced into the darkness away from the barn. He took the phone from his pocket as he ran and hit the send message button.

From behind him he heard the report of gunfire. Riker hoped the darkness and the distance would protect him, but he kept as low as he could and moved quickly.

The night turned to day for a brief moment before the force of a concussion wave hit Riker. He was knocked off his feet and tumbled in the grass. He looked back to see a flaming wreckage that had been the barn only a moment before. The fire must have reached whatever chemicals were inside the tanks.

Flaming boards rained down around the yard. A shaft of flames shot up into the night sky like a Roman candle. Riker's ears rang and he heard faint muffled shouts. He glanced back to see other men stumbling to their feet. With the light of the flame, he knew that he would be an easier target. He needed to move.

Once he was back on his feet, he sprinted towards the opening he had made in the fence. Pain shot through his leg. He worried that any step could finish off the fracture in his leg and he would feel the bone snap. If that happened, he'd fall to the ground and have no choice but to wait for his enemies to find him. It was a chance that he had to take. He hoped the bone would hold and Megan would be at the pick-up point when he got there.

23

Eighteen years earlier

Matt Riker knocked on the door to Coach Kane's office and waited for the gruff voice calling for him to enter. When it finally came, he walked inside. Though he had been in this office dozens of times over the past three years, somehow it felt different this time. In the two weeks since the Iowa state wrestling tournament and the official end of the season, Matt hadn't set foot in this office. Now he felt a little like a stranger trespassing on territory where he no longer truly belonged.

But he had no choice but to be here this afternoon. He had an appointment to keep.

Coach Kane gestured to the chair across from his desk. "Have a seat. Might as well get settled in. Guys like Zalesky keep their own schedule. Three o'clock appointment or not, we might be waiting for a bit."

Matt did as asked, setting his backpack down on the

linoleum floor and sinking into the seat across from the coach.

The older man gave him an appraising look. "You nervous?"

Matt shrugged. He was terrified, but he wasn't about to say that. "Maybe a little."

"Good," Coach said with a smile. "You'd be an idiot if you weren't. Your entire future is going to be affected by what happens on this phone call."

Matt shifted uncomfortably in his seat. "Thanks a lot, Coach. You really know how to make a guy feel better."

"Just shooting you straight." He raised his index finger. "But there's one more thing you need to remember. Coach Zalesky doesn't personally make telephone calls to guys he's not trying to recruit. You impressed him in your recruitment interview. And no doubt he's seen the tape of your performance at State. He wants you for his team. The only question is what he's willing to offer to get you there."

Matt swallowed hard. That was the crux of the issue. His father had made his position on the matter clear--he'd be providing no assistance toward tuition. If Matt's dream of wrestling at the University of Iowa was going to be a reality, he was going to have to pay his own way.

Coach nodded toward the clock hanging on the wall. Three o'clock exactly. "Now we wait."

They didn't have to wait long. The phone on Coach's desk let out a trill less than a minute later. Coach scooped up the handset and held it to his ear.

"Hello." He paused, listening. "Yes, sir. He's right here sitting across from me. One moment." He leaned forward, offering the handset to Matt. "Mr. Riker, Coach Zalesky would like a word."

Matt tried to steady his hand as he took the receiver and held it to his ear. “Hello, Coach Zalesky.”

“Mr. Riker! Pleasure to talk to you again.”

Matt was struck by the difference between the two coaches’ voices. Coach Kane was always calm, spoke softly but confidently, and there was always a hint of gruffness in his voice. Zalesky on the other hand was always enthusiastic and spoke as if he was addressing a large crowd even when he was talking to one person. The differences in their styles would take some getting used to if Riker did join the University of Iowa team.

“Same here, Coach. Thanks for taking the time to speak with me.”

Zalesky let out a laugh. “After your performance at State, how could I not? You really made your case. Trust me when I say you made a lot of people sit up and pay attention. The way you slipped out of that leg ride in the finals was truly impressive.”

Matt couldn’t help but smile. Any compliment from a man like Coach Zalesky would have been welcome, but that one in particular, felt well-earned. “Thank you, sir.”

“Mr. Riker, the reason I’m calling is that I’d officially like to invite you to join us on the mats at the University of Iowa this fall.”

“That’s great news.” Matt’s voice sounded distant in his own ears as he answered. His dream was so close, but it wasn’t in reach quite yet.

“Well, I’m sure it’s not the only invitation you’ve received. But I’m confident that our wrestling program is the best in the country, and you deserve to join the best. That’s why I am offering you full academic assistance. That’s what us non-bean counters call a full-ride. You come wrestle with me, and you won’t pay a cent for college.”

The conversation went on for five more minutes, but it passed in a haze for Matt. His mind kept drifting back to Zalesky's words. *Full academic assistance.*

He'd be able to go to college. He'd be able to wrestle with the best team in the country. All the hard work. All the blood, the sweat, and the tears. It had all been worth it.

Eventually, he said goodbye to Zalesky and set the phone down on its cradle.

Coach Kane raised an eyebrow. "I wasn't trying to listen in, but it was hard not to hear Zalesky's loud voice. Did I hear the words full-ride?"

"Yes, sir," Matt said. "You sure did."

That was one of the few times he'd seen Coach Kane smile, and it was a wide, toothy grin. "I'm damn proud of you, Riker."

Matt felt an unexpected wave of emotion wash over him. "None of this would have happened if you hadn't seen me sitting outside the principal's office and invited me to join the team freshman year. You changed my life, Coach."

Coach considered that a moment, then shook his head. "I disagree. All I did was offer you an opportunity, same as I have for a hundred kids over the years. You're the one who worked your butt off. You earned this, and don't you forget it."

When Riker left Coach Kane's office, he found Luke waiting for him outside, an anxious expression on his face.

"Well?" he asked.

Matt shrugged, his face blank. "No big deal. Just a full-ride scholarship to the University of Iowa."

Luke's eyes widened and a slow smile broke out on his face. "Holy shit, dude! That is incredible! Congratulations."

He held up his hand and Matt slapped it in a high-five, a wide smile on his own face now.

"Let's get the hell out of here," Luke said. "We need to celebrate."

"Actually, I think I'm going to head home. I want to tell my mom the good news."

"Yeah, of course." Luke thought for a moment. "And your dad! Come on, I'll drive you home. I want to see the look on his face when you drop this on him."

Matt didn't bother arguing. He normally walked the two miles home after school, but riding in his best buddy's truck felt much more appealing this afternoon. He wanted to share the good news with his parents as quickly as possible. If he hurried, he might even get there before Dad made it home from work. It would be nice to tell Mom first without Dad there to suck the joy out of the room.

Luke spent most of the drive to Matt's house talking about all the chicks Matt was sure to get as a wrestling star at college. Luke wouldn't be going to college--he'd be joining his dad's construction company instead--but he quickly shifted the conversation to all the visits he intended to make to the university and how he expected Matt to provide him with plenty of alcohol and introductions to female students. Matt promised to do his best on both fronts.

When they pulled into the driveway of the Riker family's small, single-story home, Matt let out a disappointed sigh. His dad's beat-up old Bronco was there. That meant he'd either gotten fired again or just got sent home early due to lack of work. Either way, it would be a hit to his paycheck, and he would not be happy. Matt would have to be careful in his delivery of his news. His dad was volatile at the best of times, and he could interpret Matt's news as bragging, which would mean a rough night indeed. But as long as he hadn't been drinking, Matt felt as if he'd be able to navigate the situation. He had a lifetime of practice, after all.

He turned to Luke, who was already unbuckling his seatbelt. "Hey man, would you mind doing me a favor? Wait out here while I scope out the situation?"

Luke raised an eyebrow. "And miss the look on Gary Riker's face when you give him the proof that he was wrong about your wrestling skills taking you to college?"

"Just for a minute. Let me make sure he's not in a mood. Then you can come in."

Luke shrugged. "Yeah, okay. But you owe me an introduction to a hot redhead at U of I, understand?"

"Deal." Matt opened the truck's door, stepped out, and walked up to the house.

He paused on the stoop and tried to see what he could decipher about the situation inside the house. It was quiet. That could be a good thing or a bad thing. He pushed the door open and slowly stepped inside.

He was greeted by the faint sound of a Johnny Cash record, his father's preferred music when he was feeling melancholy. Matt knew from experience that melancholy could turn to anger with little warning in this house. His eyes immediately went to the end table next to his dad's favorite chair. What he saw made his heart sink. A half-empty bottle of Jack Daniels and an empty glass. It was not even four o'clock, and already his dad had put away enough whiskey to make most men pass out. But not Gary Riker. Gary was just getting started on his evening.

Matt's mind was already running through possibilities. Should he still go out and celebrate with Luke as he'd planned? That would let him avoid his father, but it would also leave his mother alone with the old drunk. Would it be better to endure a hellish night at home for her sake?

He was still considering that when he heard a loud crash

from the kitchen. It was quickly followed by a slurred voice shouting in anger.

"Look at what you did, you stupid bitch!"

Matt didn't stop to think. He sprinted toward the kitchen. The first thing he saw as he stepped through the doorway was the broken pieces of a plate on the floor. The second thing he saw was his father's fist slamming into his mom's face.

24

RIKER STUMBLED out of the woods in the dead of night. The sky behind him had a soft glow from the fire at the barn. He could hear a babble of a stream flowing to his right. It guided him to an embankment. He climbed up it and reached a paved country road. Once he stood on the side of the road, a car's headlights flipped on.

Megan drove over to Riker, and he was in the car almost before it stopped. She hit the gas and they sped away into the night.

"Holy shit! What did you do?" Donnie asked from the backseat.

"For the moment, I shut down production of a rather large heroin operation."

Donnie let out a laugh. "You make it sound like you flipped off the power. That place exploded. I mean, we could feel the shockwave in the car."

"Are you hurt?" Megan asked.

"No more than I was before the evening's festivities. My leg is throbbing like a son of a bitch, but I'll be fine."

Donnie leaned forward, putting his head between Riker

and Megan. His eyes were wide and looked clearer than Riker had seen them since he had been back.

"That was the best thing I have ever done. When those guys came out with rifles I was sure that I was going to die. It was so intense."

"You did great Donnie. Thanks for taking such a big risk."

"All I did was stand outside of the gate and acted drunk for a few minutes and it was intense. You just infiltrated a drug facility and blew it up. You did it by yourself. You're like Commando."

Megan had a shocked look on her face. "I'm shaking and all I did was drive."

"You both did great." Riker's tone was serious.

"How did you get past the guys with the assault rifles?" Donnie asked.

"Men with guns always think they have the power. They don't think that anyone will challenge them, and they let their guard down. I just took advantage."

Donnie was smiling. "You need to teach me how to 'take advantage'. We just shut down a drug operation. I want to do this all the time."

"First, I appreciate your enthusiasm, but it took me fifteen years of hard training with some of the world's best warriors to acquire my skills. I can't really just teach you some tricks. Second, we didn't shut down their operation. We just threw a wrench in the works."

Megan looked concerned. "You don't think this is enough to stop them for good?"

"There were seven men in the barn, along with twenty women. I didn't get a chance to check the house, but I would guess that it held at least that many people."

Megan's head snapped towards Riker. "Twenty women? What were they doing there?"

"They were producing and packing the heroin. I'm sure they were the night shift."

"The night shift?"

"An operation like that doesn't shut down for half the day. They work the facility in two twelve-hour shifts. That's why I'm sure there were another twenty workers in the house. One shift sleeps while the other works."

Megan paused for a minute to process what Riker had just said. "A twenty-four-hour operation that requires twenty workers at a time has to produce way more drugs than this town can use, doesn't it?"

"Yes. In fact I just destroyed enough to supply New York for about a week."

Donnie turned to Riker. "That's impossible. I thought that they were just selling locally. Why would they have such a large operation here?"

Riker stayed silent and let Megan work the problem. She spoke up quickly. "This is the perfect place to produce a huge operation. No one would ever suspect this town as a drug center. The police force is small and can be bought. They can work almost in plain sight with very little risk."

"That's right. I expected to find a local operation at the farmhouse, but this is so much more."

"Who is in charge of all this?" Donnie asked.

"I'm not sure yet, but we are going to find out soon."

"How?" Megan asked.

"You don't mess up a multi-million dollar operation without getting the attention of the man in charge. And whoever is in charge of this will be a serious and ruthless man." Riker shook his head. "I'm sorry, but I have endangered this entire town."

"I think that's a little dramatic," Megan replied.

"No, it's not. The men in charge of this scale of production cannot be seen as weak. They will need to make a swift and harsh retribution. You are both in serious danger and so is anyone related to the business. That includes family and friends of anyone involved."

Donnie shook his head. "You didn't endanger anyone. My brother was set on fire before you ever arrived. Coach Kane is dead. Kids are sticking needles in their arms. These guys were already killing all of us. They were just doing it slowly. I'd rather have them come at us full force. At least everyone will know that they are under attack."

"He's right, Matt," Megan agreed. "We were already in danger. At least we are fighting back now."

Donnie smiled. "Hell yeah. We are kicking their asses." He paused for a moment. "What do we do next?"

"I'm glad that you are both willing to fight back. I'll be with you till the end, no matter how things turn out. Just know that it will be even more dangerous from here on out."

Megan put one hand on Riker's shoulder. "We get it. We can get hurt. I believe that the question is what do we do next?"

Riker knew that Donnie and Megan didn't really understand the danger that they faced, but he admired their spirit. "We prepare for an attack. These people will retaliate quickly. Their number one mission will be to kill me."

"Do they even know it was you?" Donnie asked. "I mean, it was night. They might not have seen your face."

Megan glanced at Donnie in the rearview mirror. "He's the x-factor in town. He has already messed with them, and they wanted to kill him even before tonight. I'm pretty sure they will figure out that it was Matt. Even if it wasn't, they need someone to make an example of."

"Well said, Megan. They will come for me tonight. The good news is that they will not prepare. They will strike hard and fast, relying on numbers and firepower."

"Striking hard and fast with lots of firepower doesn't sound like good news at all," Megan said.

"We know where the enemy will strike, we know the approximate time, and we know that they will underestimate us again."

Megan and Donnie gave each other a confused look. "Okay, so how do we use our advantages?"

"First, we go shopping."

Twenty minutes later Riker, Megan and Donnie were going through the aisles of a hardware store. Riker had given everyone a list of materials to load into a cart. Both Megan and Donnie were confused by the list, but they filled their carts with the requested materials.

After the materials were loaded into Megan's trunk, they raced back to her house.

"Shouldn't we have gone to a gun shop or army surplus store?" Donnie asked.

"Guns have waiting periods, and I don't like leaving records of where I've been. Besides, I don't want to kill all of the men coming for us tonight. That's why we got the supplies we did instead of lethal weapons."

"You don't want to kill the guys coming for us tonight? Aren't they going to be trying to kill you?"

"I'm guessing that they will send the guys from Luke's crew. They may be working for a drug dealer, but most of them aren't murderers and I doubt any of them are soldiers. They are just a bunch of local guys who have taken the wrong path. I'd rather not kill them, but I will if I have to."

"You're a better man than me. I'd say anyone working for those scumbags deserves to die."

"How about a little less psycho?" Megan said. "You know a lot of guys that work for Luke. Would you really kill them?"

Donnie shook his head. "I would if they were coming to kill me." He turned to Riker. "At least tell me that you'll give them a beating."

"If I'm alive in the morning, I promise that all of the guys who come for me will be regretting their current life decisions."

Donnie smiled. "I can live with that."

The three pulled up to Megan's house. They grabbed all of the supplies from the hardware store. They included roofing starter shingle roll, nails, copper wire, work lights, adhesives and nylon rope. Riker directed them as they set up the perimeter of the house.

The three worked quickly knowing that time was short. Riker could see that Donnie was having trouble focusing as the alcohol left his body. He still worked as hard as he could. Megan was exhausted as well but she did as Riker directed.

"You weren't kidding, these guys are going to regret making a move on this house," Donnie said.

"Just because I don't want to kill them doesn't mean that they shouldn't learn a lesson. What happened to all the tough talk in the car about killing everyone?"

"It's just that I remember laughing when I watched *Home Alone*. I don't think this version will be quite as funny."

"I always wondered why people liked that movie. That kid was a total psychopath, and most of his traps were poorly constructed. I guess he was just a kid, but you should still take pride in your work."

Megan looked at the two men. "You know you have a very different take on that movie than most people."

Riker shrugged. "Sorry, I guess I have a slightly different background than most people."

Donnie laughed. "I saw you walk into a drug dealer's compound tonight unarmed and escape while the place burned to the ground. I'd say you have a much different background than most people."

Forty-five minutes later the three finished the makeshift defenses. Riker knew that it was a rush job, but he thought it would do the trick.

"Will this be the end of it? I mean if we stop the men who come tonight will that finish off what's left of the drug element?" Megan asked.

Riker shook his head. "No this is just the first step."

25

THE INTERIOR of Megan's home was mostly dark. The only light was the glow from the TV through the window blinds. Riker could see the silhouette of Megan's car sitting in the driveway in the starless night. He watched the home from down the street sitting in bushes along the roadside. He was tucked into the light brush sitting motionless. Everything about the night reminded him of the first time he came to Megan's home. A perfect small town with the sights and smells to match. The only major difference was the team of men coming to kill him.

A smile crossed his lips as he thought of his old call sign and how he got it, Scarecrow.

Riker checked his minimal gear. There were a few dozen zip ties in his back pockets. They were already made into loops with two connected to each other. He would be able to quickly tighten them to subdue any attackers. He also had a two-foot section of rebar. It was a simple weapon, but a very effective one. In close proximity he would have the advantage over anyone with a rifle. In his pocket was a remote control that controlled the lighting he had set up around the home.

Riker wondered if any of the men coming for him was the man that killed Coach. He hoped that he would not have to kill any of the men this evening, but he would make an exception for that murderer. His second thought was of Luke. The idea that his old friend might be part of the team sent to kill him sent a sinking feeling into his stomach.

Riker knew that pondering unknown possibilities would not help him survive the upcoming attack and he pushed the thoughts from his mind. Instead, he focused on the location of traps that he had set up and the advantages that he could gain from his surroundings. His wait was short as two trucks pulled up on the side of the street one hundred yards from Megan's house.

Each truck had five men in the bed. All of the men had shotguns. Once the trucks stopped the men hopped out and stalked towards Megan's house. The drivers of the trucks stayed in place with the engines running and the lights off.

Riker had guessed that they would come from the direction of town. The trucks had driven past him, and he sat on the opposite side of the road watching the attackers approach Megan's home. Riker waited until they were close to the home and then he began his attack.

Riker crouched and moved across the street. He went around to the driver's side of the truck parked farthest from the home and crouched low heading to the driver's door. The night was dark and he hoped that both drivers were watching the men approach the home and not on guard for a rear attack. He reached the first driver's door. From his crouching position, he slid a hand up and grabbed the handle. In one swift motion, he opened the door and stood up while sliding his left arm into the cab before the door had fully opened. His arm went around the driver's neck and Riker pulled him from his seat.

The driver let out a muffled sound and grabbed the steering wheel to keep from being pulled entirely from the truck. He fell sideways half out of the truck and Riker wrapped his arm around the man's neck completing the choke hold. He went limp and Riker pulled him from the truck onto the ground. Riker used the zip ties to secure his arms behind his back and rolled him under the truck hiding the unconscious man.

He closed the door softly and moved to the second truck. The driver must have been focused on the men approaching Megan's house since he was still sitting in the truck. Riker glanced up to see that the men with the shotguns had reached Megan's driveway. They were about to begin their assault on the home.

The men moved down the driveway and Riker closed his eyes and turned his head from the home. Then he hit the switch in his pocket turning on the floodlights. Four lights at five hundred lumens each clicked on. The men with the guns shielded their eyes, but it was too late to save any night vision that they had. All of them would be left with a large afterimage in their vision for several minutes. Riker switched the lights back off.

"Don't let them get away!" One of the men shouted. "Cover the back of the house; we'll take the front."

Riker opened the door of the second truck and pulled the driver out. His arms flailed trying to grab onto anything that would keep him from being pulled from the vehicle, but in his panic, he was simply pulled from his seat. His body would have hit the gravel on the side of the road, but Riker's arm was securely wrapped around his neck. His arms continued to swing wildly for a few seconds until his body went limp. Riker pulled another set of ties from his back pocket and screams echoed into the night from the direction of Megan's home.

Riker ran towards the house. His night vision was intact and he could make out four men on the porch. Three more had gone around the house on the side closest to Riker. He guessed that the other three went around the other side. They were running to the back of the home to cut off any escape. Unfortunately for them, the paths to the side of the home were lined with roofing paper with the adhesive side up. Each sheet was cut four feet in length and had rows of two-inch nails sticking up.

All three men on the side of the home Riker could see were on the ground. Their screams echoed through the night air and they struggled to remove the nails from their feet and limbs.

Riker moved swiftly and silently towards the men at the front of the home. Two stood at the base of the steps to the porch. The others moved to the front door. One of the men stumbled while climbing the steps, betrayed by his lack of vision. He reached out to catch himself with his hand, and a nail slid through the center of his palm. An inch of the metal stuck up through the back of his hand and the palm was stuck to the tar paper that held the nail.

He screamed and dropped his shotgun. When he pulled his arm back away from the nail, the paper came up with it. He swung the hand around in panic to remove the nail. Four feet of paper swung around with nails spaced five inches apart.

The man next to him stopped and tried to steady his friend. When he turned to help his friend he saw a figure approaching the men at the bottom of the stairs from behind.

Riker swiftly reached the two men at the bottom of the steps. Each held a shotgun at the ready, but they were distracted by their screaming companion on the porch. Riker moved to the side of the man on the right, putting the guy between himself and the other armed man. Riker grabbed the middle of the shotgun barrel and swung the steel rebar down towards the man's arm. The man flinched, pulling the trigger as the metal slammed into his right wrist. Buckshot tore into each man on the porch. The center of the blast passed between the men into Megan's front door, but shot tore into the side of each man. The attacker with the nail through his hand spun and fell. He landed on the tack strip of nails sending one into his side. The sleeve of the other man on the porch was torn up above the elbow. Tattered fabric and shredded flesh were exposed. He dropped his weapon and grabbed at the bleeding limb.

Riker pushed the man that he had hit with the rebar into the man standing next to him. They stumbled and fell, one man landing on top of the other. Riker took no chances and swung the rebar before they had even hit the ground. The metal connected with the hands of the second gunman. The fingers seemed to bend in odd fashion when the center of the hand crumbled.

Riker dropped to the ground and his skills as a wrestler took over. The men were stunned and easy to handle. He grabbed the broken limbs and secured them behind their backs.

He did the same with the injured men on the porch. Once they were tied in place, he moved to the side of the house farthest from the trucks.

When Riker came around the corner of the house he saw a man on the ground holding his foot which was stuck to tar paper. Two other men were trying to hold him steady and free the injured foot from the nail and adhesive. When they saw Riker moving in, it was too late.

The first swing of the steel rod connected with the jaw of one of the men helping his friend. Blood sprayed from underneath his chin as his head snapped back. He fell like a fresh cut tree, landing on the lawn with a thud. The other two men scrambled to grab their shotguns which were on the ground next to them. Riker simply stepped on the barrel of one of the guns, pinning it to the ground. He swung his rod again, bringing it down on the assailant's shoulder. The man let out a grunt of pain and Riker brought the bar into the air ready to slam it into the man with a nail through his foot.

The injured man raised his hands in front of his face and screamed out, "Don't hurt me. I surrender."

"Lay on your stomach with your hands behind your back," Riker commanded.

Moments later all three men were bound face down on the lawn. Riker could hear men yelling at each other on the other side of the house. He picked up a shotgun and made his way around the back. Peering around the corner, Riker saw one man lying on the ground attempting to pull tar paper and a nail from his foot. The other two men were shining their phone lights at the ground around them watching for other traps.

Riker fired his shotgun at the ground between the men. "Drop your weapons or the next round takes your head off!"

The man on the ground raised his hands into the air. One of the men with a phone dropped his shotgun and raised his hands in the air. The last man took off running. He only went a few steps before a nail pierced his foot and he fell forward. He tried to catch himself but only managed to put another nail through his forearm from another strip of nails.

Riker bound the three men, leaving them face down on the lawn. Two still had nails through their limbs and tar stuck to their bodies.

He stood up, breathing deep as the adrenaline surged through him, and allowed himself a moment of satisfaction. He'd successfully defended his territory from an attack; there was something primal in the act and in the way it made him feel. He took one more deep breath, then went back to work.

As Riker began to force all of the men to the front of the home he heard a siren in the distance. By the time the police car pulled into the driveway, he had twelve men lying face down in front of the home.

The car came to a stop and the door flew open. An officer got out, staying behind the door for cover and pointing a gun over the window.

"No one move!"

Riker slowly raised both of his hands above his head. "Good evening, Officer Alvarez. We need to talk."

26

"Mr. Riker," Alvarez called. "What exactly is going on here?"

Riker didn't move, and he kept his hands high. He tried not to blink against the beam of the flashlight pointed at his face and the weapon that surely accompanied it. He knew this would be a tense moment for the officers—responding to a call at night to a place where violence had clearly just occurred—so he decided to go with the short version of events. "Some guys attacked my cousin Megan's home. Thankfully, I was able to subdue them."

There was a long silence as Alvarez and her partner took in that information. Finally, Alvarez spoke. "How many men?"

"Twelve."

"Jesus!" Alvarez's partner exclaimed. "You took out twelve guys?"

"They're all alive. Some of them need medical attention, but they'll live. You'll find them lying with their hands zipped tied. I can give you their exact locations if it would be helpful. Three of them are just to my left on the lawn."

The beam of the flashlight left his face and swept over the grass to Riker's left, settling on the prone figures lying there. After a moment, Alvarez let out a heavy sigh, and her hand went to the radio clipped to her shoulder. "Sharon, it's Alvarez. We're going to need some backup. And a couple ambulances."

"Copy that, Alvarez."

The next twenty minutes went by in a flurry of activity. Riker stayed quiet and polite, speaking only when Alvarez or one of the other officers asked him a question. He gave them the location of all the restrained individuals, and he matter-of-factly and succinctly answered their queries about the strange injuries some of the men had sustained. The officers looked at him suspiciously at first, as if there had to be more to the story than he was sharing, but their attitudes started to change as they rounded up the men. All of these individuals were clearly known to the police and none of them seemed to be fans. Riker's position was also helped by the behavior of the men themselves. Most of them refused to say anything, even when the cops asked them direct questions. The ones who spoke were belligerent toward the officers. Slowly but surely, the officers started to relax their attitudes toward Riker.

When the last of the men had been loaded into an ambulance, Alvarez approached Riker. Her weapon was back in its holster, and she wore an expression that was something between bemusement and concern. "You wanted to talk?"

Riker just nodded. He figured he'd let her lead the way in the conversation.

"You've been in town, what, a couple days now?"

"Not quite four days."

She put her hand on her hip. "You want to tell me how a

guy goes about making enemies with just about every man in this town with a drug arrest on his record over the course of four days?"

Riker shrugged. "Winning personality, I guess."

Alvarez glanced over her shoulder, making sure no one else was in earshot. "Mr. Riker, I certainly admire your abilities. Taking out twelve guys who were attacking you in the dead of night is damn impressive."

Riker accepted the compliment with a nod.

"All the same, I can't help but be a little concerned. Do you think these guys are going to stop here? They'll probably be out on bail by the end of the day, and I'm kinda doubting they'll just forget what happened tonight."

Riker considered that a moment before answering. "How long have you been on the force, Officer?"

"Six years next month."

"And have you worked in any other police departments?"

"Not that it matters, but I have not. Why?" There was an edge of annoyance in her voice now.

"Because most towns the size of Kingsport don't have a criminal element like the one you've got here." He watched her face carefully in the glow of the moonlight. He had a good feeling about Alvarez, but he still wasn't completely sure he could trust her. What happened next would help determine that.

She met his gaze for a moment, then looked away. "We have our problems. I'm not going to deny that. Heroin and opioid addictions are out of control."

He wasn't ready to tell her about the facility he'd attacked outside of town, but there was no reason to beat around the bush about the root cause of the problems. "It's not just people selling and buying drugs. There's something bigger happening. Drugs are being produced in Kingsport. The question is why."

She regarded him for a long moment before answering. "Mr. Riker, as you said yourself, you've been here for four days. Don't presume that you know more about the situation here than I do."

"I'm not trying to presume anything. I'm just stating facts. What's happening here is far bigger than any small-town police force is equipped to handle on their own. You need the Feds on this. Get the DEA involved."

She let out a soft chuckle. "You think we haven't? Chief Myers has been working with them for the past two years. They are monitoring the supply chain and gathering evidence. These things don't just happen overnight."

Riker didn't bother arguing with that. Instead, he nodded toward the departing ambulance. "You have an opportunity here. Those guys are spooked. You could find out some valuable information with a little interrogation."

"Not likely. Every one of those guys has been arrested at least twice. They'll lawyer up so fast that we won't have time to ask a single question first."

Riker shook his head. "The guy with the hooked nose and the blond hair?"

"Michael Smitty," Alvarez offered.

"He was hesitant compared to the others. Didn't want to be here. You get him alone, away from his buddies, he'll talk. Maybe you could even find out who's really running things in this town."

She frowned, but then nodded. "I'll give it a try. But I want you to do something for me too."

"What is it?"

"Get somewhere safe. You might think you understand what's happening in Kingsport, but you don't. Taking down twelve guys is damn impressive, but this won't end there. You're in dangerous waters. This is my town. Let me and my colleagues handle things from here."

Riker glanced over at the front porch and saw Megan sitting on the stoop, her arms wrapped around her chest. He looked back at Alvarez. "Your point is taken, Officer. I appreciate your concern."

Alvarez stared at him for another moment, her mouth half-open, like she wanted to say more, but then she turned and headed back toward her squad car.

Riker waited until she was gone and then joined Megan on the porch. Not long ago, the yard had been filled with police, paramedics, and nosy neighbors, but now all was dark and they were alone. It was almost as if the past few hours had never happened. But the slight shake in Megan's shoulders as she sat silently told another story.

"You all right?" Riker asked.

"Yes." She paused. "Maybe. I don't know." She turned to look at him. "You were amazing tonight."

"You weren't so bad yourself."

She let out a joyless laugh. "You kidding me? What did I do? Picked up you and Donnie at the drug lab and hid inside while you took out the bad guys? You call that help?"

"I do," Riker said. "You stood in the face of evil and didn't flinch. Staying inside tonight was the right move. If you'd come out and tried to help, you might have gotten hurt. Or one of those guys might have grabbed you to use as a hostage. You did the right thing."

"I'm not so sure."

"I am. And if you ever find yourself in a similar situation, I want you to do the same thing again."

She let out another laugh. "Let's hope I never do. You beat the bad guys. This is finally over."

Riker knew she was wrong on that front, but he didn't want to take away her happy illusion just yet. The chaos of having twelve of their men arrested and their drug lab destroyed would buy Riker a few hours before the bad guys struck again, and he needed to make sure he used that time well.

He put his arm around Megan and gave her a quick hug. "Why don't you go inside and try to get some sleep."

"Not a bad idea," she said, stifling a yawn. "What about you? Are you going to get some rest?"

"Not yet. There's one more thing I need to do first."

27

RIKER WAITED until Megan was in her room before he took the car. He knew that she needed rest. She claimed after the attack that she would never sleep again. Riker knew better. The adrenaline would wear off from the last several hours and her body would demand rest.

The downside of that fact was his body demanded rest as well. He sat in the car parked in front of one of the nicer homes in town. His leg screamed at him and he wondered how many more times it could take pressure before it snapped. His eyelids felt heavy and tried to slide down, sending him into an unconscious world. He snapped them up, reminding himself that his force of will was much stronger than two small flaps of skin.

The task that sat in front of him could not wait until the morning. By that time the man in the house would be gone, and tracking a man on the run would take time that Riker didn't have. He got out of the car and closed the door without making a sound. As he crept around the home, he could hear movement inside. He considered that there might be exterior security cameras, but he doubted the occupant currently had the time to watch them.

He reached a door on the side of the garage. This one had a simple lock and turned easily with Riker's bump key. The garage held a high-end sedan with its trunk open. The door to the house was also propped open. Riker moved around the car, examining the contents of the trunk. There were several duffel bags and a suitcase. The duffel bags were lumpy, poorly concealing stacks of money within.

As Riker walked into the house, he almost collided with Doc Hanson. There was a thin layer of sweat on the man's face, and he held a duffel bag that matched the others. When he saw Riker, he let out a soft yelp.

"Matthew, what are you doing here?"

"Don't worry Doc; I'm not here to hurt you. I'm just looking for some answers."

The words did little to calm Hanson. His entire body was visibly tight. "That's good to hear, but you may not be my only visitor this evening. I'm guessing any other guest I have will not be so polite."

"Then let's be frank with one another. I think we are past the point of games."

The doctor stared at Riker, his face pale. "Any information I give you will result in my death. Since I'd rather like to live past this evening, I don't have much to say."

"Based on what you said a moment ago, you may not make it past this evening no matter what you tell me."

Doc hesitated. He pulled a gun from his jacket pocket and pointed it at Riker with a shaky hand. "That's true, but I may be able to trade your life for mine. If I turn you over to them, I may just live to see another day."

Riker slowly raised both hands and moved towards the table in the kitchen.

"Where are you going?"

"If we're going to wait around for someone else we might as well get comfortable. I do have a fractured leg after all. Getting off of it sounds nice." Riker casually took a seat at the table. He gestured to the chair across from him. "I'd love some coffee, but I'm guessing you don't have time to put on a fresh pot."

Doc kept the gun trained on Riker. His grip on the weapon told Riker that he had little to no experience using it. Doc took a seat across the table resting his elbow on its surface. "Who sent you here?"

Riker gave a slight smile. "No one, and before you ask I really am a beekeeper. I don't work for any government organization or anyone else for that matter. I'm self-employed."

"You're telling me that you just happened to come into town and disrupt a drug trafficking operation? No one sent you?"

"That's right. The only reason I came was for Coach's funeral. After that, one thing just led to another."

Hanson gave a soft snort. "You're telling me that blowing up a cartel barn was 'just one of those things'?"

Riker shrugged. "I guess I am."

"You want to tell me how you figured out I was involved?"

"I started getting suspicious when we talked in the coffee shop. You were a little too eager to have me help find Coach's informant."

Hanson gave a thin smile. "We hadn't had any luck. I figured maybe you'd be able to do better. But certainly that wasn't the only clue."

"No. After my injury, you quickly changed tactics. You pressured me to get out of town. That supported my theory, but honestly, I didn't know for certain until I got here and saw the duffle bags in your trunk." He leaned forward. "What about you? How did you go from small-town doctor to drug runner? I mean this house is nice, but I would think you could afford it on a doctor's salary."

"You're right. But having a couple million saved away for a rainy day is nice. I don't run drugs, Matthew. I just help with management."

"Is there a difference?"

"I've never shown up to anyone's house in the middle of the night with a shotgun. From what I hear, I'm glad I wasn't at your home this evening."

"Okay, you haven't killed anyone, but I'm guessing you ordered the men to show up at my cousin's place."

"Like I said, I just manage. If it makes you feel better, they were just supposed to bring you in. There are a few people that have some questions for you. Although if what you just told me is true they will be disappointed by the answers."

"How did you justify producing enough drugs for a medium-size city?"

Doc shook his head. "I got here by baby steps. It seems bad now, but I don't think you can really judge."

"You're going to have to explain that one a little better, Doc. It's pretty easy to judge someone who profits off the destruction of other people's lives. Especially if it is someone that they trust."

"Have you ever heard the stories of how Pablo Escobar made his offers to government officials?"

"Sure, silver or lead."

"That's right. Take a bribe or take a bullet to the head. It is an easy choice for most people. It worked so well that other men use the same tactic."

"But we aren't in South America? No cartel would be bold enough to set up a production and distribution facility in the States."

"Baby steps. We were simply a stop on the way to other cities in the distribution network. None of us invited a cartel into this town. We were just a regular small town with a drug problem. Then one of the generals got an ambitious idea. He wanted to corrupt a small town. Why cross a border when you can make the product here."

The last pieces fell into place for Riker. "You can't corrupt a large city. There are just too many people and elements to control. In a town like this five or six key people would do the trick."

"Now you're getting it."

"You're telling me that everyone here took the money? No one tried to stop them? This is your home. How could you all just give in?"

"We didn't. Chief Raynor was never involved. All of us were already taking money to look the other way. When they decided to increase the operation they needed law enforcement involved. They made him an offer. He and his wife ended up with a bullet in their heads."

Riker paused for a moment and then clenched his fist. "You covered that up. There was never any official report that they were murdered."

"Like you said, you only need a few key people in a small town. After I saw what they did to the chief, my choice was easy. They also convinced the new chief that the choice was simple."

"Do you even understand how many lives you have helped destroy? Don't you care about anyone?"

"People were dumping poison into their veins long before these animals got involved. What I told you the other day in the coffee shop was true. I've watched the drug problem slowly spin out of control in this town over the years. I don't make them do it, and they'll continue doing so with or without me. I could have died for a principle and changed nothing, or I could get rich and stay alive. I chose the second option."

As Hanson finished his sentence Riker shot across the table. The doctor reacted by trying to move back and away from Riker, but he was too slow. Before the older man could stand up the gun was in Riker's hand.

Hanson sat with a dumb look on his face. Riker sat back in his seat with the pistol pointed at him.

"Managers tend to lack the skills of the men with their boots on the ground. For future reference, this model has a safety." Riker flipped up a switch next to the trigger guard of the gun. "Now it's off."

Doc Hanson lowered his head. "I don't suppose you'd do me the kindness of pulling that trigger?"

"Not today Doc. In fact, I'm going to give you a shot at redemption. I'm going to clean this town up, but I need a little more information."

"What could I possibly give you?"

"Good managers are organized. They always keep records." Riker gave him a wink. "You strike me as a very good manager."

Riker took his phone out of his pocket and sent a text to Officer Alvarez.

Did you get anything from questioning the attackers?

Alvarez responded a moment later. *Actually yes. We got a name from Smitty, the man you pointed out. Thanks.*

I'm assuming that that name was Doc Hanson.

There was a long pause. Then she responded. *Why would you say that?*

I'm holding him for you at his house. You should get over here quickly. I also wouldn't mention where you are going to the chief.

Alvarez texted back. *Do not move a muscle. I'm on my way.*

Hanson looked at Riker. "I thought you worked alone. Who was that?"

"I said I work for myself. I've learned that there are times when it's better not to work alone."

"You know that they are going to kill both of us. The best we can hope for is a quick death. I assure you that it isn't always quick."

"Actually neither of us knows that. The future can have a funny way of surprising you." Riker stood up with the gun still pointed at the doctor. "I do have one more question for you, Doc, and I want you to tell me true."

"What?"

"Do you have any good coffee? I really could use a cup."

Ten minutes later, Officer Alvarez arrived to find Riker and Doc Hanson drinking coffee like old friends, boxes of records stacked on the table.

28

Riker set down the stack of papers he'd been flipping through when Alvarez walked through the door. Her face was unreadable, but something about the way her eyes flashed when she saw Doctor Hanson put Riker on alert. Every time he'd seen her so far, there'd been something reserved and careful about her demeanor. This time was different. What he saw behind her eyes was barely restrained fury.

Doc Hanson seemed to sense it too. He knocked back the rest of his coffee in one go. "Officer Alvarez. How are you?"

"Not great, but better than you, asshole." She raised her left hand, showing a paper clutched there. "This is an emergency warrant to arrest you and to search your house."

He carefully took the paper and read it. "So it is. Though the search warrant is rather unnecessary. I gave Matt here full access to my records, and I would have done the same for you."

Riker gestured to the stack of papers and the laptop on the floor next to him. "I gotta say, it's pretty interesting reading. Doc might be a lot of things, but a slouch at record-keeping isn't one of them. This reads like a complete history into the cartel's involvement in Kingsport."

"The cartel?" The anger in Alvarez's voice was even clearer now. "You brought a drug cartel to this town."

"In a way," Doc answered, his voice flat. "I didn't mean for this to happen, but I'm not going to claim to be an innocent victim either. No point in that now. I'm as good as dead, and they say that confession is good for the soul."

"You wish. Death is too good for you. You'll be rotting in a prison cell for the next two decades."

The doctor looked down at his empty coffee cup for a long moment before answering. "Officer Alvarez, if you think the cartel is going to let me live long enough to see a trial let alone prison, you are very naive indeed."

Alvarez sank into the chair across from Doctor Hanson. "Tell me how it worked. You prescribed opioids and got them hooked? Then transitioned them to heroin?"

"Not initially, no."

Alvarez leaned forward, the fury clear on her face now. Riker waited, aware that there was a fair chance she might attack the doctor at any moment.

"You son of a bitch. You prescribed Oxycontin to my mother."

He met her gaze, his eyes blank. "Yes, I did. And she took the prescribed dose after her surgery and then stopped. She had self-control. Not all patients are like that. I suppose that after I watched dozens of patients get addicted and then turn to heroin after I refused to refill their prescriptions, I figured that I might as well make some money off of them."

Riker looked at Alvarez. "If you want to hit him, I'm totally okay with that."

The officer gripped the arms of her chair hard. "Of

course I want to hit him. I'd love to do a hell of a lot worse than that. But we're not going to play it that way. I want to do this thing by the book. I can't give whatever fancy lawyer the cartel buys him any ammunition."

"Other than the fact that this vigilante broke into my home and attacked me?" Doc said with a laugh.

"He's not wrong," Riker said. "I hope I didn't screw this up for you."

"Are you kidding? Since you've gotten to town, we've made more progress in taking down this drug ring than we have in the past two years." Her eyes softened and she shot him a smile. "On the other hand, my paperwork has increased rather dramatically, so I'm not entirely happy with you."

Riker returned her smile. "I don't envy you that."

Alvarez stood up and stepped toward Doctor Hanson. "Okay, let's get you to the station. We've got a nice cozy cell waiting for you. I checked it before I left, and there wasn't a single cartel operative hiding under the bed, so you can look forward to a peaceful night where you will most certainly not be murdered."

"Perhaps not tonight," Doc said, his voice deadly serious now. "Perhaps not even tomorrow. But El Leon will come. And when he does, your bars and your guns will not protect me."

A chill ran up Riker's arm. *El Leon.* "The lion. That's the man you work for?"

Doc Hanson shook his head. "The man I work for wouldn't deem to come to our little town himself. He's not one for crossing borders. Too much exposure. But he will send El Leon, and that man is like a force of nature. He doesn't think. He doesn't feel emotions, as far as I can tell. He simply carries out his master's wishes."

Riker's mind flashed back to a story he'd heard a couple days prior, in this very house. "He's the guy who killed Donnie's brother."

"Yes. And believe it or not, that doesn't even rank among the top three most brutal things I've seen him do. "Women... children...." He turned to Alvarez. "...police officers. He doesn't care, and he shows no mercy. It brings me no pleasure to say it, but I truly believe we're all going to die at his hands."

Riker shrugged off the threat. It was hardly the first time he'd heard one like it. He'd faced his share of brutal enforcers, each of whom had made a career of striking fear into the hearts of their enemies, but he was still standing. If El Leon made the mistake of coming to Kingsport, he'd suffer the same fate as the rest of them.

"Enough." Alvarez's voice was even, but it was clear she'd been a bit shaken by Doc Hanson's words. Apparently she didn't have the same background as Riker when it came to facing off against killers. "I've about had it with your scare tactics. On your feet, Doctor. You are officially under arrest."

As she cuffed the doctor, Riker glanced down at the stack of papers on the floor next to his chair. He'd had the chance to skim through some of it before Alvarez had arrived, and it had provided quite a bit of context to what was happening in Kingsport. The good doctor hadn't been afraid to put his co-conspirators' names in writing, and there were quite a few people implicated, including Luke. But there were two names Riker hadn't seen, and he knew this could be his last chance to ask Doc Hanson about them.

He got to his feet and held up a hand as Alvarez started to lead the doctor away.

"Doc, answer me one more thing. Coach Kane. What do you know about his death?"

The doctor gave Riker a thin smile. "That's why you're getting mixed up in all of this? You really care about your old wrestling coach this much?"

"I do. And if you're right about El Leon being this unstoppable force who's gunning for you, what's it matter? You might as well tell me."

"I suppose you're right. And I'd be happy to tell you. If there was anything to tell. Truth is, Coach Kane was a nosy busybody who was digging into our business, but I'm not sure what he found. If the cartel had anything to do with his death, it happened far above my paygrade."

Alvarez shook her head sadly. "Come on, Doctor Hanson. Let's get you to your cell."

Riker followed them out to the car. Once she'd put Hanson in the back, he pulled her aside. "You need to be careful here. We're going to have to watch his cell. He might be right about the cartel ordering his death."

She raised a skeptical eyebrow. "In a police station?"

"There's something you need to know. Chief Myers is working with the cartel."

Her eyes searched his, inspecting him to see if he was kidding. "That's impossible."

"I'm afraid it's not. At best, he's been looking the other way and burying the drug cases. At worst, he might be involved in the production. Either way, that story he's been selling you about working with the DEA is a fairy tale."

She looked like she might be sick. "My God. If you're right..."

"I am."

She nodded slowly. "All right. I'll take your word for it for now. I'll watch him."

Riker watched as they drove off in the police car,

wondering if Doc Hanson was right on El Leon. Either way, Riker knew there was much more work to be done.

29

RIKER SLID into the guest bed at Megan's house as quietly as he could. He needed rest and the sun would be up in a few hours. He hoped his cousin had managed to get some sleep. A lot of work was ahead of them, and performing the required task would be hard with no rest.

Sometime later, he startled awake, hearing movement in the house. For a moment he was disoriented. He didn't remember falling asleep, and now the sun lit up the shades in his room. He sat up and recognized the sounds in the house as meal preparations in the kitchen. The smell of bacon hit his nose and he relaxed. He could also smell himself and decided a shower would make breakfast more pleasant for all parties.

After he was clean and dressed he found Megan putting the food on the kitchen table. It was a traditional breakfast of eggs, bacon, toast, hash browns and coffee.

"Thanks. You didn't have to do all this."

"Well, you didn't have to save our lives. I figure breakfast makes us even."

Riker smiled and took a seat. "Even Steven."

"Where did you go last night? I saw that the car was in a different spot this morning."

Riker chewed on a piece of bacon for a moment. He wanted to share a normal meal before talking about what he'd discovered that night. By the time he finished his bacon, he'd decided there was no point in delaying the inevitable.

"I went to see Doc Hanson. He is a part of everything that has been happening here."

Megan shook her head. "That's impossible. Doc is on the city council. He looks after everyone in town. He's a good man."

Riker told her all about the previous evening. His conversation with Doc and the confession he provided. When he finished Megan's mouth was half-opened and there were tears at the corners of her eyes.

"I'm sorry that he betrayed the people of this town."

Megan wiped her eyes with the palm of her hand. She drew a breath and sat up tall. "I'm sorry about that too, but I'm glad that he's going to get what he deserves. Most of all I'm glad that this is all over. Now that we weeded out the problem we can give the people of this town the help they deserve."

Riker saw the determination in his cousin's eyes. She reminded him that there was still good in the world and some people are worth fighting for. "I know you will put in the work to get this place back to the way it used to be. There is one last problem that we need to deal with. It's a rather large one."

Megan raised an eyebrow. "I thought blowing up the lab and finding the man who was running everything would be the end of it."

"It is. The problem is Hanson wasn't the one running the

operation. He was working for someone much worse. The production here represented a major investment from a cartel leader. I have a feeling that he will not just let my actions go."

"The cartel? Like a South American drug cartel? They were here in our town?"

"I'm afraid so. I'm guessing that they are sending a force here to try and salvage the operation. Even if they decided to let this operation go they will want to make an example of the people that destroyed their business."

"You think they will come after you out of spite?"

"I think they will come after all of us out of spite. They work in a business that relies on fear and cruelty. Even if attacking the people of this town doesn't make any logical sense they will do it just to keep from looking weak. We are dealing with the worst of the worst."

"So what now?"

"Finishing breakfast sounds like a good first step. After that we need to figure out who is coming and when. I'd love to figure out who is pulling the strings from south of the border and pay them a visit, but I think we need to take care of the immediate threat first."

"Is that the kind of thing you do? Go into foreign nations and kill bad people."

"It was the kind of thing I did. I thought that I had gotten out of it, but life never seems to go along with your plans."

Megan smiled. "I suppose that's true. I never thought that dealing with a drug cartel would be on my to-do list, but there it is. Item number two after cleaning up the dishes."

"I'll be glad when we can check that off the list," Riker said with a laugh.

For a brief moment, time seemed to stop for Riker. He

looked at Megan sitting across from him with a smile on her face. Steam rose from the coffee and caught the light of the morning. Danger was on the horizon, but for this moment they were safe. He realized this was the first breakfast he ever had with family.

Megan caught the distant look in Riker's eyes. "You okay?"

"Yeah, I'm fine. I just realized that I've never done this before."

"Done what?"

"Sat and had breakfast with family."

Megan laughed. "You can't be serious."

"I never really thought about it until this moment. My dad hit the sauce hard every night. My mom and I always moved around the house like mice in the morning so we didn't wake a grumpy bear. Clattering around in the kitchen was out of the question. After I left I joined the military and then lived on my own. It's just never happened for me until I came back here. You are my only real family left."

"I'm sorry Matt. That's horrible."

Riker shook his head. "It's really not that bad; it's just the way things turned out for me. I just wanted to say thank you. You showed me something that I didn't even know I was missing."

"I know it's been a long time, but home is home. Now let's finish this extravagant meal that I made for you," she said with a wink.

He ate for a few minutes before he spoke again. "I wish I would have come back here years ago. Maybe I could have helped make a difference. Maybe things would not have gotten so bad."

"Sometimes people take the long way home. Your path

was just a little longer than most. I'm glad that you made it back."

"Me too."

Before their plates were emptied there was a pounding on the door. Riker stood up and grabbed a knife from the block on the counter. He palmed the handle and the blade faced backward along his forearm. "Wait here. I'll see who it is."

He went to the window in the living room and crouched low. The pounding came again on the door in a frantic series of knocks. Riker carefully pushed back the blind enough to peer at the front door. He saw Luke pounding on the door. He wasn't holding a weapon that Riker could see, and he looked panicked.

Riker moved next to the door and spoke loud enough for Luke to hear him. "Fair warning, Luke. I'm done holding back."

"I know things are really messed up right now, but I need to talk to you. Things have gotten out of hand. I don't know who else to turn to."

"Sorry to tell you this, but you knocked on the wrong door. I know you were there the night Coach died."

Luke's eyes widened in surprise, but he quickly recovered. "I'm sorry I lied to you about that, but I didn't have anything to do with his death. I can explain."

Riker eased the door open and peered out at his friend. "I think we're a bit past that point. I don't believe a word you're saying. You're in trouble and you're just trying to save your own ass."

"No man, this isn't about me, it's about who's coming to Kingsport." Luke stared at Riker, his eyes pleading. "It's the cartel. They are on their way, and when they get here they are going to kill every one of us."

30

Eighteen years ago

As Matt saw his father's fist smash into his mom's nose, the rest of the world seemed to fade away. The smell of stale cigarette smoke that always permeated their small house, the fragments of the broken plate on the floor at his mother's feet, the distant sound of Johnny Cash, the record skipping now—all of it disappeared. All he saw was his dad hitting his mom.

It was easy enough to piece together the broad strokes of what had happened here. Dad had come home early, probably laid off from his job again, and taken a bottle to the living room to start drinking. He'd turned on his music and proceeded to get completely and thoroughly day-drunk. Then he'd come to the kitchen for a snack and stumbled across his wife. Maybe she'd said something that annoyed him. Maybe she'd just made a noise he didn't like—two plates clacking together as she stacked them perhaps—and it had set him off. Now here they were. And Matt made three. The happy family was together once again.

Matt's hands clenched into fists and his body began to shake with rage. "Get away from her!"

Gary Riker looked up suddenly, like a startled animal, and for a moment Matt imagined he saw a flash of shame on the older man's face. Then his eyes settled on Matt, and the shame disappeared, replaced with a wicked smile.

"Matty. Your mother and I are just having a little conversation. Go to your room. I'll get to you in a few minutes."

Matt took a step forward, the anger inside outweighing his mounting fear. "I'm not going anywhere. Get away from Mom."

Gary's smile widened. He was actually amused by his son's attempt to interfere. "I know your heart's in the right place, kid, but this is adult stuff. Go to your room right fucking now, or you're going to get hurt."

Matt's rage was so strong now that he could only utter a single word in response. "No."

Now Gary's eyes went cold. "Sure about that? Remember what happened last time?"

Matt certainly did remember. He'd spent days afraid that his jaw might be broken. His father, on the other hand, easily rebuffed his attempted attack and had left without a single bruise. Still, that had been over a year ago. How many hours had Matt spent in the weight room since then? How many hours on the wrestling mat?

What his father said next made Matt wonder if his face was so easy to read.

"You might be hot shit on the mat, son, but here in the real world, there aren't any rules. Ain't no referee to make sure we fight clean. In a world like that, your old man can still lay you out without breaking a sweat. So I'm going to tell you one more time. Go to your room."

Matt paused for a moment, then nodded, doing his best to make it appear his spirit was broken. He saw the beginnings of the smile returning to his father's face. Then he charged.

He covered the three steps between them in an instant, moving with a quickness earned from years of conditioning with Coach Kane. But somehow, impossibly, his father reacted even more quickly. Despite being drunk, Gary Riker had impressive reflexes. He brought his hands up in a boxer's stance and threw a quick jab. The fist connected with Matt's chin, sending him staggering backward.

"Tried to tell you, boy." Gary stalked toward his son as he spoke. "It may have been twenty years since I served, but the Army boxing team taught me well. Your old man can still throw a punch."

It was so powerful a blow that Matt had to blink away the tears from his eyes. He was so angry now that all conscious thought was gone. That was okay. That left the other part of him in control. The part of him that had gone all the way to the wrestling state championship. The warrior.

His father was right—in a boxing match against him, Matt wouldn't stand a chance. But he was right about something else too. There were no rules here. This wasn't a boxing match. He could use whatever means necessary.

Matt dropped low and sprang forward again. This time, Gary wasn't ready. His son had challenged him a few times over the years, but a single punch was all it had ever taken to stop him. Gary wasn't expecting this second attack.

Matt wrapped his arms around his father's legs and pressed forward, driving him to the ground in a vicious takedown. The old man's head hit the linoleum with a thud. Matt brought back his fist and drove it into his father's stomach, forcing the air out of his lungs. As the older man gasped, Matt hit him again, this time punching him in the eye.

"Whoa, Matt! Hold up!"

The voice came from behind him, but Matt ignored it. He punched again, and his fist connected with his father's nose.

Arms wrapped around Matt's chest, pulling at him, attempting to drag him off his father. Matt threw an elbow back at his attacker and felt it connect. He looked over his shoulder and saw Luke staggering backward, his hand going to his nose.

"Shit! Luke!" Matt's conscious mind was beginning to return now. He got up off his father and took a step toward his friend.

"It's okay, man. I'm good." Luke blinked hard as he surveyed the scene in the kitchen. "What the hell is going on here?"

Matt stammered, not sure how to even begin to explain. Luke's life was different from Matt's. His dad was caring. Affectionate. Matt would be willing to bet his scholarship that the man had never laid a hand on Luke or his mother. How could he even begin to explain the domestic war that took place in his home on a regular basis?

Out of the corner of his eye, Matt saw his father struggling to his feet. And his hand was reaching out toward the stove and the cast-iron pan waiting there.

Matt's focused again, sharper than ever. He'd stood up to his father, even got the better of him. Gary Riker would not let that stand. He'd put Matt or his mother in the hospital as payback. Maybe both of them. Matt couldn't let that happen.

As his father reached for the pan, Matt charged. Once again he went for the legs, wrapping his father up, taking him to the ground where he didn't stand a chance against his wrestling champion son. Matt tackled his father hard and fast, and mid-takedown, he heard a loud, terrible sound, like a thud and a crack. For a split second, he thought it might be a gunshot. Then he saw the strange angle of his father's neck, and he realized with mounting horror what had happened.

His father's head had hit the edge of the counter at exactly the wrong angle. That had combined with the downward force Matt was applying resulted in his snapping his neck.

Matt let go of his father, and the man sank the rest of the way to the floor, his head rolling loosely, as if all the muscles supporting it had melted away in an instant. A strained wheeze escaped the man's mouth. Then the light went out of his eyes, and he lay still.

Matt's eyes went to his mother, who hadn't moved since he entered the kitchen. Blood seeped from her split lip, and her left eye was already beginning to swell, but the horror was still clear on her face. "My God, Matty. What did you do?"

Though he didn't want to, Matt turned back to his father. His strangely twisted head lay on the linoleum, and his wide, vacant eyes gaped at Matt, as if they wanted to swallow him.

He didn't know how long he sat there, motionless and afraid. It felt like hours, but it must have been far less than that. He had no idea what to do next. It was as if he was waiting for someone to come fix this problem. But no one could.

And then someone did.

Luke marched back into the kitchen, something clutched in a kitchen towel in his hand. The light flashed against the object, and Matt recognized it. His father's pistol. Luke wrapped his arms around Gary Riker's limp body and lifted him, leaning him against the kitchen counter and holding him there in some semblance of a standing position. Then he put the gun into the man's right hand and carefully inserted the limp index finger through the trigger guard.

"Cover your ears," Luke said. Then he aimed the gun at the far wall and pressed down on Gary's index finger hard. The pistol went off, its report echoing through the small kitchen, its bullet punching a hole in the drywall.

Then Luke carefully slid Gary Riker back to the floor. He left the gun where it fell by the older man's side.

"Okay, we're going to call the police," Luke said, turning to Matt and his mother. "But first, we have to remember what we all saw. Mr. Riker was drunk and beating on you when Matt and I came in, Mrs. Riker. Matt tried to stop him, and they fought a little. But then Mr. Riker pulled this gun out of his waistband and started waving it around. He took a shot at Matt, but he missed. He started to aim again, but Matt tackled him. His head hit the edge of the counter on the way down and we heard his neck snap." He turned to Matt. "Is that what you remember happening?"

Matt drew a deep breath and felt his mind begin to clear under the conviction of his friend's story. "Yeah. That's exactly what happened."

"Good." Luke turned to Mrs. Riker. "And we witnessed it

going down just like that. It was self-defense. Matt saved his own life and probably ours too. Isn't that right, Mrs. Riker?"

Sharon Riker stared at her husband's limp body for a long moment. Then she nodded weakly.

"Good," Luke said. "Then I'll make the call."

31

RIKER STEPPED out onto the front porch causing Luke to step back. Once Riker got a good look at him in the morning light it was clear his old friend hadn't slept recently. He looked as if he was on the verge of a panic attack.

"Put your arms out to the side."

Luke shook his head. "If I was here to kill you I wouldn't have knocked on the front door."

"Maybe, but I'd rather be certain that you aren't bringing any weapons into the house."

Luke did as he was told and lifted his arms. After a quick pat down, Riker was satisfied and let him into the house. Riker pointed to the couch and he took a seat.

"What the hell is he doing here?" Megan said as she entered the room.

"That's a great question. What the hell are you doing here?"

"I'm looking for help. I know I fucked up bad, but like I said this isn't about me."

"Okay, who is this about?"

Luke took a deep breath. He looked from Riker to

Megan trying to decide how to continue. "This may sound crazy, but you have to believe me. The operation in Kingsport is being run by a major drug cartel."

"You're always a little bit behind," Megan said in a bitter tone. "We already knew that."

"What? Who told you?"

Riker gestured to the couch, then sat in the chair across from it. "Let's just say we figured out the cartel connection. I guessed that they would not take the loss of their production facility lightly and that they would retaliate. If you have more specific information, I'm all ears. But first, you need to tell me the truth about the night Coach died."

"Yeah, of course." Luke sank down onto the couch, his eyes hollow. "There's this guy on my crew named Eric Underwood. You know him?"

Riker said nothing. He wasn't about to reveal anything to Luke. Not until he knew the truth.

Luke sighed. "Okay, I get it. Point is, I knew Eric had been unhappy for a while, and I suspected he might be talking to someone. Obviously, I couldn't have that. But I didn't want the cartel to know. They are the kill first and validate later types. So I decided to follow him that night. He spotted my truck while he was parking, and he took off. Guess I spooked him. But the other car didn't see me. The moment I realized it was Coach, everything changed."

"How so?" Megan asked.

Luke leaned forward, a pained expression on his face. "If Coach was the one Eric was talking to, that meant Coach might have some sort of a plan to help him. And if Coach could help Eric, maybe he could help me too. For the first time in over a year, I saw a possible way out. That was when I saw someone walking toward Coach's car."

Riker's face betrayed nothing. He could tell it was difficult for his friend to tell his tale, but he wasn't in the mood to make it any easier.

"There were no other cars. This guy was on foot. It was dark, so I couldn't get a good look, but I could tell he was big. I couldn't say who it was for sure, but I had my suspicions. In that moment, I was almost certain it was El Leon." He visibly shuddered as he said the name.

"El Leon?" Megan asked. "The same guy who killed Donnie's brother?"

Luke nodded. "He's the cartel's top enforcer. The worst of the worst. When I saw him, I didn't hesitate. I threw the truck into gear and raced out of there. The next morning, I heard that Coach died in that very spot." He paused, looking Riker in the eyes. "I'm sorry, Matt. If I wouldn't have been such a coward, I might have been able to save him."

"Perhaps," Riker allowed. "The question is, what are you going to do about it? Are you ready to be brave?"

Luke gave the question serious consideration. "I'm not going to lie. I'm scared shitless. If El Leon is coming here..." He trailed off, his eyes distant.

"What is it about this El Leon?" Riker asked. "I've never seen you scared of anyone. Not like this."

Luke was quiet for a long moment before he answered. "I've never told this story to anyone, and putting words to what I saw is just about the last thing I want to do now. Maybe telling you will help you understand what we're up against."

"Telling us what?" Megan asked.

Luke squeezed his eyes shut and drew a deep breath. "The first time I met El Leon was in a bar fifty miles outside Mexico City. Quiet place in the middle of nowhere. This was when we were simply moving product and were just starting to talk about production. The cartel picked the location and instructed Doc Hanson and me to come alone. We made the trip down, not really sure what we were getting ourselves into. We walked into the bar and got our first look at El Leon."

He paused, shifting in his seat.

"He's a big guy. Maybe six-five and rock solid. Handsome, I guess. He's got this calm demeanor, like he's above whatever is going on around him. And his eyes... I'm not sure how to describe them other than to say they are cold. Not lifeless exactly. I guess I'd call them reptilian. Anyway, we sat down and started negotiating the details. It went surprisingly well. Both Doc and I were impressed by the terms. They were generous. If this worked out, Doc and I would be set for life."

"This story isn't making you any friends so far," Riker growled.

"I doubt this next part will either. I wanted to be respectful, so I asked El Leon to pass a message to the cartel boss. I said, 'Please give our regards to Nicolás Marcillas and tell him we look forward to our partnership.' El Leon didn't react. He stood up calmly, walked to the front door, and turned the deadbolt. Then he reached into his jacket and pulled out a pistol. He proceeded to put a bullet through the head of every man and woman in that bar other than us."

"My God," Megan said, a hand going to her mouth.

"When they were all dead, he sat back down. His shirt was splattered with blood, but he was just as calm as he'd been the moment we walked into the bar. He looked me in the eye and said, 'We don't speak that name.' Then we went over the details of the arrangement one more time. Doc and I had to sit there surrounded by fifteen dead bodies, brains and blood pooling on the floor all around us, the smell of death and shit heavy in the air. When we'd finished our discussion, El Leon politely shook our hands and walked out of the bar." Luke looked up at Riker "That's the kind of man we're dealing with. The kind who can execute fifteen innocent people and then sit back down like nothing happened. He's coming here, and he's bringing a small army."

A chill ran through Riker. He'd seen some terrible things, horrendous acts he'd never be able to wipe from his mind, but what Luke was describing still shook him. He'd had run-ins with men like El Leon before, men who treated killing with a cold indifference. Men who believed the dispatching of human lives was just another task to be done for their masters. Such men were beyond dangerous.

It was silent for a long while before Riker finally spoke. "Why come here? We already destroyed the production facility and the heroin."

Luke shook his head. "That was just the tip of the iceberg. The silos on the farm hold most of the supply. They hold grain on the top but there is a second door to the hidden storage rooms. There is easily three hundred million worth of product in those silos right now."

"Holy shit. They made that much here in Kingsport?" Megan asked.

"I know it's really messed up. But it gets worse. The cartel guys are coming here to recover the heroin, but they are also going to clean up loose ends. They want me to assemble my entire crew at the farm. I have a feeling that after we help load up the drugs we are all going to end up buried in the field behind the farm. It isn't going to stop there. Anyone who knew about what was happening here is in danger and so are their families."

Megan glared at him. "If you hadn't brought them here, we wouldn't be in this mess!"

"I get it. I'm a total piece of shit, but I never thought that it would come to this. I was just trying to make a little money on the side. By the time I realized who I was getting involved with it was too late."

Riker could see that Megan was about to lose her cool. He spoke before she could. "We will have time to decide what kind of punishment you deserve later. Right now I need to know how many are coming and when."

"Let's just say the odds are going to be against us. I've seen you beat some long odds over the last few days, and I'm hoping that you can do it again."

32

An hour later, Riker and Luke approached the front door of the Kingsport Police Station. Luke paused a moment before opening the door. "Do you think this will work?"

"There's only one way to find out." Riker pushed open the door and stepped inside.

When they entered Riker noticed that Ed was missing from the reception desk. He could hear a bit of commotion coming from the main room. Riker and Luke went down the hall to find Ed, Alvarez and another officer each sitting at their desks typing on their computers.

"Looks like the Kingsport police are hard at work this morning," Riker said, announcing their presence.

Alvarez glanced up from her computer. "Actually we're still hard at work from last night. We haven't even finished processing the men who attacked you." Her eyes shifted from Riker to Luke. "Are you adding him to the list of people I need to lock up?"

"He's actually here to help us with something. I assume the doctor's still in custody?"

"Yep, he is alive and well." She turned her computer

monitor so Riker could see it. A small window with a video feed showed Doc Hanson sitting at a table in an interrogation room. "I've been keeping an eye on him all night."

"Is Chief Myers in?"

"Yeah, he got here a few hours ago. He went straight into his office and he hasn't come out."

"So he doesn't know what was in the files we took from Doc Hanson's house yet?"

"No. I told him that I wasn't sure what Hanson knew. Just that he was somehow involved with the drug dealers."

"Great. We need to meet with him."

"You want to meet with the chief?"

"I want you and Luke in there too. There are some bad things coming for this town and if we don't get the support of the entire police department right now, I don't think we stand any kind of a chance."

Alvarez glanced from Riker to Luke. "I thought you said the chief might not be on our side in this situation."

"We need to get him on our side. If not, we need to get him out of the way."

Alvarez's eyes widened and she drew a quick breath. Riker could tell that the idea of arresting her chief had seemed distant until this moment. Now the thought of walking into his office and confronting him was hitting home.

"Hey, we are all in this together. Hopefully he will be rational and do the right thing." Riker put a hand on her shoulder. He needed everyone calm in that room or things could quickly go south.

"Okay, let's go have a word with the chief."

She led the way to the office with the words Chief Myers written on the door. The shades were drawn and there was no way to see inside. Alvarez knocked lightly on the door and waited a moment with no response. She knocked again louder. "Chief, I've got some people here that need to see you."

After a moment of silence, his voice came through the door. "Not now. I'm busy."

"This can't wait."

"It's going to. I'm busy right now."

Riker pushed by Alvarez and opened the door. When he stepped into the office Alvarez and Luke followed. Chief Joe Myers stood up from his desk and glared at the intrusion. Riker glanced around the room. There was a box of papers on the floor by his desk, and a shredder next to it. His desk was empty but for a handful of items: his computer monitor, his service revolver, a glass filled with brown liquid, and a picture of his son.

His face was stone as he regarded Riker. "I should have known. You keep popping up where you don't belong, Mr. Riker."

"What can I say? It's a gift."

"I'm glad that you are here. I was going to have my officers pick you up anyway. Officer Alvarez, arrest that man."

Riker took a step forward. "There's no need for theatrics Joe. No one is going to arrest me."

"I have a report of arson from a farm outside of town. Witnesses can place you at the scene. Last I checked, that is a crime."

Riker stood directly across from the chief and looked him in the eye. "Part of your responsibility is to protect that farm, isn't it?"

"It's my responsibility to protect everyone in this town."

"Yes, it is. The question is, why haven't you? There was no official report filed about that fire. In fact, I'm guessing that you had to tell the fire station to ignore any calls about it. It would be a bit of a problem if the fireman noticed one of the biggest drug operations on US soil."

"Alvarez, I told you to arrest that man."

Alvarez shut the door behind her. "Chief, Doc Hanson told us everything."

The color left Myer's face. He slowly sat down at his desk. One hand reached for the glass of bourbon, and the other rested on the gun. Riker saw the look of defeat in the man's face. He was at a crossroads, and he could turn a very dark direction at any moment.

Riker spoke in a calm and soothing voice. "I can tell that you are a good man at your core, Joe. When I saw that gun on your desk I wasn't sure if it was for you or for Doc Hanson. An evil man would have found a way to kill Hanson by now. You're still fighting the will of the cartel in every way you can."

Joe took a long sip of the bourbon. "They did ask me to kill Hanson. I figured that he's already in custody. What's the rush? I'm more evil than you think."

"No, you're not. I'm sure that the reason your son goes to Brown and the reason that you are no longer with your wife is because you care about them. You distanced yourself from them as much as you could to protect them, didn't you? You knew that the cartel would leverage them against you more if it seemed like you cared about them."

The chief finished his drink. He slid open a desk drawer, pulled out a bottle of Johnny Walker, and refilled his glass, keeping his other hand on his weapon and his eyes on Riker.

"These people can't be reasoned with. There is no way to beat them. They killed the last police chief, and they approached me with an offer the day I took the position. They would pay me for my cooperation or they would kill my family. I could tell that they were indifferent about my answer. They were just as happy to put me on the payroll as they were to murder my wife and son."

"I understand that these men cannot be reasoned with, but they can be beaten. I have fought men like this in the past and I am still standing. Many of them are not. The only chance you have at getting your life back is to help me fight these men. It is your only chance at redemption. If you use that gun on yourself now, your soul will be marked with the guilt of what you have done forever."

Joe glanced over at the gun in his hand. "If I fight back and fail, they will find my son and they will kill him."

"This isn't just about you and your family anymore," Alvarez said. "I know you. I've seen you in the community. You are a good man. It isn't just about protecting your own. These people are coming to clean house."

"It's true," Luke added. "Now that the production facility is destroyed, they are sending a crew to pick up the remaining supply. Once they have it, they are going to get rid of any evidence they were ever here. That includes anyone who had any information about what was going on. I've seen these men in action. They don't leave loose ends. They will kill any person that might know who they are or what they have done. Who knows how many people they'll kill."

"We can stop that," Riker said, "but we will need people and supplies. With your help, we stand a chance."

"How many men are coming?"

"He told me that my crew should be on site to load the product tomorrow morning," Luke answered. "I'm guessing that there will be at least four transport trucks. They aren't going to put all the product in one place in case it gets busted. Generally, each truck has two guard cars. So there could be as many as fifty guys. El Leon will almost certainly be leading them."

Myers let out a bitter laugh. "We have a total of five officers. There is a fifty percent chance Ed will have a heart attack the moment I tell him that a group of killers is coming to town. You really think we stand any chance?"

Riker looked him dead in the eyes. "A battle is always about much more than numbers. With your help, we control the information. They don't know that you or Luke have turned. We know where and when they will be. We have some time to prepare. These are advantages that we can use to even the odds. It will still be dangerous, and we may not win, but we do have a chance."

Luke grinned. "I'd listen to this guy. He did take out the entire production facility and get the better of twelve armed men all by his lonesome."

The chief thought for a moment. "Say I agree to help in your suicide mission. What happens afterward?"

"Are you asking if you go to prison?" Riker asked.

"Yeah. Is that how I redeem myself?"

"Frankly I don't know and I don't care. You may deserve to rot in prison for the things you've done, and you might not. It isn't my call. I just want to save the people of this town and make sure that the men coming here get what they deserve. Your future lies in the hands of the courts and Officer Alvarez. The real question is, what kind of man will you be today?"

Joe Myers finished his drink in one long sip. He took in a long sharp breath, and he looked Riker in the eyes. "You were right about the gun. It was for me. I planned on using it after I finished that bottle. I suppose I'm on borrowed time now and the odds of us living through the next twenty-four hours are close to zero." He extended a hand towards Riker.

Riker shook it. "I'm in for redemption and for saving as many people as we can."

"Glad to have you on the team."

The entire room seemed to breathe a sigh of relief.

"So what do we do next?" Luke asked.

"I'd like to talk to the man himself, if I can," Riker said.

Luke raised an eyebrow. "You want to speak with El Leon?"

"No. His boss. It's time for me to talk to Nicolás Marcillas."

33

RIKER WAITED, arms crossed over his chest, while Alvarez unlocked the jail cell. The big metal door swung open with a loud creak, revealing the sole prisoner inside. He sat on his cot, eyes on the floor. After a long moment, he looked up and his head tilted in surprise at the sight of Riker.

"Not who I expected," the doctor said. "Did they make you a deputy or are you my new roommate?"

"Neither. I need your help."

Doc Hanson smiled at that. "Well, I currently find myself with lots of time on my hands. How can I be of assistance?"

"Nicolás Marcillas. I need to speak with him."

The doctor stared at Riker hard, as if trying to figure out if he was kidding. Then he turned to Alvarez. "Officer, my professional opinion is that Matthew Riker is at serious risk of self-harm. I recommend putting him on a twenty-four-hour suicide watch."

Alvarez frowned. "What the hell are you talking about, Doc?"

"He says that he wants to talk to Don Marcillas. And

speaking with the leader of a cartel without an invitation to do so is no different than putting a gun to your own head."

Riker took a step into the cell, pushing down his mounting frustration. Chief Myers hadn't had the cartel boss's number. All communication went through Doctor Hanson. "Listen, you told us yourself that you were as good as dead already. What's the harm in putting us in touch with Marcillas?"

Doctor Hanson raised a finger, as if he were a teacher about to give a lesson to a pupil. "Ah, but there are degrees of death. If I am killed simply to keep me out of the justice system for fear that I *might* talk, my death will be relatively easy. Perhaps a slit throat or a number of shanks to the torso before they let me bleed out."

"That's your idea of an easy death?" Alvarez asked.

"Comparatively. If they know that I talked, or worse, gave you Don Marcillas' phone number, they will hand me over to El Leon. Then my death will be very slow indeed."

Riker took another step forward. He was only two feet from Doctor Hanson now, and his long shadow fell over the older man. "Listen to me, you son of a bitch. You brought this force of evil into our town. I personally hold you responsible for every death the cartel has caused so far and every one they're going to cause when they get here tomorrow. Stop thinking about yourself for once and do the right thing. You think you can remember how to do that?"

Riker reached into his pocket and held out Doctor Hanson's phone, which Alvarez had taken from the evidence locker. Hanson stared at the phone for almost thirty seconds. Finally, he spoke.

"I don't have the number in my phone. They made me commit it to memory."

"Then dial."

Hanson reached out with a shaky hand, took the phone and tapped at the screen. Then he handed it back to Riker. "There. I've ensured my own torture and death. All you have to do is push Send."

Riker drew a deep breath, then pressed the button.

The phone rang three times, and then a voice answered. To Riker's surprise, the man on the other end spoke English.

"You are very lucky that I answered."

"Am I?" Riker replied, careful to keep his voice even.

"Indeed. Doctor Hanson is in jail, and even if he wasn't, he wouldn't be stupid enough to call me after fucking things up so badly. No one who works for me would. So I assume this is the man who has been causing all the trouble."

"Matthew Riker at your service." Riker shifted the phone to his other ear.

The man on the other end let out a soft grunt of disapproval. "Well, Mr. Riker, either you are very, very good, or the men I left in charge of my operation in Kingsport are very, very bad. Either way, you have my attention. May I ask why you're calling?"

"First, let me thank you for speaking with me," Riker said in perfect Spanish.

Marcillas let out a sharp laugh before answering in Spanish himself. "Perhaps I underestimated the schools of Iowa. Your accent is quite good."

"I didn't learn Spanish in Iowa," he said in English.

"Then where did you learn it?"

"Juarez mostly."

There was a long pause. "Are you DEA, Mr. Riker?"

"No. I don't work for the government, mine or yours. What I am going to ask you now is a personal favor."

"And what favor is that?"

"Your operation in Kingsport is functionally shut down.

The key players are either under arrest or soon will be. The production facility is destroyed."

"This I know," the drug lord answered.

"There is a substantial amount of product here, but it is not more than you can afford to lose. I would like to respectfully ask that you forget Kingsport, Iowa, exists. Tell the men who are on their way here to turn around and go home. Write off your losses and continue on with your life."

Riker looked up and saw both Alvarez and Doctor Hanson staring at him, both of their faces drawn with surprise.

There was another long pause. "Forgive me if I'm not up-to-date on American customs, but my understanding was that a favor was something like driving a friend to the airport. What you're asking is significantly larger than that. Tell me why I would agree to such a thing."

"Because if you don't, I'm going to make it my personal mission to destroy you and your entire organization."

Marcillas let out a long, deep laugh that came from the belly. "Mr. Riker, you are an amusing fellow, I'll give you that. But I believe you are in a bit over your head on this one. The list of men, governments, and organizations that have tried to bring me down is lengthy. Your name wouldn't even rank in the top hundred things I'm worried about at the moment. If you somehow managed to locate me, you'd be dead before you got within a mile of my compound."

"I'll bet Javier Herrara felt the same way."

"Herrara?"

"I assume you've heard of him?"

"Of course I've heard of him." Marcillas' voice was serious now.

"He had quite the operation," Riker said, thinking back to the mission he'd carried out for QS-4 against the drug lord. "Major distribution network. Army of enforcers. Underground compound near Mexico City. *Had* being the operative word. He didn't have any of those things when I was done with him."

"Bullshit." For the first time, there was a hint of anger in Marcillas' voice.

"I assure you it is not. Ask around. I'm sure you have connections to people who worked for Herrara. Ask them about how he disappeared from his compound, never to be seen again. Ask about me. They'll remember if they were involved in that incident. Ask them about Espantapájaros."

"The Scarecrow," Marcillas said in English.

"Yes," Riker confirmed. "But it doesn't have to go that way for you. I have no interest in ending your business or your life. All you have to do is tell me you'll leave us alone. Just say the words, 'I'm done with Kingsport' and we will never speak to each other again."

This time the pause was so long that Riker thought the drug lord might have hung up. Then Marcillas spoke in slow careful English, his voice thick with fury. "Let me tell you what is going to happen. My men are coming to your little, insignificant town, and they are going to take back what is mine and destroy everything that stands in their way. I don't know what happened with Javier Herrara, but I do know our current situation. You have a drug-addicted town with an incompetent police department. I have many, many men, each trained and experienced in combat and willing to die to carry out my wishes. I have a team of your own townspeople who will do my wishes. I have military-grade weaponry. I have El Leon. My lion will kill you and everyone who stands with you, Officer Alvarez included. But your deaths will not be the end. Your families will be next. Then your friends. Then anyone I suspect gave you even the slightest bit of aid. Finally, I will order El Leon to bring me back your decapitated head so that I may piss into your dead mouth. You will rot with the taste of my urine on your tongue. Let that knowledge be your dying thought, Mr. Riker."

"So I guess that's a no, then."

"Goodbye, Riker. We will not speak again."

There was a click and the line went dead.

"Oh Jesus, what did you do?" Doctor Hanson asked. "What the hell did you do? You just made it so much worse. He's going to burn Kingsport to the ground."

Alvarez raised an eyebrow. "I hate to say it, but Doctor Heroin has a point. Was it really a good move to piss him off?"

Riker gave a shrug. "He was already coming to kill us. Besides, I needed to hear his voice. I wanted to find out what he knows."

"And did you?" Alvarez asked.

"Yes, actually. Chief Myers said he hadn't informed anyone up the chain that Doctor Hanson was in custody, but Marcillas knew about that. That means there's someone else in this town in contact with the cartel."

"Great, just what we need. Another enemy."

"But there's good news too. When he was running down his list of the people he was going to kill, he didn't mention Luke. That means he doesn't know Luke is working with us. That's an advantage we can use."

Alvarez smiled weakly. "Well, I suppose that's something."

"Indeed it is." Riker thought for a moment, considering their next move. "Okay, let's circle the wagons. We have a hell of a lot of work to do before the enemy arrives."

34

TIME WAS GOING by too fast. Riker guessed that he had no more than sixteen hours to bring his plan together. That would be hard with a crew of professionals. What he had was a willing but unprepared group of misfits.

A clock in the shape of a cartoon cat, its eyes moving back and forth with the swing of its tail, guarded the wall of Megan's living room. The time was almost noon. Conversation buzzed from five other people in the room. Megan had picked up sub sandwiches for everyone and the scent of freshly baked bread drifted through the air.

Riker took note of his team. Donnie, a drunk who was looking to avenge his brother. Joe Myers, a disgraced police chief with a lot to lose. Luke, his old friend who had gone astray. Officer Alvarez, a good cop who still held her optimism. Megan, a school teacher with spunk, and the last of his family. These people were not battle-tested. Riker knew that some if not all of them would be dead in the next twenty-four hours.

A whiteboard propped up on the couch displayed a roughly drawn map of the farm. Riker stood in front of it and cleared his throat. "I need everyone's full attention for the next few minutes. We all have a part to play and if things go wrong, we will die."

The conversations in the room stopped and all eyes turned to Riker. Luke and Joe nodded like the possibility of their deaths was old news. He could see that the others still didn't truly understand the stakes of the game they were about to play.

Riker continued. "I know that sounds dramatic, but it's true. Even if we all perform perfectly, we may not live through this. I'm telling you this because I need your complete focus. We do have a chance but only if we all work together, and only if we all do our parts correctly."

"I'll do whatever you need. I'm fine with dying if I take some of these assholes with me," Donnie said with conviction.

"Thanks, Donnie, but the goal is to keep all of you alive and stop these guys."

Megan frowned and turned to Chief Myers. "What about outside help? Shouldn't we be calling the DEA or the FBI or something?"

The chief raised a skeptical eyebrow. "By tomorrow morning? If I call now, maybe they'll send a guy out tomorrow or the next day to investigate. The wheels of bureaucracy turn slowly. Once we're under attack, sure, they'll send people. But they aren't going to scramble a fighting force because I suspect some cartel guys are headed my way."

Megan's eyes fell. "So we really are alone."

"Maybe so," Riker said with a grin, "but at least we're alone together. Luke, give me a breakdown of the men who are currently in town."

Luke was sitting on the couch next to Joe. He awkwardly

looked around the room and then stood before he spoke. It was apparent that he was not comfortable with public speaking, even in a small group. Luke looked at Riker "Should I go up front, or just talk from here?"

"Where you're at is fine. Just go over the resources that the cartel has here in town."

Luke nodded and drew a breath. "Well, my team is pretty thin right now. Between the twelve guys you took out last night and the other guys you injured since you've been in town, there are not a lot left. I've got five guys left at the construction company who are still able to fight, and there are eight guys out at the farm." He paused, glancing at Megan. "Then there's Blake."

Megan grimaced at the sound of her student's name. "I saw him getting into it with Eric Underwood's son David the other day. I figured he was working with your crew. We have to keep him out of this."

"Agreed." He turned back to Riker. "The women who work the production side of things are already gone. Most of them barely speak English, and I suspect they were here against their will. I gave them enough money to get home after you burned down the barn. I told the others the cartel was calling them back."

Riker nodded, glad he didn't have to worry about getting the women somewhere safe before the next morning.

"Our one advantage is that no one knows the cartel is coming except for me," Luke continued. "It's my job to get them out to the farm tomorrow morning. Seems I've failed to mention it to them so far."

"Good. Let's keep it that way." Riker thought for a moment. "Anybody left that you can trust completely?"

Luke considered that, then shook his head. "There's not

one of them I could guarantee wouldn't sell us out to save his own hide."

"Do you think any of them know you are helping us?"

"I don't think so."

"Excellent. Do you have any heavy equipment at the construction site?"

"Of course. We do run an actual construction company. What kind of equipment are you talking about?"

"A bulldozer and an excavator. Bring both of them to the farm."

"They are going to ask why I'm bringing equipment there. What do I tell them?"

Megan shook her head as if Luke were one of her slow students. "They were storing a bunch of drugs in an underground lab that just burned up. There may be things down there worth salvaging. Just tell them you had the brilliant idea to dig it up with your big equipment."

Luke nodded his head. "Right, right, that makes sense." He turned back to Riker. "Why do you want the equipment?"

"When the cartel arrives at the farm I don't want them to have the option to leave. We will use the equipment to block them in or destroy their vehicles. That will be phase two."

Alvarez asked. "So what's phase one?"

"The cartel is sending between twenty and fifty men to this town. According to Luke, there are an additional thirteen local operatives. We need to secure the farm so we can prepare it for the arrival of the cartel."

Megan spoke up. "Are we sure that the cartel's going to the farm?"

Joe Myers answered. "At the end of the day, it's always about the drugs and the money. They have a lot of product at that farm. Getting it will be priority number one."

"I agree, but killing Doc Hanson will be a close second," Riker interjected. "He knows too much, and they are already aware that he is in custody. If there is a second target, it will be the jail. They may send someone straight to the station to take him out. We will need to leave at least a team at the station to protect him."

The chief nodded. "I guess it makes the most sense for that to be me and Officer Alvarez."

"Agreed. Just be ready. El Leon may walk in the front door with a smile on his face before spraying the room with an automatic weapon."

"Got it. We will have a mandatory vest rule for the next twenty-four hours."

"Speaking of vests, how much gear do you have at the station? This is going to take all the firepower we can get our hands on."

Joe smiled. "Honestly, we have way more gear than you would expect. Our supply room is filled with SWAT gear. We have automatic rifles, tactical shotguns, two sniper rifles, vests, and a host of miscellaneous gear. When they sent us all that stuff, I thought it was a major waste. We don't even have a SWAT team. I guess it's nice to have it when you need it."

"I don't recall them sending us a bunch of great equipment that we didn't ask for at the school," Megan said. "In fact, I had to buy my own stapler and hole punch this year."

"I don't think we need to debate budgetary politics. I'm just glad that we don't need to make another run to Home Depot for supplies to fight the cartel," Donnie said.

"Same here," Riker said. "Boards with nails work just fine on small-time drug dealers, but I'd rather have some real weapons for this fight. After we secure the farm, I'll go to the storage locker with Joe and Alvarez to get us some gear."

"What about me? Do you want me running around with a shotgun?" Megan asked.

Riker wanted to tell Megan to get out of town before the fighting started, but he knew where that conversation would end. "Strong communication is going to be essential, especially because we are fighting on two fronts, the farm and the police station. I need you to help coordinate everything. You're our command center and the rest of us will communicate through you."

For a moment it looked like she was going to object, but then she uncrossed her arms. "I can do that. Honestly. I was scared that you were going to hand me a shotgun, pat me on the back and say go get 'em, tiger."

Luke laughed at the thought. "If only your students could see you running around with a shotgun defending the town. I bet none of them would ever goof off in class again."

Joe did not laugh; his face was solemn. "Let's try to focus on the task. This is no joke."

"Chill out. I always joke around when I'm nervous." Luke returned his attention to Riker. "What's next, coach?"

"When you bring the construction equipment to the farm I'm going to move in and clear out any hostiles. I'll try not to kill your crew, but this will be a winner take all fight."

"What's my role in phase one?" Donnie asked.

"Phase one is going to be up to me and Luke. It will be a quick surgical strike. I'll move through the house clearing out any armed men. Luke will have my back."

"So I'll just be waiting around?"

"Your moment will come when the cartel arrives. Those men will be expecting trouble. They will also greatly outnumber us. We will need to keep them confused and off-balance if we want to have any chance to beat them. You and Luke will be positioned around the farm with assault rifles. We will keep you just outside of the fence. You can take one or two shots at a time and then move quickly. Then take another shot. The two of you will be spread out. This should give the illusion of a larger force attacking. If we properly block their exit with our equipment we should force them into the main building as a defensive position."

"What will you be doing?"

"I'll be using one of the sniper rifles. I'll keep them from getting to any of you, and I'll thin their numbers. I have some ideas for the rest of the plan, but I want to see what we have to work with on that farm before I make the final strategy."

The room was silent for a moment; the members of the team, exchanging nervous glances.

Luke broke the silence. "That is a pretty good plan."

Riker smiled. "Thanks, Star-Lord."

Everyone in the room looked confused. Luke waited for a moment and then asked, "Star-Lord? Is that like a code-name or something?"

Riker shook his head. "I thought you were quoting *Guardians of the Galaxy*. Sorry that none of you are familiar with one of the best movies the MCU has to offer."

Megan laughed out loud. "Hardened killer and movie dork; that is an unusual combo. I think I have the trump card for the strangest family."

Everyone in the room laughed. Riker turned a light shade of red. "Laugh all you want. It's still a great movie."

"Don't worry coach," Luke said. "We'll follow your instructions. It's just nice to know that you are actually human."

The word coach struck Riker. It was the second time

Luke had used it. Apparently he was filling in for his fallen mentor in both action and name. He hoped that his team wouldn't be let down by his leadership.

"If anyone has questions about what they need to do next, now is the time. We have until morning before they arrive. We will prepare in every way we can, but these men will not hesitate to kill any of you. When the fighting starts. I need all of you to remember that. Do not hesitate and do not try to spare them. We will have one shot at this. Let's make it count."

35

The afternoon sun beat down on Riker as he waited crouched in the bed of Luke's truck. The trailer with the small excavator rattled and clattered as it thumped along the uneven stretch of road behind them. Riker kept his body relaxed and his breathing easy, his thoughts drifting back to the many types of transports he'd ridden to various combat missions. There had been cargo planes, helicopters, transport trucks, trains, and ships of all shapes and sizes. But hiding in the back of a vehicle hauling construction equipment was a new one.

He glanced up and saw Luke in profile through the truck's rear window. It felt strange going into battle with his old friend, but he much preferred being on the same side. They'd been through too much together to be enemies now.

Luke glanced back as if he could feel Riker looking at him and spoke through the rear window, which was slid open. "I'm going to ask one last time. You sure about this, man? There are eight guys in there. I'd feel a hell of a lot better if I was going with you."

"I'm sure. This is how it has to be. Just keep the ones at

the gate occupied for five minutes or so. It shouldn't take longer than that."

Luke shook his head and let out a chuckle. "I like your confidence."

As much as Riker would have liked to have someone by his side when he attacked the compound, it simply wasn't feasible. This would require stealth and taking out the enemy quickly, quietly, and hopefully via non-fatal means. That was a big ask, and Luke simply didn't have the training for it. Riker knew from painful recent experience that the man could throw a solid punch, but this required more finesse and a skillset only Riker possessed.

"Here we go," Luke said a moment later.

Riker felt the truck slow and turn. He knew that they had arrived at their destination.

"'Sup, Luke?" a low male voice said. "What the hell is all this?"

"Doc's orders," Luke replied. "Wants us to dig through the wreckage of the place. Recover what we can."

"So you brought a freakin excavator." This was a new voice, and it came from the other side of the truck.

Though Riker was crouched too low to see anything, he'd been here recently enough to be able to clearly picture the scene in his mind. The gate to the compound was in front of them, and the two men guarding it stood to either side. According to Luke, these two were the best men left on the crew, so it made sense to have them guarding the entrance. Anyone who wanted to proceed inside would have to get through them before dealing with the others. Theoretically. Riker planned to bypass them completely and save them until he was done with the others.

"I figured the excavator will make short work of it.

Unless you'd prefer to dig through the charred remains by hand."

"Not especially," the second man said. "I'm not complaining. I'm just wondering how we're going to get her through the gate."

Luke opened the door to his truck. "I was thinking about that myself. The trailer isn't going to fit through the gate very easily. I say we unload her and drive her through on her own." Luke stepped out of the truck, leaving it running, and headed back toward the trailer. "Help me get these straps off."

There was a moment of silence. Then Luke spoke again.

"Careful you don't smash your fingers."

That was the signal phrase Riker had been waiting for. As soon as he heard it, he threw a leg over the passenger side of the truck, slipped over, and dropped to the ground on the far side. A quick glance over his shoulder told him the two guards were both busy releasing the straps tying down the excavator and were paying him no mind. Even Luke was not looking in his direction. Riker quickly made his way to the front of the truck and through the open gate, favoring speed over silence. The truck's diesel engine would cover any sounds his feet made as they crushed over the gravel.

Once he was through the gate, Riker didn't bother looking back. His targets were ahead of him, and he needed to put his focus there. This job would require speed and precision. He clocked the position of his targets. Two silos stood just past the burnt facilities Riker had so recently destroyed. According to Luke, a pair of men would be guarding each silo, with a final pair sitting in a truck between them, radio in hand, and ready to assist either if the need arose.

Riker moved quickly, keeping near the tree line as he made his way past the house and to the silo on the right. Two men stood leaning against the silo, both looking bored. Both had pistols on their belts but neither was holding a weapon. The truck was just where Luke had said it would be--just between the silos. Riker could just see the back of the bed from where it stood, and he figured that if he played the angles right, he could take out these two men without the ones in the truck being able to see.

Using the silo to block him from the sight of the guards, Riker headed toward them. He reached the silo and slowly worked his way around it. When the first guard came into sight, Riker saw that this was going to be easy. The man was staring off into space, his eyes distant.

Riker attacked suddenly and viciously, slipping an arm around the man's neck and squeezing, cutting off the air and any chance for a scream. A moment later, the man was unconscious. His partner glanced over, and his eyes widened at the sight of Riker attacking his friend.

Riker let the unconscious man fall and crossed the ten feet between him and the other man in an instant. The man's jaw dropped, but he didn't have time to utter even a shout before Riker's hand slammed into his throat. He dropped to his knees, hands going to his injured windpipe. In an instant, Riker had those hands bound behind his back with a zip tie. He quickly bound the man's ankles the same way. He pulled out a bandana from his pocket, one of several he'd brought for this purpose, and tied it around the man's head, forming a gag. He did the same to the unconscious man, and then he moved on.

Crossing the space between the two silos was going to be the trickiest part of this operation. He needed to double back and make his way behind the truck so that the men inside didn't see him. He did so carefully, his eyes on the two figures inside the cab. If they spotted him in their rearview mirror as he passed, they gave no indication.

Riker hurried to the second silo, taking the same approach as he had the first time, carefully working his way around the structure to hide his approach. When he spotted these two guards, he shook his head in disgust at their lack of professionalism. They were sitting on folding chairs and playing cards on a crate placed between them.

This time, Riker didn't even bother with subtlety. He grabbed the first man from behind, choking him out in full sight of his partner. By the time the other man got to his feet, his buddy was unconscious.

Riker charged ahead, knowing that he'd have to handle this fourth guard slightly differently. As he reached him, he grabbed the man's right shoulder with one hand and punched it hard with the other. He heard an audible crack as the shoulder dislocated.

The man started to cry out, but Riker quickly drove the air from his lungs with a punch to the stomach. A moment later, Riker had him on the ground, hands and feet zip-tied. The way his hands were tied behind his back would be quite painful with that dislocated shoulder, which was exactly what Riker was counting on. When he put on the man's gag, he left it loose, knowing the man would be able to work it even looser with his tongue, and eventually, he'd be able to push it aside.

Riker secured the unconscious man, then worked his way around to behind the truck with the final two guards and waited.

Attacking two men in the cab of a truck wasn't an ideal situation. They had the protection of the vehicle, and there was no easy way to get inside to take them out, at least not without killing them. So Riker would have to draw them out.

He didn't have to wait long. Less than two minutes later, the man with the dislocated shoulder began shouting loudly now that he'd worked his way free of the gag. With Luke's diesel engine still running, there was no chance the men at the gate would hear it, but he hoped that the men in this truck would.

"The hell?" one of the men asked as he opened the driver's side door and stepped out.

"It's Riker!" the injured man shouted. "He's here!"

Riker waited until both men were out of the truck, then he moved in. Less concerned about silence now, he slammed his foot into the side of the first man's knee. The man let out a shout of pain as he staggered, his leg giving out under him. Riker turned his attention to the other man, attacking with a flurry of jabs to the face, knocking the man back. An uppercut sent the man sprawling to the ground. Riker descended on him like a pouncing lion, rolling him onto his stomach, securing his hands and ankles.

The other man was still on the ground, and he was pulling his pistol from its holster. Riker slammed a foot into the man's wrist before he could extract his gun. The man cried out as his wrist snapped. A moment later, he too was bound.

The urgency gone, Riker made his way back to the gate casually, taking the most direct path now. When he reached it, he saw the two guards were still working on getting the excavator off the trailer. Only Luke was looking in his direction, and his eyes lit up in surprise and delight at seeing his friend return so quickly. His hand went to his waistband, pulling out his pistol.

"Hey guys, change of plans," Luke said.

The two men looked up from their work to see a pistol pointing at them, and Matthew Riker stalking toward them.

"You're going to stand very still, and my buddy Matt is going to tie you up."

The men were so surprised that they didn't even put up a fight.

A few minutes later, Luke and Riker exchanged a fist bump.

"I can't believe you actually did it," Luke said. "You took out six guys by yourself in what? Six minutes?"

Riker shrugged. "Give or take."

"That's damn impressive, my friend."

"It's what I do." He paused. "Or what I did. I retired from that life."

Luke smiled. "Tell that to the guys bound and gagged on the ground."

"Turns out I'm not very good at retiring."

Luke looked at his friend for a long moment, and his smile faded. "You know, I used to wonder what happened to you. Where you were now. I hoped you had a wife and maybe a couple kids. A boring job somewhere. I hoped you'd managed to avoid a life of violence."

"I guess neither of us were able to pull that off." There was a hint of sadness in Riker's voice.

"Well, I guess we'll need that experience for what's coming." Luke let out a sigh. "You do realize that this is going to be the end of us, right? I mean, the battle that's ahead... Our chances of surviving are incredibly thin. And even if we do survive, the cartel is not going to let us walk away. They'll keep coming until we're dead. Those guys are relentless."

Riker couldn't argue with anything his friend had said. On the other hand, he had a bit of experience when it came to relentless organizations wanting him dead. "I wouldn't count us out just yet. Our odds aren't great, but I never was much of a math guy."

"That's for damn sure," Luke said with a chuckle. "I carried your ass through Algebra 2 junior year."

"No argument there." Riker slapped his friend on the shoulder. "Come on, we have work to do. You have to get these guys over to the station and set everything up here."

"Me? What are you going to be doing?"

Riker didn't answer. He wasn't ready to share absolutely everything with his old friend just yet. There was something he needed to do before the coming battle.

36

RIKER SAT in Luke's truck outside a small house on the east side of Kingsport. It was late—too late for a casual visit to someone he barely knew—but he didn't have the luxury of following etiquette tonight. There was a good chance he was going to die tomorrow. If he was going to do this, he needed to do it now.

But first, he needed to make two phone calls. He fished his phone out of his pocket and tapped Megan's number. She answered on the third ring.

"I hope you're calling to tell me we've defeated the cartel and can all go home now."

"That's still a work in progress," he said. "How are things going there?"

"Good. Chief Myers is freaking out a little, but I think he'll be able to hold it together. Alvarez is barking orders at him now. I thought he was going to push back the first time she did it, but he actually seemed a little relieved."

That made sense to Riker. Sometimes when things felt as if they were spinning out of control, you just wanted someone to tell you what to do. That appeared to be where the police chief was at currently.

"Listen, Megan, I need you to do something for me."

"Of course. What is it?"

"Tomorrow morning, I need you to forget about all this and go to work."

There was a long pause.

"Matt, we've been through this. I'm not going to sit back while my town is being—"

"And I'm not saying you should," Riker said, cutting her off. "You've already done more than I ever should have asked of you. But tomorrow's going to be a fight against trained killers, not local hardasses. It's going to be messy and bloody."

"Which is exactly why you need me."

"No. Your kids need you." Riker paused, shifting the phone to the other ear. "Look, this whole thing started because a high school teacher wanted to make a difference. I wouldn't be the man I am today if not for Coach Kane, and I'm sure there are dozens of others who could say the same thing. Your kids need you. They just attended one funeral. Don't make them go to another."

Megan sighed. "Damn it cuz, I hate it when you make sense. All right, I'll go to work tomorrow morning. Though I'm not sure how you expect me to teach world history while I know you're in the fight of your life."

"If anyone can do it, it's you. I gotta go. We'll talk soon."

He hung up, then stared at his phone. The call to Megan had been necessary, but this next one was just for him. Maybe he shouldn't be spending his time on something like this while there was still so much work to be done. On the other hand, he thought he deserved a little something of his own before he sacrificed everything.

He touched another phone number and waited while it rang.

"So Matthew Riker does know how to use a telephone," Jessica said.

The sound of her voice brought an immediate smile to his face. "Indeed. I've also heard that modern telephones actually work both ways. You could even call me if you wanted to."

It had been a little less than a month since Riker had left California and seen Jessica for the last time. They'd spoken three times since then and exchanged a few texts. It always felt comfortable when they talked, but both of them seemed hesitant to do it too often, as if their new relationship were a fragile thing that might be crushed if either of them applied too much pressure.

"How's the bee-keeping game?"

"Solid. I named one of the bees after you."

"I hope it was a queen."

"Of course it was. But I'm actually back in Iowa right now. My hometown."

"Really?" she asked. "Visiting family?"

"Funeral. My old wrestling coach passed away."

"Oh Riker, I'm so sorry."

"Thanks." He swallowed hard. "How about you? How's the leg?"

"Well, I'm pretty darn fast on my crutches these days. It will almost be a shame to get the cast off."

"Maybe you could give me some tips. I hurt my leg the other day, and I've got some crutches myself."

"Yeah?" There was a hint of concern in her voice now. "Let me guess. Rugby injury?"

"Something like that."

There was a long pause. "Riker, whatever it is you're up

to, I'm sure you have a good reason for it. I'm not going to ask you to be careful. But I will ask you to be smart."

Riker smiled again. They'd only known each other for a month, and yet she already saw right through to the heart of him. "I think I can do that. Listen, I've got to go. I just wanted to hear your voice."

"And did it live up to your expectations?"

"I'd say it exceeded them."

"It wasn't entirely unpleasant to hear your voice as well. Maybe give me a call when you get back to North Carolina."

"You can count on it. Bye, Jessica." He hung up and set the phone down on the passenger seat, promising himself he'd do everything he could to stay alive to make that phone call.

He walked up to the house and pressed the doorbell. A moment later, the door opened and Patricia Kane stared out at him.

"Can I help you?"

"Hi, Mrs. Kane. I'm Matthew Riker. I was on your husband's wrestling team a long time ago."

The woman's expression softened. "I remember you. Oscar talked about you a lot. Both when you were on the team and after. He always thought it was a shame you weren't able to accept that scholarship to the University of Iowa."

"No arguments there. I wish I could have." It was something Riker thought about sometimes. Not often, as there was no reason to dwell on such things, but occasionally. How would his life be different today if he'd been able to follow the original plan? There would have been no Navy SEALs for him. No QS-4. Maybe his life would have been better for it. Maybe the world would be worse. Maybe Li never would have gotten home to her parents. Maybe Simon and Jessica would be dead. Such speculation was worthless, though. There was no way to know for certain.

"It's a little late, Matthew. I was getting ready to turn in. Was there something I could help you with?"

"I just wanted to pay my condolences. I didn't get to do so at the funeral. Coach meant the world to me. He changed my life, and I thought you should know. I'm very sorry for your loss."

She nodded, her eyes suddenly filled with tears. "Thank you. It's not the first such sentiment that I've heard today, but still means a lot. I can't help but think how many more lives he might have touched if he hadn't thrown his life away on that naive obsession of his."

Riker tilted his head in surprise. "Mrs. Kane, I know it might not seem like it now, but Coach didn't throw his life away. What he did made a difference. It's still making a difference. He stood up for what's right, and that's never a mistake."

"Perhaps," she said carefully. "But I'd much rather have him be wrong and here beside me than right and dead in a box. If that's selfish, then so be it."

"It's not."

She gave him a long look. "There's something else you want to say. I can tell."

"Yes ma'am," he allowed. "It's a difficult question."

"Son, I just buried my husband. I can do difficult. Ask away."

"I noticed there was a closed coffin at the wake."

She crossed her arms, her expression suddenly unreadable. "That's not a question."

Riker hesitated. He felt awful broaching this topic with the victim's widow, but he needed to know. Ever since Luke had told him the story of Coach's death, something had been nagging at him, and he needed to know for sure. "I don't know how to ask this delicately, so I'm just going to say it. I heard that Coach was shot. Was he shot in the head?"

"That's half right. He was shot twice, both in the head. The killer put a bullet through each of his eyes."

A chill ran through Riker.

"Now will there be anything else? It's late."

"No ma'am. Thank you. And once again, I'm sorry for your loss."

Patricia eased the door shut without responding.

Riker stood on the darkened stoop for another moment, listening to the sound of her footsteps retreating into the house. It would be a long night for Patricia Kane, he knew. He doubted sleep would come easily for her.

He turned and walked back to the car. It would be a long night for him as well, followed by a long morning tomorrow. With the information Mrs. Kane had just given him, Riker knew he had no choice but to survive the coming battle so that true justice could be done for Oscar Kane.

37

Eighteen years ago

Matt stared out the window as the truck sped down the country road. He'd seen all of this—everything from the old barn they'd just passed to the broken warning light at the railroad crossing—a thousand times, and he was suddenly aware that this might be the last time he ever saw it. Kingsport had been a rough town to grow up in. He'd seen his share of hardship, especially recently. But it had also been home. And leaving home was never easy.

"You know what Stephanie said when I told her where I was driving you today?" Luke asked. He was leaning back in his seat, one hand casually draped over the steering wheel and the other hanging out the open window. "She said I should get on that bus with you. You believe that?"

Matt felt a sudden jolt of hope at the idea. Leaving was scary, and leaving to enlist in the military was even scarier. It would be very nice indeed to have a friend by his side. But he knew that would never happen. Luke's future had been decided long ago. He'd stay in this town, work for his father for ten years or so, and then take over the business. That had always been the plan, and Luke had never pushed against it.

"Not a bad idea if you ask me. The two of us in military uniforms? We step into any bar in San Diego and the ladies would be falling all over us."

Luke let out an abrupt laugh. "Right. You wanted me to join you, you should have signed up with a real branch of the military, like the Marines. The few, the proud, all that shit. I'd be down with that."

"Can't be a SEAL in the Marines."

"Yeah right. Somebody from this town becoming a SEAL? Can you imagine that?"

They drove in silence for a few miles, neither of them knowing what to say. The last two months had been intense, and the weight of the lie they'd shared hung heavy around both of their necks. But they'd stuck to their story. Self-defense. The inquiry that had followed had been terrifying; despite the way his family feared him, it turned out that Gary Riker had quite a few friends in Kingsport. Spending five nights a week in the bars will do that. These friends put enough pressure on the police that the district attorney hadn't felt comfortable dropping the matter entirely. Matt's public defender lawyer had ultimately worked out a deal. To avoid going to trial, Matt needed to plead guilty to involuntary manslaughter. Though the DA couldn't technically force Matt to join the military, he made it clear that the options were military service or jail. The prison time would be waived if he agreed to enlist. Ultimately, the DA just wanted Matt out of town. He figured that would be enough to get all of Gary Riker's lowlife friends off his back.

Matt had considered the deal for only an hour before accepting. He'd signed the plea deal and kissed his hopes of wrestling for Coach Zalesky at the University of Iowa goodbye.

In the month between signing the plea and graduating from high school, Matt had spent much of his time researching his upcoming career. Though it hadn't been his decision to enlist, he intended to make the most of the opportunity. He'd serve his country with everything he had, and he'd do it on the toughest team of hardasses on the planet. With his dream of wrestling at U of I gone, he embraced a new dream. He wanted to be a Navy Seal.

As the countryside rolled by, Matt considered how quickly his life had turned upside down. He'd gone from heavily recruited wrestler to the killer of his own father. Even though his dad's death had been accidental and it had happened because Matt was protecting his mom, he still had trouble sleeping at night. He supposed he would for a very long time.

"Coach came to see me yesterday," Matt said. He hadn't intended to share this with Luke, but for some reason, it just felt right.

"Yeah?" Luke raised an eyebrow in surprise.

"He told me he was proud of me for enlisting to serve my country." Matt paused, glancing over at his friend. "I want you to know that I didn't tell him what happened, but I did thank him. I thanked him for giving me the tools to stand up to a bully who was hurting my mom."

Luke gripped the wheel hard, staring at the road ahead of him. "Did you think he put it together? You don't think he would tell—"

"No. Never. Not Coach Kane."

Luke's face was unreadable as he considered the news.

He glanced down at his fuel gauge and let out a curse. "I gotta stop up here for gas."

Matt checked his watch. They had plenty of time.

Ten minutes later, Luke pulled the truck into a Shell station. Matt hopped out and pumped the gas. He dug a ten out of his pocket and handed it to Luke.

"You sure?" Luke asked.

"Please. You're driving. I can at least chip in for gas."

"I won't argue. But if you're buying, I'm flying." He turned and headed into the gas station to pay for the fuel.

Matt watched the numbers roll on the fuel pump as his mind wandered with thoughts of what the next few days would bring. Three days on a Greyhound bus to San Diego with boot camp waiting at the other end. For a boy who'd never been farther west than Kansas, that was a lot of unknowns. He couldn't help but think of his mother's parting words to him. "Goodbye, Matt. I'm not much of a letter writer so we probably won't talk again for a while. Be safe."

"Riker."

The gruff, unfamiliar voice woke him from his thoughts, and he looked up. A short man was shambling toward him, slowly but purposefully.

The man smiled when Matt looked up. "Yeah, I knew it was you. Matt Riker. Gary's son." He glanced to his left. "Told you it was him."

A second man, this one tall and thin, stepped around a beat-up old truck and glared at Matt. "What are you doing out here, son?"

"Just pumping gas." Matt's voice sounded weak in his own ears. "On my way to enlist. Joining the Navy."

The shorter man raised an eyebrow in mock surprise. "Is

that right? You're leaving us?" He glanced at his friend. "Guess this is our last chance to have a little talk with Matt."

The tall man nodded. "See Matt, we're old buddies of your father's, so we know Gary wasn't big on reading the good book. I'm guessing you never had much in the way of a religious education."

"No, I guess I haven't." Matt suddenly realized the tall man had worked his way around to the other side of him so that the men were flanking him. The truck on one side, the fuel pump on the other and two men boxing him in. There was nowhere to run.

"Well," the tall man said, "let me give you a little education now. See, there are these things called the Ten Commandments. You might be especially interested in the sixth and the seventh. You know what those say?"

Matt shook his head.

The short man turned a bit, and Matt saw that he was holding a tire iron down next to his leg. "Honor your father and mother. And thou shalt not kill. Seems to me you broke both of those."

The men were inching closer now, and Matt was growing more desperate. His options were slim. Sure, he could charge one of the men, probably the short one, but how would the court feel about him being involved in another altercation? Would his plea deal suddenly go away? Wasn't there something in there about no further violations for the next three years?

The more he thought about it, the more Matt realized he was going to have to take a beating. He could only hope that they didn't kill him.

"The good book is clear," the tall man said. "Justice must be done. The price must be paid."

"It must," the short man agreed.

"What the hell is all this?" Luke stepped around his truck, coming up alongside the tall man.

The man didn't take his eyes off of Matt. "Son, you are going to want to walk away."

"And why would I do that?"

The short man lifted the tire iron, making sure both younger men could see it. "'Cause if you don't, you'll get the same as your friend."

Luke considered that a moment. Then he shrugged. "I get that. You know Matt's heading out of town, and you want to throw him a beating on his way out the door. It's not like he can ever get revenge, right? He'll be gone."

The two older men exchanged a glance.

"It's not like that," the tall man said. "It's about justice being done. We can't let a killer go unpunished."

"The thing you didn't consider is me," Luke said, ignoring the man's response. "See, I'm not leaving. Not ever. And if you lay your hands on me and my friend, I will not forget. In fact, I'll make it my life's mission to make sure you never forget either."

The tall man gave him an appraising stare. "That a threat? Trust me, kid, I've got more friends in this town than you do."

"Maybe. But are those friends there when you're sleeping at night? Because I will be. You'll wake up to me standing over your bed with a crowbar. That's if you wake up at all."

The tall man flinched. His face flickered between disbelief and horror. "Kid, you don't even know where I live."

"You're right about that. I don't even know your name." Luke took a step toward him. "But here's what you don't understand. You might have more friends, but I have more time. I'm younger, I'm more diabolical, and I've got nothing on my schedule but finding out everything there is to know about you." He paused. "Or we can just get on with our days."

The tall man stared at him for a long moment, then shook his head. "Let's get out of here. These two assholes aren't worth it."

Luke and Matt watched them until they pulled out of the gas station, and then they got back into Luke's truck.

Once they were back on the road, Matt let out the laughter he'd been containing since the two men walked away. "Dude, that was amazing!"

"Please, don't even give me that."

Matt suddenly realized that his friend wasn't laughing. In fact, his face was as serious as he'd ever seen it.

"I wouldn't have done that for anyone else."

"I know. And I appreciate it. What you did for me with my dad, I won't forget it, Luke. If you ever need anything, just call and I'll come running. That's a promise."

Luke shot him a smile. "You'll be too busy making the world safe for democracy to think about me. You'll forget Kingsport ever existed."

"Never going to happen." There was earnestness in Matt's voice. "Whether I like it or not, this will always be home."

"Damn right it will."

They pulled into the bus stop five minutes later. Luke got out and grabbed Matt's duffle bag out of the truck's bed and tossed it to him. Matt was surprised by how light it felt. Everything he owned in the world, and he could carry it with one hand.

The two friends shook hands without a word. Matt headed into the station and Luke headed back into Kingsport. A new life awaited them both.

They wouldn't see each other again for eighteen years.

38

A COOL WIND blew across Riker's cheeks as he looked out the second-story window of the old farmhouse. It had been a long night of preparations, and he'd somehow managed a few hours of sleep. But now the sun in the eastern sky announced that the day had arrived, and Riker knew that battle would soon be arriving to join it.

One of Chief Myer's men had spotted the caravan just west of town. Five large trucks, each carrying maybe as many as eight men. The officer had made no move to stop the men, just as instructed. He'd simply passed the message on to Chief Myers who had passed it on to Riker.

Somewhere in the neighborhood of forty armed men were coming toward the farm that had served as the drug cartel's production facility. Chief Myers and Officer Alvarez were at the station, the cartel's likely secondary target. That left just Riker, Luke, and Donnie to defend the farm. It would have to be enough.

Donnie was off in the woods somewhere preparing, but Luke stood next to Riker.

Luke cast a nervous glance at the horizon. "What's the over/under on us being alive an hour from now?"

"Tough to say. But I like our odds of taking quite a few of these bastards with us."

Luke chuckled and shook his head. "I was really hoping for a motivational speech or something."

"Stick to the plan, and we have a shot at surviving. That's the best I've got."

"Guess it'll have to do."

Riker glanced over at his old friend. "Can I ask you something? How come you never took me up on my offer?"

"What offer is that?"

"The one I made on the day you dropped me off at the bus station. Remember what I said? If you ever need help, just call and I'll come running."

"I didn't even have your phone number."

"Yeah, but did you even try? Did you ask Megan if she had it? Or my mom when she still lived around here?"

Luke's expression answered the question for him.

"So why didn't you? When you realized you were in over your head with the drug cartel? I would have moved Heaven and Earth to help you."

"I know." Luke's voice was distant, as if he were thinking back to better days. "I considered it, but only briefly. Thing is, I guess I liked the idea of you remembering me like I was back then. Back when I took no shit. Back when I was free. I didn't want you to see what I'd become."

Riker gave his friend a long look. "You're still that guy, same as you ever were. You're still the kid who stood up to those drunks who wanted to kick my ass at the gas station the day I left. You may have lost your way for a bit, but you're here now."

Luke slowly nodded, not meeting his old friend's eyes as

the emotion threatened to overtake them both. "I'm glad you came back, Matt. And if this is the end, I'm glad it's with you."

"We're not dying today. Coach would kick both our asses in the afterlife."

"True that." Luke suddenly tensed, his eyes on the horizon. "Right on schedule."

Riker followed his friend's gaze and saw a large truck rolling down the country road, its silhouette barely visible in the early-morning sun. Another vehicle quickly followed.

"Showtime. Better get to your station. And remember what we talked about. Trust Donnie on the route. He knows these woods better than any of us."

Luke gave a quick nod, his gaze still fixed on the approaching vehicles. Then he left the house and headed towards the front gate.

Riker drew a deep, cleansing breath and reached for his weapon. Once the battle started, this would all happen very quickly, but he knew from experience that the time between now and the first shot would drag on for what felt like an eternity. Waiting for battle was always difficult, even for a man who had once borne the codename Scarecrow.

The M24 SWS sniper rifle had come straight from the Kingsport Police Department weapons stock where it had sat unused for the past ten years. Riker had spent an hour with it the previous night cleaning and oiling it and sighting it in, making sure it was ready to function. It was a solid weapon but he was taking no chances today. With the odds stacked this high against them, he needed to make sure every shot counted.

From his vantage point on the upper floor of the house, he could see the entire farmyard along with the road past the fence. Since the barn was leveled nothing obstructed his view. He watched the approaching trucks through the open window. He could see all five of them now, and when he looked through the scope he could make out the individual men in the first vehicle. All male. Looked Colombian to Riker. He could have put a bullet through the driver at this distance, but that would throw their plan into all sorts of chaos. He needed to wait.

Reaching into his pocket, he pulled out his phone and tapped a number on his contact list.

"Riker, how's it going there?" Officer Alvarez sounded stressed but not near the breaking point. He had a feeling she was going to make it through this if any of them were.

"It's like they read our plan. They just showed up at the farm. Coming from the west too, so the sun will be in their eyes."

"All five trucks?"

"Yep, all five."

"Damn it, I should have stayed out there with you."

"No," Riker insisted. "We need you and Chief Myers at the station. Could be a smaller team coming to take out Doc Hanson, or it might even be another large team we haven't spotted yet."

"I hear you. Waiting isn't my favorite."

"I understand that. Just stay frosty. I'll let you know as soon as we have things cleaned up here."

"Thanks. Good luck, Riker."

"Same to you."

The first truck reached the closed gate. Luke stood in front of it with an AR slung over his shoulder. He approached the drivers' window and nodded at the driver. The window rolled down and a Colombian man glared at him.

"Open the gate. We want to make this quick."

Luke watched as the other trucks lined up behind the first. "We're all ready to get you loaded up and back on the road. Head around the right side of the barn. They are waiting for you at the silos."

Luke pushed open the gate to the farm and the trucks went through. As the last one passed, he hopped into the bulldozer that was parked just inside of the fence. He moved the large piece of equipment into the opening of the fence. With the dozer parked there it was impossible to get a vehicle around through the entrance. Luke got out and ran along the outside of the fence.

Riker watched from his vantage point in the house. The room that he was positioned in was on the southwest corner. There were several windows facing south and west. He watched Luke move along the outside of the fence and disappear into the woods.

The caravan of trucks followed Luke's instructions and drove towards the silo. When the lead truck reached the side, the ground gave beneath the front tires and the front of the truck dipped down into a ditch. Luke had spent the previous night digging an impressively deep ditch with the excavator. Once he was done, they covered it with sheets of plywood and then dirt. The driver never even slowed down before the truck crashed.

The other four trucks stopped and the driver of the second truck got out to see what had happened. Riker watched through the scope of his weapon and forced himself to wait. Men started to climb out of the back of the first truck. The driver and front passenger attempted to climb out of the eight-foot-deep pit.

The men that excited the truck were armed with assault rifles. They scanned the area and tried to determine if this was an accident or attack. One of the men looked back at the gate and pointed at the bulldozer that was blocking the exit. Riker took that as a sign to start the attack.

He fired a single shot through the driver's window of the truck at the end of the line. The bullet made a small hole in the window and a large one in the side of the driver's head. The men outside of the trucks crouched and looked around the farmyard for the source of the shot.

Riker fired again. This time the driver of the third truck met his maker. Shouts came from the men around the trucks and they were able to determine that the report of the weapon came from the farmhouse. The men exited the back of the other vehicles and took cover behind them. Riker continued to fire his weapon killing three more men before the first round of return fire sprayed the side of the house.

He ducked back into the house and crouched low to the floor. The men who were firing at him were in motion looking for cover. Their shots were wild, but bullets still managed to shatter windows. Riker moved to another window and shot twice more.

The men on the ground moved to the far sides of the trucks using them for cover. A few men dared to peek around the ends of the truck looking for the sniper. As they set up, automatic fire came from behind them.

Donnie and Luke watched the events happen just like Riker explained they would. The trucks were stopped in the open and when the men took cover from Riker they were exposed to Donnie and Luke who were waiting in the woods on the south-side of the property.

Luke was the first to fire. He fired rapidly hitting three men. After a few shots he stopped firing and ran to a new position ten feet away. As soon as he stopped shooting Donnie started to fire. He shot a few bursts and then moved his position while Luke fired. From their cover in the forest, it seemed as if a large force was attacking.

A dozen men were down before the panic firing started. Bullets tore into the forest. The shots were wild and Donnie and Luke ran through the woods to their next position. The Colombians started to charge the farmhouse. They fired as they moved and advanced their position towards the only structure that could shield them from the attack.

39

Almost thirty men survived the initial assault. Riker had hoped that the men sent for the drugs would be little more than hired help. Just warm bodies to load the drugs onto trucks, these men were much more than that.

They were caught off guard with the ambush, but now their training and skill showed through. Four men would lay down cover fire on the farmhouse while four others watched for attacks from the rear. The others would move as a group. Then their leader would call out a command and the shooters would charge. The result was quick movement and a relentless stream of bullets tearing into the farmhouse.

Riker was forced to army crawl out of the room. Bullets were cutting through the walls and windows. The objects in the room shattered around him as he crawled through splinters and over broken glass. Riker had planned to escape through the rear door of the house, but he was pinned down by the fire. He knew that he needed to exit the home before the remaining men entered.

Luke's voice spoke through the radio on Riker's belt. "You need to get out of there. They are almost to the house."

Riker hit the button as he continued to crawl. "If you could get me any kind of distraction it would be greatly appreciated."

"Roger that."

Luke followed Donnie through the woods. They were on a path that was hardly more than a game trail. Branches snapped against Luke's arms and face as he ran. Luke could see glimpses of the farmhouse through the trees and brush; some of the men were already at the front of the house and the others were approaching quickly.

"We need to draw some fire," Luke said as he slowed down and moved towards the fence. Donnie followed his lead and the two fired in unison at the men. They were a few hundred yards from the house and the distance was greater than their skill with the weapons. The fire drew the attention of the men approaching the house, but instead of stopping they moved faster towards the building.

"We need to get closer. Follow me," Donnie yelled as he ran back into the woods."

Riker reached the top of the stairs when he heard the front door crash open. They made it inside before he even got to the first floor. Half of his plan had worked. He had lured the men into the farmhouse. The part where he escaped before they got inside didn't go as planned. When he heard the men rush into the house, he knew there was only one escape possible. He just needed to be sure the remaining men entered the trap before he left.

Riker lay prone at the top of the stairs. He tossed the sniper rifle to the side and gripped his pistol. In the close quarters, it would be a better weapon. He waited and listened as more and more footsteps entered the house. Riker watched the barrel of a rifle slide around the wall at the base of the stairs. Riker waited with pressure on the trigger of his 9mm. Above the barrel, an eye peeked around the corner. Before the man with the rifle got a view of the top of the stairs a bullet tore through his skull.

Riker yelled out, "Alpha team, they are in the house. Cover the exits."

He heard a man yell in Spanish from the first floor. "The first floor is clear. They are all upstairs. Clear the level but take one alive if you can."

Riker moved back from the stairs to a room at the end of the hallway. He shut the door and moved to the window. If he could get out of the back of the home, it was only twenty yards to the fence and his escape in the forest. He pulled back the curtain to see if the area was clear. At that moment, bullets tore through the window. Riker hit the deck and glass rained down on him. It seemed that the attackers had reached the back of the home and were ready for anyone trying to escape. He accepted his fate and hit the button on his radio.

"Are all the men in the house?"

"There are a few guarding the exits, but most of them are in," Luke said.

Riker heard a creak on the stairs. Some poor soldier was making his way up to the second floor. "Blow it."

"Are you clear?" Luke asked.

"Sorry man, it looks like I'm going to be taking hell from Coach today."

"Screw that. I'm not blowing it while you're in there."

"I'm not making it out of this one. Don't let me go down for nothing. Take these guys out."

Donnie and Luke continued to move closer to the back of the house while Luke spoke.

Donnie turned back to Luke, "Don't you dare push that fucking button."

Luke stopped in his tracks and grabbed a remote detonator from his belt. "You heard the man; we can't let him die for nothing."

"We're not going to. Git ready to blow that thing. I know how to get him out. As soon as we're clear hit the button. Let him know I'm coming."

Luke stood with his finger hovering above the button of the detonator. He moved through the forest until he could see the farmhouse. "Riker, Donnie is coming your way."

"That's a negative Luke, it's too dangerous. Just hit the button."

"He's already on his way. I can't stop him."

"Make him stop."

Before Luke could respond Riker heard gunfire from outside of the house. There was immediate fire returned. Riker didn't hesitate he jumped through the broken window. For the brief moment that he was in the air, he saw Donnie firing at the four men outside of the rear of the house. Donnie was on the other side of the fence, but he had no real cover. All four men were returning fire.

Riker used his forward momentum and rolled once when he hit the ground. The moment he came to a stop he fired his weapon at the men shooting at Donnie. One of the men was already down, Riker's shots didn't require any thought; he moved with the speed of muscle memory and years of training. Three rapid shots and three head snaps were followed by a moment of silence.

Riker sprang to his feet and ran towards the opening they had prepared in the fence. He reached it and slid through. Behind him he heard the report of a rifle and an instant later he was knocked down by the force of a concussion wave.

Luke had hit the detonator the moment Riker cleared the fence. The team had rigged all the chemicals left on the farm in the cellar of the old farmhouse. The result was an explosion like the one that destroyed the barn.

Riker's ears rang and he stumbled back to his feet. Leaves were drifting down all around him from the surrounding trees. The wave of the blast was strong enough to knock them from the trees. It made the forest look like a peaceful fall day. Riker turned back to see the house and the scene changed completely.

Debris and fire rained down from the sky. Half a mangled body was smashed into the fence not far from where Riker stood. The ringing in Riker's ears started to lessen and he could hear a muffled version of Luke's voice.

"Are you okay? Can you hear me?"

Riker turned and saw Luke running towards him. "Yeah, I'm okay. Where's Donnie?"

Riker looked around. He started to move towards the last location that he had seen Donnie. He remembered seeing him firing at the men from the other side of the fence.

Riker and Luke found him leaning against a tree. Blood was seeping into his clothes from three different locations. One in his chest and two in his abdomen.

"Hey guys, did we get them?" Donnie whispered.

"Oh my god, Donnie." Luke dropped next to Donnie's side and started to pull back his shirt.

Riker could see how white Donnie's face was. He recognized the combination of shock and loss of blood that was keeping him calm. He had seen it too many times before.

Riker kneeled next to Donnie and took his hand. "Hey

man, you did awesome. You got them all. Sam would be proud."

Donnie gave a half-smile. "You think so?"

"I know so. You came in like the days of old with no fear. I'm alive because of you."

Donnie's smile grew wide for a moment. Then it faded and his head dropped to his chest.

"Donnie, stay with us man!" Luke said.

Riker put a hand on Luke's shoulder. "He's gone. I'm sorry."

Riker's phone buzzed. "I'm getting a message from Alvarez. They may need our help. We will have time to honor Donnie, but for now, we need to carry on."

Riker pulled out his cellphone and tapped Alvarez's number.

"Riker, how's it going there?"

"We need ambulances. Not sure if anyone survived, but we need to check."

"I take it you got them?"

"We got them."

"And yet somehow you don't seem happy."

"The price was high. Donnie didn't make it."

"My God. I'm sorry, Riker."

He shifted the phone to his other ear. "How are things at the station?"

"Nothing yet. It's totally quiet here."

Riker frowned. "The enforcer, the one they call, El Leon, he wasn't here. I gotta assume he's heading your way."

"We'll be ready. And I'll get those ambulances out there fast."

Riker felt his phone buzz as a text came in. "Thanks. Luke and I will be at the station soon."

He ended the call and looked down at the text message. What he saw made him go cold.

The text was only a single word, but it was enough to let him know he'd been wrong about El Leon's intentions. Wrong about everything. The police station wasn't the second target at all.

The text was from Megan and it said simply, *Help.*

40

Megan stood in front of her class, looking out at the seventeen faces in front of her. They stared at her expectantly, waiting for her to give them directions on that day's lesson, but her mind was eight miles away, with Matt, Luke, and Donnie on the farm just outside of town.

How was she supposed to concentrate on fifteenth-century politics when a little more than a five-minute drive away her cousin was fighting for his life? People were bleeding and dying on one side or the other, and here she was talking about events that had taken place hundreds of years ago. Coming to work and being a role model for her class had sounded sensible last night when Matt had proposed it, but now it seemed rather ridiculous.

"Ms. Carter?" a girl in the front row asked.

Megan blinked hard, trying to force her mind back to the here and now. "Yes, Ashley?"

The girl looked at her expectantly. "You were going to give us the instructions for the group activity."

"Oh. Right." Megan grabbed the instructions off of her

desk, straightening them in her hands, buying herself a moment to regain her composure. "I've broken you out into five groups. The groups are listed here." She began handing out the papers. "You each represent a European nation. Your task will be to convince the Pope that he should support your side in the conflict described on your paper. You'll have ten minutes to brainstorm, then you'll have to present your case in front of the class."

"And you're the Pope?" David Underwood asked with a smile.

"Yes. I left my Pope hat at home, so you'll have to use your imagination."

Megan sat down behind her desk as the groups gathered and began working on their arguments. The purpose of the exercise was to show the power the Church had over nations at that point in history. When she'd come up with the activity while forming her lesson plans, it had seemed like a fun and innovative way to make her point. Now, like everything else that morning, it felt a bit pointless. Her mind once again drifted back to the battle that must be going on at the farm and the second one that might be going on at the police station.

She cast an eye over the class. Matt had asked her to play a specific role: make sure her kids didn't lose another teacher. She reminded herself to stay focused on that. David Underwood was here, far away from the violence of the cartel in spite of his father's involvement. And so was Blake Mullins, who had made the mistake of getting involved in the drug game before he was even out of high school. If Matt and the others somehow managed to beat the odds and defeat the cartel, maybe Blake could start over and make a life for himself on the right side of the law.

As if on cue, Blake looked up at the clock in the corner

of the room. It was nearly nine thirty now. Megan noticed that the young man's face looked strangely pale. He turned back to his group, joining in their conversation for about thirty seconds or so, then looking back up at the clock.

Megan felt a bit of unease roiling in her stomach. Something about the way the young man kept glancing at the clock and his pale, drawn expression... It was as if he were waiting for something. She tried to push the feeling aside, but then Blake glanced at the clock again. There were a few beads of sweat standing on his forehead now. He turned back to the group.

This wasn't just paranoia on Megan's part. Something was very wrong here.

"Blake," she said.

The young's man's head snapped up, and he turned toward her, eyes wide, looking for all the world like a boy who'd been caught doing something he shouldn't.

"Would you come up here, please?"

He stood up from his chair, but not before glancing at the clock one more time. When he reached her desk, he crossed his arms over his chest and said nothing.

She spoke in a low voice so that only he could hear. "Is everything all right? You seem a little distracted this morning."

"Yeah." His answer was immediate, but there was no conviction behind it.

"You sure? You keep looking at the clock. You waiting for something?"

He shifted his weight to his other foot. "Yeah, I just... I've got a test next period in Language Arts. It's on *The Odyssey*, and I'm a little nervous about it. Those sentences are like half a page long."

Megan pressed her lips together in a thin line. In the two

years she'd known Blake Mullins, she'd never once seen him stressed about school work. He always seemed to have other things on his mind. "You know, if there's something bothering you, you can talk to me. I'm a pretty good listener. And I don't judge."

Blake's mouth opened a little, as if maybe he wanted to say something, but then it closed, and he seemed to be reformulating his thoughts. He leaned forward and spoke softly. "Listen, Ms. Carter, you should get out of here. Go to the teacher's lounge for the next twenty minutes or so. Or the bathroom. Or, I don't know, get in your car and drive. Just don't be here."

Megan tilted her head, not sure what to think of the strange words. Blake's eyes were more earnest than she'd ever seen them. "What do you mean? Why would I do that?"

He stammered in frustration. "I know I'm not the best student, and I've lied to you before. But this once, I need you to listen to me. Please get out of here."

She stared at him blankly, utterly confused. Then, all at once, she understood. Her body tensed and her mouth went dry, not wanting to believe what Blake was implying. Her hand slipped into her purse, pulling out her cellphone. "They're coming here, aren't they, Blake? They are coming to hurt us."

"Not they. *Him*."

She glanced down at her phone and quickly tapped out a single word text message. Her mind was racing so fast that it took a moment for what the boy had said to sink in. "What do you mean by him? Who is *him*?"

A loud, cracking sound erupted in the distance. Megan wasn't positive, but she thought it was a gunshot.

Blake's head spun toward the sound, and then his eyes settled on the wall clock. It was exactly nine thirty.

He looked back at Megan. "El Leon. He's not just coming. He's here."

41

Riker clutched the phone to his ear as Luke's truck bounced over the gravel surface of the country road. Luke was driving way too fast for the conditions and the winding nature of the road, but Riker wished the vehicle would go even faster. Every moment longer it took them to get to the high school meant another moment where El Leon and his fellow enforcers could be hurting Megan or one of the students.

The phone rang three more times before Megan's voicemail message kicked in. "Hi, it's Megan. I'm probably shaping young minds at the moment, no big deal, but I'll get back to you when I can."

Riker tapped the button to end the call, perhaps a little too aggressively. He couldn't help his frustration.

Luke glanced over at him, a concerned expression on his face. "You've tried her three times, man. If she hasn't answered by now, she's not going to."

Luke was right. Besides, there was another call he should be making, one he should have made immediately after Megan's text. He cursed his own stupidity as he found the number he was looking for and dialed.

"Still nothing, Riker," Alvarez said dryly. "Same as when we talked two minutes ago."

"The cartel guys aren't coming to the station. They're at the high school."

"Shit." There was a long pause. "We're going to put the school on lockdown immediately. The station's only a couple blocks from the school, so I'm going to head over there myself now."

"We're right behind you, Officer Alvarez." He swallowed hard. "I think they're going after Megan."

"I'm headed there now. We're going to stop these guys." The resolve in her voice almost made Riker believe it was possible.

He hung up the phone and tapped Megan's number again.

"Hi, it's Megan. I'm probably shaping young minds at the moment, no big deal, but I'll get back to you when I can."

Riker hung up and forced himself to put down the phone. Luke was right. If she hadn't answered by now, she wasn't likely to. Could be she was hiding from the cartel guys, or… No. He wouldn't allow himself to think of the alternative.

He glanced over at Luke and saw his old friend was gripping the steering wheel hard as the truck rumbled over the gravel.

"Luke, I'm sorry about all of this. Donnie's dead, the high school is under attack, and chances of either of us surviving beyond today are slim. If I hadn't come back to Kingsport, none of this would have happened."

Luke's jaw clenched as he stared at the road in front of him. "You're a damn fool, Matt Riker. You think we were better off before all of this? I was living under the thumb of a Colombian drug cartel. And Donnie? He was a broken man. I'm not sure you can call what he was doing living at all. You reminded us that it's possible to fight. And I don't want to hear you apologize for that. Not ever."

Riker let Luke's words sink in for a long moment before answering. He could tell that his old friend meant every word. "Let's make sure Megan and the students at the high school are safe before we start patting me on the back too hard. If a single kid gets killed, this thing is pretty far from a success."

"You have a point," Luke allowed. "Let's just make sure that doesn't happen."

They drove in silence for a while, finally pulling the truck onto a paved road. Luke stepped on the gas hard, pushing the vehicle to its limit. The truck shook as it careened down the state highway.

"I always knew the cartel people were bad. I wasn't under any illusion that I was working for saints. But what kind of people go after high school kids?"

Riker didn't answer. He'd seen a few things during his time with the SEALs and QS-4 that reminded him of this brand of evil. His last job with QS-4 came to mind, the one that had convinced him to walk away once and for all. He didn't allow his mind to go to that place often, but it went there now, if only for a moment. He reminded himself that he'd survived that brutally dark time; he'd survive this too.

Still, this felt different. It was his hometown that was under attack. His family. Something primal roused within him, the innate drive to defend his home from those who would do violence to it.

"We're going to make them pay," he told Luke, his voice even. "By the time we're done, that drug lord is going to shudder anytime anyone mentions the name Kingsport, Iowa."

A thin smile crossed Luke's face. "I like the sound of that. And I'm damn glad to be battling at your side instead of against you."

It took another two minutes before they reached the school. Luke pulled into the main parking lot, cruising toward the front door. For the most part, things appeared normal to Riker, not all that different from when he'd visited the school three days ago. The cars were lined up in the student's lot, and the facility lot appeared normal. There was no one outside, but that made sense--classes had started an hour ago and everyone would be in class.

"Matt, look." Luke nodded toward the front door of the school. A man in a security guard uniform lay still on the ground, his head resting in a pool of blood.

A chill ran through Riker. He'd known the cartel men were most likely inside the school, but seeing it with his own eyes made it all too real. The sun reflecting off the front door made it difficult to see through, but he thought he caught a glimpse of motion inside. Did El Leon have a guard at the door?

Riker considered his options. They could go in that way if they needed to, but he'd much rather find a less conspicuous way of entering.

As his eyes scanned the parking lot, he noticed something else out of place. A police car was parked alongside the building near a side door. Riker smiled. Apparently Officer Alvarez had the same idea as he had.

"We need to find a door we can enter without attracting too much attention. We don't know how many men they brought with them, but they'll most likely have their strongest defense at the front of the school. That means we go in another way."

"I know just the place."

Luke angled the truck around the parking lot, circling to the north end of the school. Riker couldn't help but smile when he saw where his friend had brought him. The exterior door to the wrestling room.

Luke turned to him and said, "I figure if there's one place we know in this school, it's this one."

"You're not wrong."

Luke parked the truck a little way from the door and the two men hopped out. They hurried to the door. Riker's injured leg was screaming at him now. He'd pushed it way too hard that morning, and it was objecting very strongly to him making it go to work again so soon. He let the pain wash over him, not ignoring it but not letting it control him, just as Coach Kane had taught him to do on the wrestling mat.

As they reached the door, Riker turned to Luke. "Ready?"

Luke nodded.

Riker reached for the door handle, but the door opened just before his hand made contact. A Colombian man stared out at them, just as surprised to see them as they were to see him.

Riker caught the edge of the door with one hand before the man could close it. He raised his other hand, the one holding the Glock, and pointed it at the man's face. "Don't move. We have a few questions to ask you."

42

"El Leon. *He's not just coming. He's here.*"

Blake's words hung in the air, and Megan found herself unable to respond.

Megan knew very little about the mysterious Colombian man, but she knew enough to be terrified. The stories she'd heard over the past few days had made her blood curdle. And now the subject of those stories was coming here. Coming for her. Worse, maybe coming for her students.

Taking a deep breath, she forced herself to her feet and strode quickly to the classroom door. It was open a few inches, and she pressed her hand against it, easing it closed. Then she reached down and pressed the lock.

As she turned back to the class, she heard shouting in the distance. A couple of the kids looked up, but most of them quickly returned to their group conversations. Only David kept staring. His eyes drifted to the doorknob and lingered there, noticing the depressed lock button.

"What's going on, Ms. Carter?" he asked.

A few others glanced up at this, and their expressions

grew more serious as they took in their teacher's ashen complexion.

The crack of another gunshot sounded in the distance, but closer than before. Now every eye was on Megan. The room was silent.

Megan swallowed hard, composing herself. "We've all been through the drills. You know what to do. Get under your desks."

For a moment, no one moved. A few of them wore amused smiles as if they thought she was joking.

There was no time for subtlety. "Get your asses under your desks!"

Ms. Carter wasn't one to swear, and she never raised her voice. Doing both at the same time provoked an immediate reaction. As one, they all slid to the floor. Even Blake rushed back to his desk and took position under it.

"You too, Ms. Carter," David called.

"I'm on it." She started making her way around her desk, but hesitated when she felt something on her neck almost like a physical weight. Turning toward the classroom door, she saw a face staring in through the window at her.

The man was tall and his dark hair hung to his shoulders. He had a broad nose and cold emotionless eyes. He wore a dark expensive-looking suit. He was the picture of calm; his was the face of a man observing a pond of ducks rather than a classroom full of potential victims.

El Leon's eyes locked with Megan's, and she froze with sheer terror. If he noticed her fear, he gave no indication. His expression remained placid.

The doorknob turned a fraction of an inch to the left before it was stopped by the lock. Then a fraction of an inch to the right before it stopped again. *Click click.*

The man shrank in the window as he took a few steps back. He raised something in his right hand, though Megan couldn't make out what the object was.

A series of rapid-fire blasts echoed through the classroom, and this time the roar of gunfire was unmistakable. The wood around the door frame splintered as bullets tore through it from the hallway. Then El Leon stepped forward and raised a heavy boot, slamming it into the door. The frame buckled and the door swung inward on its hinges.

El Leon paused in the doorway, putting his pistol back into the shoulder holster under his jacket. He sauntered inside and nodded toward Megan. Two other Colombian men, similarly dressed, followed him in, stopping just past the doorway and waiting on either side of the door.

"Apologies for the interruption, Ms. Carter." El Leon spoke slowly, his heavy accent showing through, but his careful pronunciation of each word was perfect.

Megan took a step back and her thighs banged against the cold metal of her desk. She had no idea how to respond, and she would have been too afraid to even if she had known what to say.

One of the students let out a soft whimper, and Megan turned her head toward them. Seventeen faces, every one of them terrified. This man had entered her classroom and was threatening her students. There was no one to protect them. No one but her.

Riker's words echoed in her mind: *Don't make your students attend another teacher's funeral.*

She didn't know if that was possible, if she could protect both her students and herself, but she was going to try.

Her cell phone buzzed on the desk, and its screen lit up, showing the name Matt.

El Leon frowned at it, though there was still no real emotion behind the facial expression. "Thought he'd be dead by now." He shrugged and turned to Megan. "I expect you know that you are coming with us."

Megan forced herself to look him dead in the eyes. He was close enough that she could smell the heavy scent of his cologne. "I'll go peacefully as long as you don't hurt any of the kids. If you hurt anyone else, I'll fight you all the way."

"Fight or don't. It makes no difference to me." He turned to the class. "David Underwood. Step forward, please."

None of the students moved.

"Very well. Blake, would you please point out David Underwood to me?"

Again, no one moved.

El Leon let out a short, joyless chuckle. He turned to the two men waiting by the door and shook his head, coworkers commiserating over the daily tribulations of their work life. He reached into his pocket and pulled out his phone, fumbling with it for a moment before bringing up a photograph. From her position, Megan could see it well enough to tell it was a photo of Blake. El Leon studied the photo before turning back to the students. His gaze quickly settled on Blake.

"Ah, there you are. Come, young man. It's not the time to be shy."

Blake reluctantly climbed out from under his desk and stood before the large man.

El Leon put a meaty hand on the boy's shoulder. "Please, point out your classmate David so that we can be on our way."

Blake said nothing.

El Leon raised an eyebrow. "Come now. You are the

reason we are here, young man. You've been calling me and passing on information for days. When we spoke on the phone, you indicated this room number and this time as the place where I could find both Megan Carter and David Underwood together. And now that you've brought me here, you balk at your duty?" He let out a tisking sound, as if he were scolding a young child.

A wave of anger ran through Megan. Blake had brought them here? He'd sold out his classmates and his teacher? And for what? The favor of a drug cartel who would likely kill him in the end?

Still, Blake said nothing.

"I had hopes for you, boy." El Leon's hand snaked up, grabbing Blake by the throat. Blake let out a cry of surprise and pain. El Leon quickly twisted his arm, sending the boy sprawling onto the ground on his back.

Megan gasped and started toward her fallen student, but El Leon held up a hand, and she froze.

"I very much hope that you will reconsider answering my question, Blake. Where is David?"

Blake was breathing heavily, his hand on his bruised throat. He stared up at El Leon, eyes wide with fear. But he did not answer.

El Leon strolled forward a few steps until he stood at Blake's side. Then he raised his left boot into the air and brought it down hard, stomping on Blake's left shoulder exactly where the arm bone connected. There was a sharp, loud crack, and Blake screamed in pain.

"I have a policy of only asking the same question a certain number of times." El Leon's face was still expressionless. "Hear me when I say, this will be the last time I ask. Where is David Underwood?"

Blake gritted his teeth as he looked up at the big man. He was quivering with pain and rage, but he did not speak.

"Very well." El Leon raised his boot again, this time positioning it over Blake's skull.

"Wait!"

The voice came from the back of the room. Megan's head snapped up, and she saw that it was David who had spoken. He climbed out from under his desk.

"I'm the one you want. I'm David Underwood."

El Leon set his foot down and regarded David. "Is that so? Please. Approach."

David stumbled forward on shaky legs. His brow was covered with sweat, and the terror was clear on his face.

"You don't need him," Megan said. "You have me. That's enough."

El Leon ignored her. He took a step toward David, and the two of them stood face to face. El Leon put both hands on the younger man's shoulders. "I want you to know that you have my respect. And because you have my respect, I will tell you the truth. You are going to die today, David Underwood, and you will die in a very unpleasant manner. This is no fault of your own. It is a necessary part of our business. Your father betrayed us, and so his son must die. This cannot be changed. It is simply the way of things. I thought you should know."

Megan knew the moments of her life were ticking away. She had to do something, and fast. "We can work something out if you'd just—"

El Leon once again held up a hand, and she fell silent. "Please. Take a lesson from your student and die with honor." He nodded to the two men by the door. They quickly marched forward.

The first man grabbed David, gripping him by the upper

arm. The second man grabbed Megan's right arm and pulled her toward the door. He was strong, and there was nothing she could do but go where he dragged her. She took one last look at her student's shocked faces, and the man pulled her out of the classroom and into the hallway.

43

Riker inched the gun forward, speaking in Spanish to the man inside the wrestling room. "Lower your weapon."

The man was holding an assault rifle at a forty-five-degree angle to the ground. He'd have to raise it to get a clear shot at Riker, and if he did that, Riker would have time to fire first. He could see that the man was making the same mental calculation and coming to the same conclusion. He crouched down, gently setting his weapon on the hardwood floor next to the wrestling mats.

"Bueno. Now back up slowly."

The man stood back up, hands raised, and took a step back. His eyes were wide and they were focused on the barrel of Riker's pistol. Just for the briefest of moments, the man's eyes flickered to his left, and Riker knew there was another man out of his line of sight.

There wasn't time to think—Riker just reacted. He knew his sole advantage was that the enemy was unable to see Luke, and he needed to use that. With his left hand, he threw the door open wide, and he charged forward, wrapping his arms around the man in front of him, tackling him to the ground. As long as he was tangled up with this man, the other enemy wouldn't be able to get a clear shot.

As Riker and the man he was attacking tumbled to the ground, he saw movement out of the corner of his eye. The second man had his weapon trained on Riker, but he didn't dare take a shot. Just as Riker had hoped, the man stepped around, trying to get a better angle, thus exposing himself to Luke.

Luke didn't hesitate. He fired three quick rounds into the man's back. The report of the gunshots echoed loudly in the empty gym, and Riker grimaced. So much for their stealthy attack. Everyone in the school would know they were coming now.

By the time the man Luke had shot hit the ground, Riker had the other man flipped over and face down on the mat.

He shouted at the man in Spanish. "How many of you are there in the school?"

The man made no reply but to futilely struggle, trying to free himself. This guy wasn't going to break easily; he hardly seemed fazed that his buddy had just been shot in front of him. And every moment that Riker spent questioning the man was another moment Megan was in danger. She'd asked for his help, and he intended to give it to her. He needed to end this fast.

Riker released the man with his right hand, allowing his right arm to go free. Just as Riker had expected, the freed arm shot out, the fingers clutching at the slick mat for leverage. As soon as it did Riker raised his pistol and fired, putting a bullet through the center of the man's hand.

The man screamed in pain, instinctively pulled the hand back toward his body, but Riker caught the wrist with his own left hand, keeping the man in place with a knee to the back.

He jammed the barrel of his pistol into the bullet wound, and the man cried out again.

"How many are here?" Riker shouted in Spanish.

The only reply was a whimper of pain.

Riker twisted the pistol, grinding the barrel into the wound.

"Ocho!" the man shouted.

Eight. Not great odds, but not impossible either.

"Where?"

The man replied without hesitation this time. "Two at the front door. Two here. Three to take the woman and boy."

Riker blinked hard, trying to make sense of the man's words. "What woman and boy?"

"La families." *The families.*

That had to mean Megan.

Riker raised his pistol, considering firing a round into the back of the man's head, but instead snaked an arm around his neck and applied pressure. When the man was unconscious, Riker struggled to his feet.

"We've got to move. They're going after Megan. And a boy."

Luke grimaced. "That'll be David. Eric Underwood's son."

"I met him. At the wake."

"It's my fault. I told the cartel that Eric refused to help us at the funeral. This is payback."

"You'll have time to feel bad about that later. We need to move." Riker made his way toward the door that led to the interior of the high school. He did his best to walk normally, but still, the injured leg dragged, creating a bit of a limp that slowed his progress.

As they passed through the room, he noticed he was carefully keeping his feet on the hardwood, unconsciously following Coach's rule of no street shoes on the mats. He couldn't believe the path to saving Megan and ending this led through this room where he and Luke had spent so much time.

"That was hardcore back there," Luke said. "With the hand. You done that kind of thing before?"

Riker didn't see the point of lying to his old friend. "Yeah, unfortunately, I have."

"Damn." He paused. "That was a pretty good takedown. Never thought I'd get to see you wrestle in this gym again. I think you might have a future in the sport."

"Let's save Megan and David. Then we'll plan my big comeback."

The two men moved quietly out of the wrestling room and into a long hallway lined with classrooms. Despite Riker's fear that the gunshots may have given them away, no one appeared to be heading for the gym. The hallways were empty and quiet. Riker was glad he'd paid a visit to the school the day of the wake; otherwise he wouldn't know which classroom was Megan's.

Riker stayed focused, trying not to think about all the kids and teachers in the classrooms they were passing, probably terrified at the lockdown. Had they been able to hear the gunshots? He hoped not.

He glanced over his shoulder and saw Luke six feet behind him, pistol clutched in a two-hand grip. Luke might not have military training, but he was doing well, going on instinct and following Riker's lead.

They came to a place where the hallway intersected with another one, and Riker slowed. Off to his right, he heard a thump, like someone stomping on the ground. Instinctively, he turned toward it, and he caught a glimpse of a man crouching behind a gap in the lockers.

With a sickening feeling, he suddenly realized the noise had been intentional, meant to distract him and draw his attention away from—

He spun to his left, raising his pistol, preparing to fire at the man he knew would be waiting down the other hallway. A gunshot erupted before Riker could fire, and he tensed, expecting to feel the impact of a round hitting him.

Instead, the man down the hallway let out a grunt and collapsed. As he fell, Riker saw a figure behind him, holding a pistol. Officer Alvarez.

Riker didn't stop to offer his thanks just yet. Instead, he spun back toward the man down the other hallway. He was leaning out from behind the lockers now, preparing to take his shot, but Riker fired first, putting a round through his forehead.

He turned back to Officer Alvarez. "Thanks for the assist. He would have had me if you hadn't been there."

"Serve and protect," she said with a forced smile. "It's what I do. You okay?"

He nodded. "You?"

She returned his nod, but he could see she was shaken up. He couldn't blame her. It wasn't every day a small-town cop gets into a shootout with members of a Colombian drug cartel.

"Come on. They're going after Megan. We have to hurry."

The three of them headed on down the hallway, Riker running the numbers as they went. If the man in the gymnasium was telling the truth, there were only four cartel members left. Hell of a lot better odds than Riker was used to facing. They just might be able to pull this off.

They reached Megan's classroom, and Riker peered through the rectangular window in the door. Inside, he saw students huddled under their desks. He didn't see any gunmen, but he didn't see Megan either. He threw open the door and rushed inside.

"Everybody all right?" he asked.

He saw some nods.

"We are now that you're here," one girl answered.

Near the front of the room, he saw one boy clutching his right shoulder.

"Blake," Luke said, stepping forward. "Are you all right?"

"They stomped on my shoulder. I'll be okay." He stared at Riker, his eyes pleading. "You're going to save them right?"

"Save who? What happened here?"

Blake's gaze shifted to Luke. "It was him. El Leon. He took David and Ms. Carter."

44

RIKER CHARGED DOWN THE HALLWAY, pushing away the pain in his leg, his sole focus on Megan. The cartel men had her, and if he didn't stop them, they would get away with her. Images from the story of what had happened to Sam, Donnie's brother, flashed through his mind. A steel barrel. Gasoline. A match. He had to imagine they had something similar planned for Megan. And why? All because Riker had dared to stand up to them? She shouldn't have to pay the price for that. He was just as responsible for David's safety. After all, it had been David's father's refusal to go after Riker that had put them on the wrong side of the cartel in the first place.

Riker and his friends were the only chance Megan and David had.

These thoughts fueled him, making the pain in his leg feel like a small thing by comparison.

Luke and Office Alvarez were to his left, matching him stride for stride. Blake had said the men had gone right when they left Megan's classroom, which indicated to Riker they'd been heading toward the school's main entrance. They needed to catch up before they reached the parking lot and whatever vehicle waited for them there.

They rounded a corner and spotted two men up ahead, one gripping David's arm and the other holding on to Megan. They were only ten feet from the exit. Riker pushed himself even harder, all his attention focused on the two men.

Suddenly something collided with Riker's face, and the world went topsy-turvy. His feet continued forward even as his head and torso stopped, and he landed flat on his back. The hallway swam before his suddenly watering eyes.

A foot slammed into his wrist, causing the hand to go instantly numb. He heard his pistol skid across the floor and clang against a locker.

Riker didn't allow himself even a moment to wonder what had happened. He pushed himself quickly to his knees, struggling to maintain balance and not collapse again. As his vision began to clear, he saw a towering figure step out from the cross hallway, his face expressionless. From where Riker knelt, the man looked about seven feet tall. He was broad shouldered, and he held his massive hands raised in front of him. Riker knew immediately who stood before him. It was El Leon.

A blur of motion behind El Leon snapped Riker back to reality. The other two men still had Megan and David, and they would be gone soon. He turned toward Alvarez and Luke. "Go!"

Luke nodded and took off down the hall. Alvarez cast a wary glance at El Leon before following.

The big man paid them no mind; his sole focus was on Riker.

"You conversed with my employer on the telephone." He

spoke the words carefully, like a man hesitantly stepping out onto a frozen lake.

Riker struggled to his feet. His leg was still screaming, and his nose had joined in the chorus as well now. He flexed his fingers, the feeling returning to his right hand, though the movement brought sharp pain along with it. El Leon had delivered a hell of a blow when he'd knocked Riker to the floor. Blood poured out of his nose, and some of it leaked into his mouth, coating his tongue with the unpleasant taste of copper.

The big man waited while Riker stood up, patiently watching. Though Riker could see the bulge of a pistol under his jacket, the big man made no move for it. Riker could tell El Leon was the type of man who liked to work with his hands.

Now that Riker was on his feet, he saw that El Leon was only a couple inches taller than he was. He still looked like he'd been carved from granite though; perspective did nothing to change that.

"Yeah, I spoke to your employer." Riker's words came out a bit muffled due to the blood clogging his nose. "Gave him a chance to back out of this. Shame he didn't take it."

"He wishes me to tell you that you have cost his organization a great deal of money. He considers this a personal insult. For that reason, you and your loved ones will pay with your—"

Riker twisted at the hip, attacking with a sudden, lightning-quick right hook intended to hit El Leon in the jaw. Somehow—impossibly—El Leon snapped his torso backward, leaning at the waist and protecting himself with both forearms like a boxer. Riker's blow missed completely.

Riker let out a grunt, his momentum carrying him forward as his fist flew harmlessly past the big man's shoulder. He moved with the momentum, taking a shaky step forward, planting the foot of his good leg on the floor, and driving a left-handed uppercut into El Leon's chin. This time, the fist connected, and it was as solid of a blow as Riker had thrown in his life. A jolt ran up his arm as his knuckles slammed into the jawbone.

El Leon stumbled backward, his eyes suddenly wide. For a beautiful moment, it seemed he was going to fall. Then he recovered. For the first time, his face betrayed emotion. Anger flashed in his eyes.

He took a big step toward Riker, his long gait making the distance between them disappear in an instant. His left hand came up, intending to repay Riker's uppercut with one of his own. Riker clocked the punch and leaned backward, moving out of the path of the massive fist. But as the hand whizzed past his face, Riker realized his mistake. El Leon had taken note of his opponent's injury. The punch had been a trap, and Riker had fallen for it. In leaning back, he'd exposed his legs to attack. El Leon brought his foot up and stomped downward, driving his boot into Riker's injured shin with the force of a sledgehammer.

Pain exploded and Riker heard his own voice crying out in pain as his vision tunneled. He suddenly found himself on his hands and knees, the hallway around him swimming. He drew a breath, trying to get his bearings, trying to center himself for the fight. As he forced himself upward, something pressed against his throat.

El Leon was behind him, his arm wrapped around Riker's neck. And his hold was tightening.

MEGAN STUMBLED FORWARD, moving her legs fast as she tried to keep her balance. Ever since they'd left the classroom, she'd been struggling to remain upright, unable to regain her footing in this world turned upside down. But she was still standing, and that was something.

The man's hand was like a vise around her upper arm, his long fingers wrapping almost all the way around. He marched down the long hallway, gripping her arm like the handle on a piece of luggage. He paid about as much mind as he might pay a piece for luggage, too. He had yet to so much as look her in the eye or speak to her. He simply kept wordlessly moving forward.

She heard some commotion behind them and struggled to get her head turned around without falling over. She twisted it just enough to see who was behind them--Matt! For the first time since El Leon and his goons had stepped into her classroom, she felt a spark of hope. She just might be able to make it through this.

Then, while she was still looking, El Leon stepped out from the shadow of another hallway and punched Riker square in the face. She let out a whimper as her cousin fell.

She suddenly went cold with fear. Fear for herself. Fear for David. Fear for Matt. If these men could take out Matthew Riker, what chance did she have of survival? Two others charged past El Leon—Officer Alvarez and Luke.

An especially powerful tug on her arm caused her to turn toward the front just as her captor slammed into the crash bar on the front door and pushed it open. He dragged her over the threshold and out into the sunlight. Up ahead, she saw a black SUV parked in a handicap spot near the door. The third man who'd come into her classroom already had the car door open, and he was forcing David inside.

She cast a glance backward as she was dragged toward

the SUV, but the doors to the high school were still closed. Alvarez and Luke were too far back. She'd be in the SUV and gone before they even got outside.

The terrible knowledge hit her like a fist—no one was going to save her and David. It was up to her.

But the man was so much stronger than she was. She needed something. A weapon. Then she remembered Matt's words to her a few days earlier. *Plenty of things can be weapons.*

Her hand went to her back pocket, grabbing her keys.

As they reached the car, the cartel man waiting there stepped aside. Looking inside the vehicle, she could see David already in the backseat, his expression drawn, defeated.

Megan sighed, letting her posture droop. The man reached up and placed a hand on her head to guide her down, and that was when she struck. Keyring clutched in her fist and keys protruding from between her fingers, she punched the man in the face with all of her might. She felt an instant pain in her hand, but a gratifying thrill ran through her as she pulled back her hand and saw blood on the teeth of the keys.

The man let out a yell and his hand went to his face, covering the puncture wounds. He looked at Megan with wide eyes, his expression a mixture of disbelief and disgust that someone like her had actually hurt him. She brought her right knee up, driving it into the man's crotch. He grunted and doubled over.

The other man, the one who had led her down the hall, was raising his gun, an equally shocked expression on his face.

"Get in!" he said in a heavy accent, nodding toward the car.

Megan crouched, positioning the injured man between her and the gunman.

His face reddened with anger. "Get in!"

She shifted even farther behind the injured man. There was no way the gunman could shoot her without hitting his buddy. He took a few steps to the right, trying to find an angle, but Megan moved with him, making sure he didn't have a clean shot.

The gunman strode forward, muttering in Spanish, his total attention on Megan. He never even noticed Luke walking up behind him, gun raised and pointed at his head.

RIKER STRUGGLED TO BREATHE, squirming as El Leon tightened his arm around his neck, fighting to avoid being choked out. If he lost consciousness, he was a dead man, and Megan and David would be dead right alongside him.

"I have very specific instructions from my employer." The breath from El Leon's words felt hot on Riker's ear. "I am to take you to a predetermined location. Not in Iowa. Somewhere else we have in the United States. There we will spend the next few weeks together."

Riker reached up and put his hands on El Leon's elbow. He tried to push it up, but it was like steel.

"You may be asking yourself," the big man continued, "why I am wasting breath telling you this. It is because I have so little regard for you and your abilities. You have killed many of my employer's hired men. I am significantly more skilled. As I have already proven, defeating you is not a problem."

Riker pulled down on the elbow. Again, it did not move.

And that was a good thing. The arm was tightening, but Riker's lips curled in a tiny smile.

"As you go to sleep, remember this. I am bigger than you. Faster than you. And much stronger."

Riker's hands clamped down hard, locking on El Leon's elbow. He dropped his body down, dragging the arm. With a grip this tight, where the arm went, the body had to follow. Riker dropped his right shoulder and pulled as hard as he could. El Leon slid over his back with a grunt. The big man's shoulder hit the floor and his body flipped over the top. He landed on the ground with a thud.

Riker scooped his Glock off floor where it had fallen and leveled it at the big man's head. "Maybe so. But you're clearly not a wrestler."

He pulled the trigger, putting a round through El Leon's forehead. The rapport echoed through the empty halls.

When he was certain El Leon was dead, he pushed himself to his feet, using the wall for assistance. By the time he was standing, Megan, Luke, and Alvarez were running down the hall toward him.

Megan reached him first. "You all right?"

"Yeah. I may take Doc Hanson up on some of those pain pills though." He looked her up and down and was relieved to see she didn't appear to be injured. "You?"

"Fine."

"She's better than fine," Luke said with a grin. "She stabbed one of those bastards in the face with her car keys."

Riker let out a pained laugh. "Where's the kid?"

"We made him wait outside," Alvarez said. She gestured to El Leon's body. "Didn't want him to see, you know, something like this."

"Good call. So what happens now?"

Before Alvarez could answer, a soft ring tone interrupted her.

Luke bent down and gingerly pulled a cell phone out of El Leon's jacket pocket. He looked at the screen and frowned. "Unknown number. Bogota, Colombia."

"Give it to me," Riker said. After Luke passed it to him, he pressed the answer button and held it to his ear. "Hola."

There was a long pause before a familiar voice answered in English. "Not who I'd hoped would answer."

"No. I expect not." Riker closed his eyes, his mind going over what was surely going to come next. The drug lord would vow revenge, still not understanding what he was up against. Riker would be forced to take the fight to him. Going up against a cartel boss on his home turf would be difficult, but Riker had no choice. This would not end until one of them was dead.

But what the drug lord said next surprised him.

"Mr. Riker, I am done with Kingsport."

Riker waited for a long moment, wondering if there would be more, some caveat or threat that put conditions on what he'd just said. But there was only silence.

"In that case, I don't think we have anything left to say to each other."

This time, the response was immediate. "Agreed. Good-bye, Mr. Riker."

With that, the line went dead.

Megan looked at Riker, her eyes hopeful. "Is it over?"

"Yeah," he said with a smile. "It really is."

45

Riker hobbled into the Kingsport police station on his crutches a few minutes after six the following evening. The last day and a half had been a whirlwind of activity, mostly consisting of answering the same questions again and again to representatives of different law enforcement agencies. He knew that as hectic as it had been for him, it had been even crazier for the person he was there to see.

He found Officer Alvarez sitting at her desk in the police office, loading items into a cardboard box. She noticed him approaching and nodded to him. From a single glance he could tell she was even more tired than he'd expected her to be.

She placed a final item into the cardboard box and closed the lid flaps just as Riker reached her.

"Need a hand carrying anything?" he asked her.

She shook her head. "I travel light. This one box will do me, and if I can't lift this myself, I'm not sure what I'm doing with my life."

"Fair enough."

She gave him a look up and down. "How's the leg?"

He shrugged. "Better than it was yesterday. Worse than it was two days ago. But they tell me it'll heal."

In truth, he'd walked away from the fight with El Leon in relatively good shape. His nose wasn't broken, nor was his hand. He would need to stay off the leg for a while—for real this time. But at least his brains weren't sprayed all over the floor of the Kingsport High School, like his opponent's were.

"How about you?" he asked. "Holding it together?"

"Just barely. Between the FBI and DEA asking me questions, I'd barely had time to breathe. Hell, even ICE wanted to get involved."

"Did my name happen to come up during the questioning?"

"You know I can't comment on that." She paused, looking around the small bullpen. There were only two other officers present, and they were both on the phone. She spoke again, this time in a much softer voice. "Your name came up quite a lot, actually. They were especially curious how you got your hands on a Glock registered to the police department."

"They asked me about that as well. Multiple times."

"Chief Myers is taking full responsibility for arming you. Among other things. And Luke stuck to his story. You weren't even at the farm. He called you when he found out your cousin was in trouble, and you two met at the high school."

Riker frowned. He hadn't asked Luke to do that. Of course, he hadn't asked Luke to help him cover up what had really happened the night of his father's death either. Luke seemed to be making a habit of helping Riker stay out of legal trouble.

"The questions aren't that bad though," Alvarez said. "You know what I really hate? The paperwork."

Riker chuckled. "Pretty sure you've been complaining about paperwork since the day I met you."

"We didn't have much of it before you came to town." She picked up the cardboard box. "Walk with me."

Riker did as asked, following her across the office. When they reached the door marked Chief Myers, Alvarez sighed.

"Guess there's no use trying to avoid it."

She opened the door and carried her box into the empty office. The walls were blank and the picture of Chief Myers' son was no longer on the desk. She set her box down on the desk with a thud.

"Welcome home, Chief," Riker said.

Alvarez frowned. "Interim Chief."

He met her gaze, his expression suddenly serious. "They'll bring you on as the permanent chief."

"I don't know. After all this..."

"They will. Trust me. You're a damn good cop, and everyone involved in this case is going to realize that by the time they are done investigating. And once they do, they're not going to want anyone else in that seat."

Alvarez smiled. "Thanks, Riker."

"I mean every word." He paused. "I'm leaving town."

"When?"

"Tonight. As soon as possible. I just wanted to say goodbye to a couple people first."

"And I made the list? I'm honored." She held out her hand and the two of them shook.

"Take care of my hometown, Interim Chief Alvarez."

"And you take care of yourself. Now get out of here. I'll have Officer Jenkins get the prisoner."

Five minutes later, Riker was sitting in interrogation room B when the door opened and Officer Jenkins led in Luke Dewitt.

"How do I look in orange?" Luke asked.

"Manly as ever," Riker said with a smile.

Officer Jenkins cocked a thumb toward the door. "I'll be right out there if you need anything."

They waited until the police officer left before speaking again. Even then, Riker knew the room was wired for sound and video. They would have to watch what they said, lest they accidentally make another mess for Interim Chief Alvarez. There would be no talk of what went down at the farm.

"They treating you okay?" Riker asked.

"You kidding? I've got Doc Hanson in the cell next to mine and Chief Myers in the one next to him. It's a party." He paused. "You know, Doc is still convinced that the cartel is going to have us all killed."

"How about you?"

"Nah. I believe what Nicolás Marcillas said. I think he's done with Kingsport. I think we'll live long, healthy lives in prison."

Riker saw the hint of sadness in his friend's eyes. "Don't give up, Luke. You may be able to strike a deal. You'll serve some time, but it may not be a lot."

"Oh, I'm not worried about the time. I did what I did. I'm man enough to take the punishment. I'm only sad about all the years I wasted under the thumb of the cartel. I was a prisoner long before I put on this jumpsuit." He met Riker's eyes. "You got me out, man. Whatever debt you owed me, you repaid it and then some."

Riker stared back at his old friend. Luke had lost his way for a long time, and he'd done some things that were arguably unforgivable. But in the end, he'd come back into the light.

"Consider us even. But that doesn't mean I won't call in a favor or two when you get out."

"From what I saw over the past few days, I don't even want to know what kind of favors you ask from your friends."

"Tough to say. I don't have many friends."

"Then let's make sure you keep the ones you have."

"It's a deal." Riker held out his hand, and the two men shook.

Just as Riker was about to turn to go, Luke spoke again.

"Hey, I think I figured out what I want to do with my life after all this is over."

"Yeah?" Riker asked, genuinely curious. "What's that?"

Luke gave a sheepish smile. "Assuming I ever get out of here, and assuming I can find someone who would let me, I think I want to honor Coach Kane's memory the best way I know how. I want to be a wrestling coach."

MEGAN WAS WAITING on her front porch when Riker pulled up to her house. He grinned when he walked up and saw his packed duffle bag sitting on the porch next to her.

"Wow, are you really that eager to get rid of me?"

"Not at all," she said. "But I've seen the way you've been ever since yesterday morning. You can hardly sit still. I'm thinking it's you who's eager to get rid of me."

"Not on your life. But you're right. It is time for me to be moving on. There's something I need to do." He took a seat next to her on the stoop, groaning as he stretched out his injured leg and set his crutches down next to him. "How are the kids holding up?"

"Pretty well, actually. We've got trauma counselors on-site and there have been a few justified freak outs. I spoke to David and his parents. I think his dad is more upset about what happened than David is."

That made sense to Riker. After all, it had been his father's actions that had put the boy in harm's way.

"What about Blake?"

Megan considered that a moment. "He wasn't in school today, so I stopped by the hospital. Physically, he's going to be in a cast for a couple of months. Emotionally? He's having a hard time dealing with the role he played in what happened. Before yesterday, it was all theoretical to him. He'd never seen any real violence. El Leon somehow got his number and contacted him. He felt like it was his big opportunity. Somehow, he didn't consider the consequences."

Riker thought back to his conversation with Luke. In many ways, Blake was like him. He'd behaved terribly and caused great damage, but in the end, he'd stood up for what's right, despite the massive danger to himself.

"I hope he's going to be okay," Megan said. "I hope they all are."

"With you as a teacher? How could they not be?"

A sly smile crossed Megan's face. "I also had an interesting conversation with Mr. Harlen today."

Riker grimaced, remembering how the high school principal had kicked him off campus the day he'd visited to have lunch with Megan. "Let me guess. He wants to sue me for the property damage I caused while fighting El Leon?"

"Not exactly. He wants you to speak at a school-wide assembly."

The blood drained from Riker's face. "That's way worse."

Megan laughed and put a hand on his arm. "Don't worry, I told him you wouldn't be able to make it. But believe me when I say, Mr. Harlen is a big Matthew Riker fan. I overheard him using you as an example of what Kingsport students can accomplish when they put their minds to it."

Riker shook his head and chuckled in surprise. "This town, man."

Megan's face fell. "Yeah. Honestly, I'm having a hard time dealing with the fact that so many people looked the other way or even profited from this stuff with the cartel. I thought the people in my town were better than that."

"It is shocking," Riker allowed. "But look at it another way. It was the bravery of the people that stopped the cartel in the end. Luke, Chief Myers, even Blake. They all did the right thing when it came down to it. And then we've got people like you and Officer Alvarez who never stopped fighting for what's right. All of you were willing to die to protect Kingsport. You fought even in the face of seemingly insurmountable odds. And you won."

Megan squeezed his arm. "Thanks, but you're leaving one important character out of the story. None of this would have been possible without you leading the charge."

Riker considered that and shrugged. "That's true, but I'm the product of years of world class training. Uncle Sam invested a lot of money in preparing me for scenarios like this. The rest of you didn't have that. But you did have your morals, your courage, and good old fashioned Iowa stubbornness. Turns out, that was enough."

With that, Riker pushed himself to his feet. It took far longer than it should have, but he made it.

"Want me to help you with your bag?" Megan asked.

"No," Riker hoisted the duffle bag over his shoulder, then held out an arm. "You can give me a hug though."

She stood up and pulled him into a tight embrace.

"Thank you for coming, Matt. I'm glad to know I still have a family member out there, and he's actually a good guy."

"Thank you, Megan. For everything." He pulled back from the hug and regarded her. "I've been meaning to ask. You ever hear from my mom?"

She shrugged. "I get a Christmas card every year. She's still in Florida. Do you?"

He shook his head. "I've tried to reach out many times, but she won't talk to me. That doesn't mean I'm going to stop trying."

"She's stubborn," Megan said with a smile. "Just like her son."

Riker couldn't disagree with that. He started down the sidewalk, then paused. "Keep sending your Thursday messages. And check your email on Friday mornings, because I'm going to start writing you back."

He'd gone a few more steps when Megan spoke again. "You did real good here, Matt. You finished what Coach Kane started, and you took down his killer."

"Thanks." He said it even though he knew the second part of her statement wasn't true. He hadn't taken down Coach Kane's killer. Not yet. But he intended to do so very soon.

EPILOGUE

When Riker was ten miles outside Kingsport, he picked up his phone and tapped a number on the contact list. Franklin answered on the second ring.

"Scarecrow? Is everything all right?"

"No, Franklin. It really isn't. I wish this was a social call, but I need you to get a message to Morrison for me. It's urgent."

There was a long pause. "You know you're not supposed to be contacting him. You wanted out, and you are out. The things he's working on are—"

"Just pass him the message. It's up to him what he does with it."

"All right. What's the message?"

"Fraction is back."

Another pause. "That's it?"

"That's it."

"And he'll know what that means?"

"Very much so."

"I'll get him the message."

"Thank you, Franklin. It was good hearing your voice." Riker hung up without waiting for a response.

Now that he was free of Kingsport, his mind was turning to other matters, things he'd needed to wait until after he was done in his hometown to attend to.

He'd suspected that the cartel wasn't responsible for Coach Kane's death the moment Luke had first told his story of that night. The man in the shadows stalking the car and killing Coach Kane. That wasn't the cartel's style. Coach Kane was very publicly messing with them, and they would want at least their partners in Kingsport to know it was they who killed the troublemaker. They would have wanted to use his death to make a statement.

But it wasn't until Riker spoke with Patricia Kane that he'd known for certain. The method of execution—a bullet through each eye—was all too familiar to Riker. He knew only one man who used that as his calling card.

Charles Fraction. The last time Riker had faced him, he'd ended up quitting QS-4 and swearing off a life of violence. Charles Fraction was like no other man he'd ever gone up against. And now, he was back and sending Riker a message.

The thought that Coach Kane had died simply because a psychopath wanted to send Riker a message made him sick to his stomach, but it was an undeniable truth.

Riker's phone rang three minutes after he'd hung up with Franklin. He didn't even bother looking at the caller ID before answering. "Yes?"

"Is it true?" There was an urgency in Morrison's gruff voice. And maybe a little fear.

"It's true. He killed my high school wrestling coach. A bullet through each eye."

"Good God."

"That means he's gunning for people I care about. Could be he's targeting my mentors. You could be in danger. And we need to get some protection for James Halder, my CO from my SEALs days."

"On it." There was a pause. "Riker, if he's back, we need to deal with him before more people die. We need to finally end this once and for all."

"Agreed. I'm in Iowa, but I'm driving east. I'm coming to you, Morrison. We're going to end this thing together."

AUTHOR'S NOTE

Not only was LONG WAY HOME a personal story for Riker, it was a very personal one for me as well. Kingsport is loosely based on my own hometown, and while there is no secret, cartel-funded heroin production facility there (to my knowledge), the courage of the people is just as real.

I'm hard at work planning the next book in the series, and I hope to have it to you soon. I'm both terrified and excited for you to meet Charles Fraction and to finally reveal the truth about Riker's last job with QS-4. It promises to be an epic ride where no one is safe. Riker is going to be put to the ultimate test.

In the meantime, I suggest checking out the prequel story, NO LOOSE ENDS, which introduces some of the members of Riker's QS-4 team. It also tells the story of how Riker and company brought down the drug lord Javier Herrara, which Riker referenced in his phone conversation with Marcillas in this book. You can get the novella by joining my email group. It's also included in as a free bonus with the audiobook version of THE IMPORT, which I highly recommend checking out; the wonderful Jay Snyder narrates, and he gave one hell of a performance.

Finally, thanks again for reading this series. Your reviews, feedback, and emails are a big part of what keeps me writing Riker's adventures. Writing is a solitary act, but your kindness and enthusiasm make it feel like I'm telling stories around a campfire to a group of close friends. I can't imagine a better feeling than that.

Thanks again, and happy reading.

J.T. Baier

CPSIA information can be obtained
at www.ICGtesting.com
Printed in the USA
LVHW030909100921
697444LV00008B/769